LEE BROOK

The Killer in the Family

MIDDLETON
PARK PRESS

First published by Middleton Park Press 2023

Copyright © 2023 by Lee Brook

All rights reserved. No part of this publication may be reproduced, stored or transmitted in any form or by any means, electronic, mechanical, photocopying, recording, scanning, or otherwise without written permission from the publisher. It is illegal to copy this book, post it to a website, or distribute it by any other means without permission.

This novel is entirely a work of fiction. The names, characters and incidents portrayed in it are the work of the author's imagination. Any resemblance to actual persons, living or dead, events or localities is entirely coincidental.

Lee Brook asserts the moral right to be identified as the author of this work.

Lee Brook has no responsibility for the persistence or accuracy of URLs for external or third-party Internet Websites referred to in this publication and does not guarantee that any content on such Websites is, or will remain, accurate or appropriate.

Designations used by companies to distinguish their products are often claimed as trademarks. All brand names and product names used in this book and on its cover are trade names, service marks, trademarks and registered trademarks of their respective owners. The publishers and the book are not associated with any product or vendor mentioned in this book. None of the companies referenced within the book have endorsed the book.

First edition

This book was professionally typeset on Reedsy.
Find out more at reedsy.com

*For the admins of the UK Crime Book Club Facebook group—
Thank you for creating a safe place for us indie authors.
I appreciate everything you all do.*

Contents

Prologue — iii
Chapter One — 1
Chapter Two — 6
Chapter Three — 13
Chapter Four — 26
Chapter Five — 32
Chapter Six — 44
Chapter Seven — 50
Chapter Eight — 59
Chapter Nine — 67
Chapter Ten — 74
Chapter Eleven — 84
Chapter Twelve — 87
Chapter Thirteen — 95
Chapter Fourteen — 103
Chapter Fifteen — 112
Chapter Sixteen — 120
Chapter Seventeen — 127
Chapter Eighteen — 133
Chapter Nineteen — 142
Chapter Twenty — 148
Chapter Twenty-one — 157
Chapter Twenty-two — 168
Chapter Twenty-three — 177

Chapter Twenty-four	184
Chapter Twenty-five	189
Chapter Twenty-six	198
Chapter Twenty-seven	206
Chapter Twenty-eight	212
Chapter Twenty-nine	214
Chapter Thirty	220
Chapter Thirty-one	228
Chapter Thirty-two	236
Chapter Thirty-three	246
Chapter Thirty-four	256
Chapter Thirty-five	264
Chapter Thirty-six	273
Chapter Thirty-seven	282
Chapter Thirty-eight	293
Chapter Thirty-nine	297
Chapter Forty	301
Epilogue	306
Family Tree	308
Also by Lee Brook	309

Prologue

April 2023

Detective Inspector George Beaumont opened his eyes and breathed in Isabella Wood's floral scent. "I can't wait to go home," he said breathlessly.

"Are you sure you're ready?" Wood asked. She pulled away from his embrace and licked her lips. She'd missed kissing him, and kissing him gently instead of passionately was hard for her.

But at least he was alive.

He grinned at her, noticing she was looking flustered. George was glad he could still have that kind of effect on her. He himself could feel the beginning of arousal. But he wasn't sure how long it would take for his broken body to heal fully. If it ever would.

The fall had caused bleeding on the brain, as well as two skull fractures, a punctured lung, a broken collar bone, broken ribs and a fractured wrist.

The ribs had already healed, as had his two skull fractures, but his wrist and clavicle were only about halfway there. His lung was also much better. Unfortunately, he'd probably never recover from the bleed. Not entirely, anyway.

"I'd like another kiss," he said with a grin. "I've missed this."

Isabella, her bump now showing slightly, bent over the

hospital gurney and kissed her fiancée on the lips, long and slow, savouring every second.

"What the hell is this?"

Isabella pulled away and turned towards the voice.

George opened his eyes.

Standing in the doorway was Mia, Jack's hand in her right and a string of balloons in her left.

When neither George nor Isabella said anything, she repeated her question. "What the hell is this?"

"You know Isabella, Mia?"

"I do, yeah." She furrowed her brow and stormed towards her child's father.

Wood stood up from the chair and said, "I'll get a coffee and give you two some time to talk."

But George shook his head. "I want you here. Please don't leave." He turned to Mia to try and appease the situation, but she wasn't looking at him.

She was looking at Isabella's swollen stomach.

The beautiful curve of pregnancy.

"Is—is that yours?" Mia asked, letting go of Jack's hand and pointing.

Beaumont nodded. "I was going to tell you—"

"Oh, were you?" She shook her head and let the balloons go. They slowly floated towards the ceiling. The tension was palpable. Mia folded her arms across her chest. "When?"

"We didn't tell you earlier because of the accident," Wood explained. "Surely you can be a bit more understanding?"

"I wasn't talking to you, love; I was talking to George," Mia replied. "How long has this been going on for?"

"Does it matter?" George asked, trying to shift position. He grimaced in pain, and Wood stepped forward.

Jack was playing with the doctor's board at the foot of the bed, oblivious.

"Of course, it matters." She pointed at Jack. "Does Jack know who she is?" The word 'she' was laced with poison. "Has he been seeing her without me knowing?" Again, the word 'her' was pure venom.

"I'd appreciate it if you lightened your tone, Mia," George said, "otherwise I will ask you to leave." He smiled at his son. "I don't want you to go. I've missed my boy. But I don't appreciate your tone at all."

Then he started coughing, and Isabella helped him take a drink. Jack looked up, concerned.

"Can Daddy have a hug?" George asked Jack, who grinned and held his arms out.

Both George and Isabella looked at Mia, who raised her brow. "Oh, I see; you expect me to lift him up to you?"

"Please, Mia."

"You're not being fair," Wood cut in. She walked over to Jack, picked him up, and gently placed him down next to his dad on the bed.

"Tiss, Izzy," Jack said to Wood and kissed her on the forehead once she'd bent over.

"Tiss, Dada," he said to George, who offered up his right hand to be kissed. George couldn't wait to be able to hug and kiss his son.

"Tiss, Mama?" The young blond looked up at his mother, who grinned as she stepped closer, cutting in between her son and Wood and bending close to George.

Mia kissed her son on the lips and then also stole a kiss from George. "I know you think I'm mad, but you have to understand that you've kept this from me."

"It just wasn't the right time, Mia," George explained.

"Is there anything else I need to know?" Mia turned to Wood again and inspected every inch of her body. "Like that, for instance." She pointed at Wood's engagement ring.

"We were going to tell you when we were ready," George explained.

"I don't believe you." Mia took a deep breath and frantically shook her head. "You're lying to me. The only reason I know now about this is because I've found you out! And if you've lied about that, then what else have you lied about?"

"We haven't lied about anything," George said.

Mia's face contorted. "I don't believe you. Like, just how long have you two been together to be engaged and pregnant, eh?"

George went to reply when Mia cut back in. "I knew you were seeing someone. What I didn't know was who, obviously. But you two have worked together for a while now. So how long?"

"How long what?" he asked.

"How long have you two been together?"

"Does it matter?"

"So you were cheating on me?"

"What? No!" said George.

Clenching her fists, Wood shouted, "How dare you! You cheated on George, remember."

"Don't you fucking get involved," Mia said, stepping towards Wood. "This doesn't involve you. I want the truth from George. The father of my child!"

"I want you to leave, Mia." George closed his eyes to fight against his emotions but failed as a bulbous tear fell from his right eye. "As I said before, I've missed my boy, but this isn't healthy. Seeing you like this is doing me no good. Hearing you speak with my fiancée like that is also doing me no good. I want you to leave."

Mia rushed over towards George, who flinched. She picked up Jack and pulled him away as George tried to kiss his son's head. "Come on, Jack. Let's go home."

"Bye, son," George said. "I love you. I'll see you soon, yeah?"

"Don't bet on it," Mia said.

George tried to protest and reached out for his boy, but Mia dragged Jack away, forcing the young toddler's legs to go too fast. And as they left the room on the ward, George heard Jack crying and Mia screaming at him to get up and walk.

More tears streamed from George's eyes. And when he looked at Wood, she, too, was crying.

Chapter One

Four months later

Martha Lickiss sat at her laptop, clacking away at the keys and sliding her fingers against the mousepad as she searched the genealogy website. There was a glass of wine to her left, and to her right was her mobile on a dock, spewing soft music. She'd pulled the blinds down halfway, the fields beyond the house starting to succumb to the summer darkness. The failing light reflected off the glass, and she could see for miles around her. She was alone and looking up her dead ancestors. In her own home. Safe.

As somebody who was adopted, it was something she'd always wanted to do, but out of respect for her adoptive parents, she'd decided not to search for her birth family until they passed.

Unfortunately for Martha, Ted and Mavis Mook were now six feet under, having both lived long lives until their late eighties.

Her mother's death hadn't been sudden. She got terminal cancer that, despite never smoking in her life, began in her lungs and spread around her body.

And her father had died from a broken heart. Not literally, he'd fallen rather nastily, broke a hip, and died on the operating table, but he'd practically given up on life after the death of his wife. Martha knew the only reason her father had lived as long as he had was because of the twins.

Faith and Hope Lickiss, her wonderful daughters. The apples of her eye. The apples of Ted's eye, too. And Geoff's, too, unfortunately. Her ex-husband, Geoff, was a proper arsehole who believed in outdated gender roles. Martha blamed Geoff's father, Geoff Senior. And most likely, the blame lay with Geoff Senior's father, Geoffrey Lickiss.

The woman married to the Lickiss men was expected to stay home, rear children, cook and clean. They weren't expected to have an education. Which is what Martha always said she'd wanted. And that had been an issue for Geoff.

Hence the divorce papers.

During their years together, Geoff had kept telling her she was stupid, and at one point, she almost believed it. But she knew it wasn't really true. She'd proven that to him tenfold. The occupation order had succeeded, and the house was legally hers to reside in. Geoff had really hated that. He knew she'd got one over on him. It had been a sweet victory.

Smiling to herself, she swallowed a large gulp of wine and started adding members to her tree.

Then the front door opened and slammed shut.

"Hope, is that you love?" Martha shouted, not bothering to look over her shoulder. Faith was upstairs in her room. It was just after ten, and whilst Hope had promised to be home before ten, she was nearly sixteen and Martha could remember what it was like when her own parents gave her a curfew at that age. Still, Hope was beginning to take liberties with her curfew, so she made a mental note to have a sit-down together.

When Hope didn't answer, Martha said, "You're late. It may only be ten past but late is late. Come in here, and please explain."

But Martha was met with silence.

Which was unusual.

Unlike Faith, no matter how much trouble Hope got into, she always stood her ground, a trait inherited from her father.

Or maybe not, Martha thought with a grin. She knew precisely where Hope got it from.

Picking up her wineglass and standing up, she turned to the open kitchen door and stared into the hallway. The wineglass fell from her hand.

The glass shattered, spraying crimson everywhere.

* * *

George Beaumont turned over onto his back, his breathing shallow and his eyes flickering rapidly. He was dreaming. It was the same dream as last night and the night before that. Over and over, it was always the same, like a demented Groundhog Day. It was always the dead of night, raining hard, with George running at full pelt through the deserted Georgian building, feet pounding, the sounds echoing, deafening. Then it was him taking the stairs three at a time—the thick, suffocating darkness devouring him as he climbed. Then he'd reach the third floor, fire in his lungs, his heart hammering, senses in overload, the sound of a woman shrieking. The knife would come at him, slow enough for him to avoid but unbalancing him. The next instant, his dress shoes would slip on the greasy surface, and then he would pitch backwards, over the balcony railing and into the air, plunging towards the ground far below.

But somehow, he'd always manage to hold on. And he would hear Isabella shout, "Come on, George, give me your hand."

But no matter what he does, his body doesn't move.

"You need to give me your hand now, George; otherwise, you'll fall! Our baby needs you!"

And, like always, his fingers would start to slip. One by one. And then he'd fall.

"George!"

Panicked and clutching at his throat, George awoke. His head was whirling like an F1 car performing doughnuts, and his heart was pounding. He searched his bedside table for the glass of water that Isabella always put there. Choking down the tepid liquid, his airway opened up, oxygen entered his lungs, and as he gulped more—his pulse rate started to slow. Then, after a short while, the nightmare's retreating memories vanished, and he exhaled a deep, worn-out sigh.

Then he felt an arm stretch across him, holding his shaking hand. Isabella.

She was sat up, a phone to her ear, nodding but looking at him. George struggled but managed to eventually sit up. Peering through the gloom, he saw the alarm clock said 11.15 pm. He'd only been asleep an hour.

"We're needed at an incident in Rothwell, George," she said.

Getting out of bed was a struggle for George, but it didn't take him long before he was in the bathroom. He splashed water on his face and hair, gently fingering the scar on his skull, then hiding it with his blond locks. He knew he was lucky to be alive and was grateful to the LGI for saving him. The scar was a gift, evidence of what he'd survived. One consultant had told him to show the scar off proudly, but he wasn't ready for that. He probably never would be.

George rubbed at the scar gently, a comfort habit he'd developed during his rehabilitation. A knock at the door signalled he'd taken too long, and his pregnant fiancée needed the loo, so he flushed the toilet and washed his hands before leaving to retreat downstairs in search of coffee.

Chapter Two

When Detective Inspector George Beaumont and Detective Sergeant Isabella Wood arrived at the farm on Royds Lane in Rothwell, the crime-scene tape was already in place. George looked around the area, noticing interested observers were being stopped and returned to their homes by two police cruisers. But other than that, the area seemed peaceful.

George turned to face Wood. She took in his new visage. He'd started wearing his blond hair longer to hide the long scar on his skull where the surgeons had operated to save his life. And where he'd once stood over six feet tall, been broad, and in great shape, he now stooped and carried some extra weight around his chest and stomach.

The change in her fiancé's appearance hadn't bothered Isabella. Her appearance had changed dramatically during the past four or five months. Their child would be born early next month, and whilst George told her she regularly looked 'incredible' and marvelled how she 'glowed', Isabella was struggling with chronic heartburn and chronic fatigue and felt like her bladder was the size of a pea. Walking was an absolute nightmare, and she wondered when the DCI would detain her to desk duty.

She was ready to have him. Or her. They'd decided to be

surprised. Or she had, at least. She knew George wanted a little brother for Jack, but Isabella wasn't too bothered. A little princess to spoil wouldn't be too bad. She could give her daughter what she'd never had.

It was pissing it down, and whilst George stood over them, umbrella high up in the air, she urged her fiancé through the outer cordon and towards the inner cordon where they'd need to suit up. The pair had been called to a house invasion. Uniform that had attended said it was possibly a 'break-in gone wrong'.

"Uniform who attended the scene don't really know much, George."

"The house belongs to the Lickiss family," he said.

"What did DS Mason say?" she asked. Despite being nearly ready to drop, she was still driving George around. He was concerned with the residual numbness and tingling on the left-hand side of his body and the loss of concentration and dexterity he was suffering with.

Still, despite all those ailments, the doctor and the psychologist agreed that George could return to work.

"Luke said Martha Lickiss had an occupation order to give her the right to stay in the farmhouse and stop her ex-partner from returning. But it looks as if Geoff Lickiss ignored the order twice, and she was awaiting a hearing on the non-molestation order."

"Doesn't prove Geoff was involved, though, George," Wood said.

George nodded as he struggled to get dressed in the Tyvek suit. Isabella waited, knowing her future husband would be embarrassed if she tried to help him in front of other people. Luckily it was PC Candy Nichols who guarded the inner cordon, and not a stranger. She handed Wood a piece of paper and then signed the two detectives in.

Once the pair were dressed and booted, they headed up the driveway towards the doorway. There was no light coming from the house. George didn't like it.

Wood read from a page covered in raindrops. "Pretty gory scene according to this, George," she said.

"How did he get in?"

"Door isn't forced, so he might have had a key," Wood speculated.

George grinned. Isabella had always loved his smile and was glad the accident hadn't affected it. "So somebody had a key, or somebody was let in?" George asked, and Isabella nodded. "Geoff Lickiss shouldn't have had a key if he was subjected to an order, right?"

Isabella mirrored that beautiful grin. "Right."

The yawning door swallowed the detectives up, and George stopped immediately, Isabella bumping into his back. She felt him wince. The injury the Miss Murderer had given him was hurting him. According to George's consultant, re-awoken pain from previous injuries was common.

"What's up?" she asked. She saw him slowly crouch down.

"Blood," was all he said.

She pulled out her phone and turned on the torch. There was a trail of bloody footprints leading along the hallway. She said this to George.

"Both ways," George replied.

"Did the culprit come back to the door to check something or to let someone else in?"

"Could even be the victims?" George pondered. "Lindsey's SOCOs will take impressions. So watch where you walk."

CHAPTER TWO

Isabella nodded and took a cautious stride down the confined hallway while George looked around the hallway. He couldn't see any blood spatter, so whatever crime they were here for hadn't happened there.

He watched as Wood opened a door, and from the light on her phone, George could see what looked like a large but outdated kitchen. Then he saw Wood stop.

"Are you OK?"

"Carnage," was all she said.

George ambled over and took in the scene.

The top of a wooden table was turned over. It had been hit by two chairs, one of which had three legs broken off. Books and papers were all over the floor, along with a phone and a laptop with shattered displays that appeared to have been stepped on. The counter surfaces appeared to be utterly devoid of any objects. The doors of the cabinets were dripping with red, and the tap was running.

"Jesus Christ..." George focused on the corpse after averting his gaze from the chaos. The body was lying face down in a little puddle of blood. Long, brown hair was matted to the skull, which also showed a gaping wound with copious amounts of blood, bone, and brain matter. The left arm and right leg were at unnatural angles. The blouse was covered with crimson. Its back was ripped open, and the skirt was torn. There was a pile of sick to the right of the entrance.

Skin that George assumed was once pale was now purple and black. "Badly beaten," George explained, pointing. He then turned to Wood. "Did that piece of paper say who found her?"

Wood nodded. "Sister."

George raised his brows. "Christ..."

"Sister-in-law actually. Geoff's sister, Jean."

"Could explain the prints?"

"I was thinking the same." She looked at the notes again. "Jean went straight to her van and called triple nine. Candy took a statement and then sent her home. She's going to come in tomorrow morning to give an official statement."

"I'd have liked to have seen her in person," George said. "I'll have a word with Candy tomorrow. The girl needs to learn."

Wood knew that her fiancé liked Candy Nichols. Before the accident, he'd often spoken about her and her potential. Isabella had told him to talk with DSU Smith, and George had agreed, but then the accident happened.

"Was she the one who chucked up her guts?" George asked, pointing at the vomit.

She pursed her lips. "Doesn't say."

"Probably was. That or Uniform." George noticed Isabella had worn a mask. "You coping OK?"

"Not really. It really smells in here."

"Go outside and coordinate with PS Greenwood. He's got uniforms on house-to-house. I'm fine waiting in here for Lindsey and Dr Ross."

Wood turned to leave when George said, "Does it say anything about the first responders on there?"

Isabella used her phone's torch, and George saw her lips moving as she read. Then, finally, she looked up and met his green eyes. "Says they came in through the back. Something about not wanting to contaminate the scene."

George nodded. First responders always contaminated scenes, no matter how careful they were.

Once Wood was gone, George looked around the kitchen again. "The husband forced entry," he said aloud. Then he forcefully shook his head. We don't know it was the husband, he thought He scratched his beard. But what if it was? he questioned. "But why? What drove him to it? He's been barred from the family home for nearly a year. If it's him that's gone mad, then why tonight?" His head was hurting, but he wasn't due more medication until one that morning. "Shit."

After rubbing his eyes and taking one more look, George left the kitchen by the hallway and, avoiding the footprints, entered the living room. He pulled out his phone and called DS Mason, who was working nights. "Has Geoff Lickiss been located, Luke?"

"No sign of him, son. Checkpoints are in place, and traffic units have the car registration. But we'll find him," Luke said.

George turned when he heard noises behind him. The SOCO team leader, Lindsey Yardley, walked into the living room, struggling with her bulky forensic cases, Dr Christian Ross hot on her heel.

"Nice to see you, son," Christian said, offering his hand.

George pulled off his glove and shook the older man's hand. This was George's first time venturing out of the office since being back at Elland Road. During his phased return, they'd put him on desk duty for a few weeks. "And you, Dr Ross," George said, grinning.

He then turned to crime scene co-ordinator Yardley, a doctor in her own right. Most people would demand you use the title, but Lindsey wasn't like that. Then again, George heard rumours that the elderly pathologist was retiring soon, and Lindsey would most likely then take over. "Lindsey."

"DI Beaumont."

"The scene's contaminated," George explained. "First responders. Plus, a relative."

Lindsey nodded. "So I've heard."

Blond American SOCO, Hayden Wyatt, was placing stepping plates down in the hallway, and when he saw George, he grinned in only the way an American could. "DI Beaumont, how amazing to see you. Are you good?"

"I'm doing better, thanks, Hayden."

George said nothing else and started looking around the living room. The CSI team got the hint and headed towards the kitchen to begin their work.

The DI stood in silence and watched for about twenty-five minutes. Finally, Isabella re-entered the farmhouse and stood behind him, her bump nestled into his back.

That was when the SOC team turned the body over.

Wood looked down at her phone, and the picture of Martha Lickiss Luke had sent her, then questioned, "Wait, who the heck is that?"

Chapter Three

"Blunt-force trauma to the back of the skull," Dr Christian Ross said as he tore off his forensic suit and stuffed it into the paper bag held out by a SOCO. At five foot five, the older pathologist made up in expertise what he lacked in height. "If you find the weapon, son, I can match it to the wound."

George asked, "Any idea what it might be?"

"Something hard and rounded."

"Any ideas?" Wood asked, and Ross shrugged.

"Anything else you can tell us?" George knew they'd get more information once the post-mortem was finished.

"I'll schedule the post-mortem for eight in the morning, son. It's possible the body can tell us something. So come along and see for yourself."

"Thanks." George watched the pathologist amble out into the rain. He turned to Wood. "We need to identify her, and quick."

They'd already had PC Candy Nichols use a Lantern device to see if the dead woman's prints were on the database, but they weren't. And Isabella had called Luke, who was at Elland Road, asking him to look through missing persons'. He was also looking into the Lickiss family to see if the Jane Doe could be one of them.

"There's a ladies' mack hanging on the newel post. It's damp," Wood said to George. They were both stood outside the front door waiting for Luke to get back in touch with them.

"Right?" he said.

"I'm guessing the coat belongs to her," Wood said, pointing into the hallway towards the kitchen. "We don't have a bag or a purse, so no ID. Maybe her DNA is on the system?"

George nodded and beckoned Hayden Wyatt over. "There's a raincoat inside, on the newel post. We think it belongs to the victim. Bag it, and get it forensically tested at the lab."

"Yes, sir," Wyatt said with a salute.

"Where's Martha Lickiss?" Wood asked.

"My thoughts exactly," George said. He turned to Wood. "Did Sergeant Greenwood's team find anything out?"

"Not yet," Wood explained. "They're still at it, waking neighbours up. But everybody knows the Lickiss family. They're a famous farming family, apparently."

George nodded. "I've heard of them. I went to school with one of them. They own the farm on the A654 that leads into the centre. Or they used to, anyway. He was called Gareth. I think he's Geoff Lickiss' nephew."

"Big family?"

"Massive."

"This might take a while, then?"

"Yeah, I don't think we can do much more tonight." He then pointed towards the kitchen. "She may have just been a friend of Martha's?"

"Possibly, but I think she looked young. Did Luke say whether Martha had kids?"

The victim's face had been beaten so much that they couldn't distinguish any identifying features.

"Yeah, twin daughters. Faith and Hope. We're trying to contact them now."

"How old are they?"

George thought for a moment, his head hurting him. "Fifteen."

"So why weren't they home?"

George shrugged. "Were you home at fifteen?"

"Of course I was."

George thought back to his youth. He was roaming the streets at that age, causing havoc, trying to pull birds. The memory made him think of Ellie Addiman, the girl he'd lost his virginity to, the woman Freya Bentley had left for dead hours before his life-changing accident.

He'd been lucky compared to Ellie. He'd heard from Wood that Ellie may never walk again because of an injury to her spine. So George made a mental note to go and visit her.

"We need to find Martha Lickiss," Wood said, interrupting George's thoughts.

"Luke's working on it with some CID detective constables. Do you want to go home?"

Wood shook her head and said, "CSI's out in the back garden. I think we should have a look. The first responders said the backdoor was also open."

The rain in the back garden, weirdly, was light compared to the front. Still, George and Wood found themselves splashing in and out of puddles as they watched the SOC team do their jobs.

"I've got something!" one of the SOCOs shouted. Lindsey headed over with a clear evidence bag.

George watched as a young lass headed over and started snapping photos of whatever they'd found. It took a while, and

George found that since the accident, his patience wore thin much easier than before, but eventually, Lindsey beckoned the two detectives over.

Wood asked, "What did you find?"

"A bloodied, metal baseball bat," Lindsey Yardley explained. "Looks as if somebody was in a hurry."

"Murder weapon?" George asked.

"Most likely, but Dr Ross will clarify for you tomorrow. The PM's at eight, right?"

George nodded.

"I've got something else, boss," Wyatt said, shining his torch towards them. Unfortunately, the bright lights they'd erected only covered half the garden, and Wyatt was knelt down at the back of the garden next to the hedgerow. "Looks like a handbag."

Again, George didn't move, which Lindsey welcomed with a grin. He'd have to wait. To be patient. But the incessant clicking of the CSI photographer made him feel as if a woodpecker was tapping at his brain.

Ten minutes later, Lindsey returned with three plastic evidence bags. She handed the smaller one to George, which had a plastic card inside. He scrutinised it. It wasn't an ID that he recognised.

"George."

It wasn't a driver's licence or provisional. Not even a blood donor card.

"George."

He kept turning it over and over in his hands, blinking fast at the lights that tried to blind him.

"George!"

He turned to Wood. "Sorry."

"Looks like a school-issued bus pass," Isabella explained, taking the bag from him. She wiped the drops of rain from the plastic with a swipe of her hand and showed it to George. "Are you OK?"

"Eyes are hurting."

"And that's it?" she questioned, her eyes furrowed. She knew George regularly lied about the pain he was in. It made her wonder what else he had lied about.

"Yep. Who does the bus pass belong to?" George asked.

"We need to speak to Martha Lickiss," she replied.

"Who does the bus pass belong to?" George asked again.

"Martha's daughter, Hope."

* * *

Jean Lickiss' damp hair hung long and limp over her shoulders. Through dark-framed spectacles, Jean's eyes followed George as he entered the room. A woman stood beside Jean's armchair.

"I'm Jean's partner, Taylor Corbyn," the woman who let them in said. "Please take a seat."

"Thanks," George said, sitting on the sofa.

He introduced himself and Wood, who said, "We've assigned a family liaison officer, Jean. She's called Cathy Hoskins and will be here soon. Meanwhile, are you OK to have a chat with us?"

Jean sat forward on the armchair, picked up a steaming mug of tea with shaking hands, and sat back. She nodded.

George noticed there were plasters wrapped around her delicate fingers. He said nothing, inviting Jean to speak. Instead, he looked around the modest living room. It was neat and tidy and smelled as if it had been recently hoovered with some of that powder Isabella liked to use.

"Yes," Jean eventually said.

"Thank you," George said.

Wood added, "We know you've had an awful shock, but speaking to us now could mean the difference between finding the culprit and not. OK?"

"OK."

"When was the last time you saw Hope Lickiss?" George asked, sitting forward.

Jean frowned as if not entirely understanding the question. "Hope?"

George nodded.

"Tea time, why?"

"And Faith?"

"I don't see Faith that much."

"What about Martha?"

"Was that… was that not her lying on the kitchen floor?"

George shook his head. "I'm sorry to tell you that Martha is missing and that we think the body you saw was that of Hope Lickiss'."

"Oh my God!" Jean gasped. "Hope? What?"

Taylor gripped Jean's shoulder.

"She was so young. Who would do such a thing?"

"I'm sorry, but we don't know yet," George said. "What did you see at the house?"

"Well, now I don't really know," Jean said as tears slipped down her cheeks. She had to remove her glasses, such was the extent of the tears, and clean them with her blouse.

"I really think we should do this tomorrow, officer," Taylor said.

"It's detective, and we need all the information now so we

can act upon it."

"But she already spoke with one of yours. Candy, was it?"

"Correct, but I want to hear the information directly from Jean."

"It may seem insensitive," Wood explained, "but DI Beaumont is right."

"Where's Martha?" Jean asked.

"We have people out looking for her," Wood explained. "Do you have any idea where she might be?"

Jean shook her head.

"So tell me what you know," George said.

"I don't know anything, honestly."

"We just need your help in establishing what happened," Wood explained.

Jean looked at Wood, eyes wide. "I already said I don't know anything."

"Tell me about today," said George. "Start at the beginning."

"Can we do this tomorrow, Detective Inspector?" Taylor asked, enunciating George's rank.

George directed his answer to Jean. "We can, but I'd prefer to do this now. I need to find out what happened to your sister-in-law and your niece. I'm sure you want the same."

"You may remember something you think is inconsequential, but it may, in fact, help us," said Wood. "Let us decide what's important and what's not, OK?"

"OK." Jean took a deep breath and then spoke hastily. "I finished work at five, came home and found Hope here. I cooked her tea. She went home. She was acting weird, and it kept bugging me, so after I cooked tea for Taylor and me, I decided to go and see Martha. But, as I headed for the farm, I decided it would probably be best to speak with Hope first, so I went to Nikki's to see if she was there, but she wasn't."

"Nikki, who?" asked Wood.

"Nikki Malin. Hope's best friend."

Wood nodded and made a note.

"What do you mean by she was acting weird?" asked George.

"Hope is…" She grimaced. "Was a lovely, bubbly girl. Tonight, she was quiet, withdrawn."

George turned to Taylor. "How did she seem to you?"

"I wasn't here, Detective. I was out."

"Where?"

"Is that really any of your business?"

"I'm running a murder investigation, so yes."

When Taylor said nothing, George stood. "Look, we can do this here, or I can take you both down to the station. Out of respect for what you've dealt with tonight, Jean, I decided to visit you in person so you could be in the comfort of your home. However, I can easily do this back at Elland Road. It's your choice."

George looked from one woman to the other.

Wood said nothing. She'd noticed since the accident that he'd been brusquer with people. She wondered whether it was permanent or just a lingering side effect.

"Fine, I was at the gym, OK? They have CCTV, and I scan my card in and out."

"Which gym?" asked George.

Wood's pen was poised, and she started writing as Taylor said, "Council one at the leisure centre."

"What time did you leave?" asked George.

"After Hope had left."

"What time was that?"

"I don't know, you'd have to check with the gym," said Taylor.

"Don't worry; we will." George then turned to Jean. "What time did Taylor come home?"

"I don't remember," she said.

George scratched his beard. His hand instinctively went to the scar on his skull, but he pulled it back. Instead, he rubbed his eyes.

"You look exhausted, Detective Inspector," said Taylor. "Perhaps this is better done tomorrow?"

Ignoring Taylor, he stared at Jean. "What happened after you went to Nikki's?"

"I came home, and Taylor told me to go visit Martha, which I did. I noticed the door was open, and so went inside..." Jean's voice trailed off, and she looked up at George. "Where is she?"

"You tell us," George said.

"I really have no idea. What about Faith?"

"Why aren't you out looking for her instead of sitting here asking my partner stupid questions?" asked Taylor.

Jean hung her head. "Sorry about her. She gets defensive."

"It's perfectly understandable," said Wood before turning to Taylor. "I appreciate you're upset, Taylor, but we need to find Martha and Faith, and we need to find Hope's killer."

When Taylor said nothing, Wood turned and stared at Jean. "I know it's upsetting, but can you tell me what you did when you reached Martha's house?"

Jean nodded and blinked some more tears into existence. She then pulled out a tissue, abruptly sniffed, and rubbed her nose with it.

George furrowed his brows. It felt as if the woman was purposely trying to delay answering the question. "In your own words, I need to know what happened, Jean?"

"I entered the house because the door was open. I shouted Martha's name but got nothing back. So I went into the kitchen, and I saw... I saw..."

"You're doing great, babe," Taylor said, kissing her partner on the top of the head.

"It was horrible," Jean eventually managed. "Seeing a body like that—on the kitchen floor, battered and broken. And now you tell me it was my young, beautiful niece. Who did that to her? Who killed her? And where is Martha?" Tears cascaded down her face.

"Then what happened?" asked George.

Dabbing her face with the tissue, Jean said, "I saw the—the body on the floor like I said. I didn't see anyone else around. It was raining and getting dark. So I got in my car, and I rang 999." The tissue disintegrated into confetti and fluttered down on the crimson carpet.

"Did you go around back?" asked George.

"Are you listening to what I said?" Jean asked, fury painted across her face. "Or are you just here to try and set me up?"

"I'm here for the truth."

"No, I left the house immediately and went to my car. I stayed there until the police arrived."

"And you saw nothing?"

"It was getting dark."

"Did you touch the body at all?" asked George.

"No," Jean shot back. "Why the hell would I?"

"To see if there was a pulse."

All the colour drained from Jean's face. "Are you saying I could have saved Hope?" Jean curled up, arms around her chest, heaving back sobs.

"No, there was nothing you could have done, Jean," George said. "If what you're saying is true, and I have no reason to doubt what you're saying, then you did exactly the right thing by leaving the premises and calling us." He looked at Wood and got up. They'd try and verify both stories using CCTV, private doorbell cameras, and house-to-house enquiries, but it was time to go home. The night shift could start dealing with all that so they could get some rest.

"We do need to take your fingerprints and DNA, though, just to rule you out of the investigation."

Jean's eyes widened to balls of fear. "Why would you need my DNA? I didn't—I didn't do anything."

"It's just procedure," George said. "9 am tomorrow. Elland Road Station. For now, though, I think you need to rest."

"I can't believe you think I'm involved," Jean said through fits of tears.

Leaning over, Taylor Corbyn squeezed her partner's elbow. "That's not what they're saying, babe."

"Taylor's right, Jean," George said. "You were in the house and may have contaminated the scene. This isn't to implicate you. Quite the opposite, in fact. This is my card with my number. Call me tonight if you remember anything else. Otherwise, we will see you tomorrow."

"Fine! Just find Faith and Martha." The woman convulsed into sobs.

At the door, George turned. "Your brother, Geoff, when did you last see him?"

Jean looked up, confusion skittering across her face. "Geoff? Surely you don't think he did this?"

"Not at all. We have to follow up with everyone. Where can we find him?"

Shaking her head, Jean shrugged. "I've no idea where he is. I don't think he's had anywhere permanent to live since Martha kicked him out."

George exchanged a look with Wood, who raised her brow. Clearly, she, too, had caught the tone in which Jean described how Martha had removed Geoff from the farmhouse.

Interesting.

It made him want to interrogate Jean further, but it was getting late, and George needed to sleep.

George handed a card to Taylor, who offered her hand to shake. "As my colleague advised, family liaison officer Cathy Hoskins will be here soon." He quickly shook Taylor's hand and then went to leave, but Taylor followed him to the door.

"I really hope you find Martha before it's too late," Taylor whispered.

George turned and furrowed his brows. "What do you mean?"

Taylor turned to make sure nobody was listening in. "Martha hasn't been well since... you know..."

George said, "I don't know."

"Since that business with Geoff."

"You mean the occupation order?" George wondered where this conversation was going.

"Yes, and the other stuff."

"Miss Corbyn, if you know something, then tell me."

"I don't. I'm sorry. I've said too much already." Taylor Corbyn turned to go back inside.

George went to put a hand on the woman's arm to stall her but stopped himself. Instead, he shouted, "But as far as I'm concerned, you haven't said quite enough. Jean's niece has been murdered, her other niece is missing, her sister-in-law has disappeared, and we have no idea where Geoff Lickiss is. So if you know something we don't, then tell me!"

"No. Sorry. I know nothing."

Wood passed by the pair, but George stood his ground. Taylor went to close the door, and George thought of blocking it with his foot but decided to speak to the pair again tomorrow.

"I think you know an awful lot more than you're letting on."

Taylor shrugged.

"Come to Elland Road with Jean in the morning, Taylor. Maybe your conscience will decide to tell me what you know."

Chapter Four

Exhausted, George and Isabella returned home to Morley. Luke had kindly offered to set up the Incident Room for them so everything would be in place to resume investigations in the morning while searches were ongoing through the night to find Martha Lickiss.

As soon as George's head hit the pillow, he began snoring, but Isabella lay there, staring at the ceiling. Her brain wouldn't switch off. So where was Martha and Faith Lickiss, and who had murdered Hope Lickiss?

Nothing made any sense.

Hopefully, Lindsey Yardley and her SOC team would find something for them to go on, but their first priority was locating Martha Lickiss and her ex-husband, Geoff. Then they might have a better idea of what had happened in that house.

She got up to empty her bladder again and returned to George struggling to breathe, his leg twitching, covered with sweat and fighting with the duvet. Isabella slowly moved towards him, pulled the duvet down, and ran a gentle hand through his blond locks. They were far too long for her liking, but she understood why he'd grown the hair out. They'd obviously shaved part of his head so they could operate. That bald patch, plus the scar, was something George struggled with daily.

CHAPTER FOUR

The alarm clock showed 3.55 am. Counting sheep, Isabella willed sleep into her brain. No use.

She sat up.

Or she sat up the best she could, anyway, and pulled out her mobile. She was reading a pretty decent crime thriller on the Kindle app set in Scotland about a killer called 'Mister Whisper'.

Half an hour later, she was fast asleep.

Outside, somebody watched the house.

They'd seen the light go on in an upstairs bedroom and a shadow move around behind the blinds.

And then the light had gone off.

They were about to leave when a dimmer light appeared.

Despite the early morning hour, it was practically the same routine as the last four months.

So they then made a phone call.

Like they had done every night for the last four months.

When they were satisfied, they switched on the engine and drove away.

* * *

Something woke George up, though he didn't know what.

He lay in the dark, listening.

He'd dreamt of falling again. Was it just that?

All he could hear was the thumping of his heart in his chest and Isabella's gentle breathing beside him.

Then George heard a low growl from below.

Rex. Their Jack Russell Terrier.

George remembered when they'd spoken about getting a therapy dog for him. He'd not long been home from the hospital and had researched online.

"I'm struggling, OK?" George shook his head and looked down. "Is that what you want to hear?"

Isabella said, "You know it's not."

"Do I?"

"George, don't—"

"Don't what? Tell the truth? I'm broken, Isabella. The accident changed me. And you're as aware as I am how broken I am now!"

She shook her head and, with tears in her eyes, threw her arms around him.

"But despite being broken, I want to return to work eventually."

"It's too soon now."

"Hence why I said eventually." George grimaced. Isabella was probably right. In fact, he knew deep down she was right.

Even now, three months on from the conversation, all he'd really done over the last few months was take some uneventful trips to the supermarket. Asda or Morrisons. That was it. In three months. He hadn't even ventured to the White Rose Centre. He felt pathetic.

"I'm going to speak to Jon," George had explained. That day was counselling day, and whilst he hated the sessions, he did like Jon, the counsellor. He'd trained as a psychologist and so helped George prepare for his meetings with the police psychologist he was forced to also visit.

"What about?"

"Returning to work." He shrugged. "I can go back one day a week. Then two days. Build up. Christ, I'll even do fucking office work if it means I can get out of here."

"Is being here so bad?"

"That's not what I meant."

"So what do you mean?"

George lightly fingered his scar and closed his eyes. "I need to get out."

"I know you do. It's why I agreed with Jon and the consultant at the hospital."

"So you think we should go see him?"

She nodded.

"But what about the baby?" he asked.

"They'll grow up together. Be best friends. It'll be great."

And it had been great—one of the best decisions they'd ever made. Rex had got George walking again and helped him strengthen muscles he'd never even realised had atrophied.

And the positive effect it had on his mental health had been incredible.

Rex howled again. Clearly, it wasn't just George's imagination; he had definitely heard something.

Slipping out of bed, he grabbed the nearest thing he could find to use as a weapon, which happened to be Isabella's curling wand, and opened the bedroom door.

"Are you OK, George?" Isabella murmured.

"Fine," he whispered, hoping that was the case.

She watched him amble out of the bedroom and heard him tiptoe along the landing. She sat up and listened, her own heart thumping in her chest.

Rex was in the kitchen, emitting a low howl.

George quietly descended the stairs, holding the wand tight and high, clenching his fist, ready to swing it down if necessary, and stood in the hallway listening without turning on any of the lights.

Other than Rex's howling; the house was quiet. What could the pup hear that George couldn't?

The DI crept down the hallway and into the kitchen, where

Rex was wide awake in his crate. "Are you OK, boy?" George unlocked the door, but Rex stayed where he was.

Rex was alert, arched low, his eyes fixed upon the backdoor.

Was somebody outside in the back garden?

No, George could hear nothing—

A gentle rustle, like something or someone, was sneaking around outside.

Pulse racing, George peered through the glass, looking for shadows, but the garden was covered only with darkness. And he could see no movement. He couldn't hear anything, either.

After a few minutes, Rex relaxed. Instead of howling, he jumped up and licked George's knee, happy at the impromptu late-night visit.

Clearly, whatever it was had gone.

Still exhausted from the late-night visit to Rothwell, George considered going back to bed but knew his hammering heart wouldn't allow him to nod off.

So instead, he made a cup of tea and sat at the kitchen counter drinking it in the dark; Rex sat on the floor by his feet, nagging on a slice of cheese.

George wondered who it was who'd been outside. Was it Geoff Lickiss? Jürgen Schmidt or one of his lackeys? Or was it Mia?

Since finding out about the engagement and the pregnancy, Mia had made life difficult for George. Whenever he wanted to see Jack, she'd make excuses so that George couldn't see his son.

It had gotten so bad at one point that Isabella had driven George to the house in East Ardsley out of the blue, meaning Mia would have no excuse and deny him access.

Despite that, she still kicked off, not wanting Isabella in the house. In one way, he understood. Whenever Mia eventually moved on and found somebody else, Jack would have another male father figure in his life. George hated the thought. It wasn't jealousy but something else. And clearly, Mia felt the same about Isabella.

But regardless of how Mia felt about Isabella, she was part of Jack's life and always would be.

As for Schmidt, he'd received a postcard after returning from the hospital that read: You're a dead man, Beaumont.

As a detective, he'd made many enemies, but he knew Schmidt had sent the threatening postcard. He just knew.

Once his heart had slowed down and he could think straight, George laughed at the situation. It was probably just a cat on the prowl that had got Rex's hackles up.

But then, he'd never acted that way before. And he knew for sure cats had been in the back garden because he'd regularly had to pick their shit up.

But if the intruder was human, how had they got into the garden? It was fenced in on all sides.

Yes, it was a detached house, but the neighbouring houses to the left and the right were in extremely close proximity.

Maybe they'd left a footprint or something. It was too dark to see now, so he'd take a look after work tomorrow.

"Goodnight, Rex," George muttered, pointing towards the crate.

The pup trotted inside and plopped himself on his bed, and looked at George, who scratched him under the chin.

"You're such a good boy, Rex." There was no more noise, and Rex seemed calm.

Everything was back to normal.

Chapter Five

"You're late," DCI Alistair Atkinson's monotone voice echoed down the hallway.

It wasn't what DI Beaumont needed to improve his mood. It was only five past nine, not that Beaumont made the point aloud. He desperately wanted to, though.

"Sorry for being woken up in the late hours to attend a crime scene in Rothwell, sir," he said instead, clenching his jaw to stop anything else coming out that he might regret.

DCI Atkinson usually stuck to his office, but with the Jürgen Schmidt case hotting up again, he'd started to appear far more regularly than George liked. In fact, since his phased return started, Atkinson had spoken with George daily, something George really didn't enjoy.

The two men had got on well initially, but his handling of the Freya Bentley case, or the 'Book Club Killer' as the press had lauded her, meant George had stopped trusting his superior.

It didn't help that the DCI had taken point on the Schmidt case ever since it had escalated with the drugs bust earlier that year. Though Beaumont couldn't blame him, not when the man had both DSU Jim Smith and DCS Sadiq breathing down his neck. But that meant the DCI put pressure on HMET, the Homicide and Major Enquiry Team George served on. Plus, shite always rolled downhill. DCI Atkinson would be first... then DI Beaumont would be next.

Luke had taken him to one side during the Freya Bentley case, asking him if he disliked the DCI because George had wanted the job. And whilst he understood his old mentor's opinions, they were wrong. George simply disliked the DCI because he was a prick, and he tried to stop him and Wood working together.

"An update came in overnight." Atkinson fell into an amble beside Beaumont, the older DCI a head taller and a man narrower by comparison.

George headed for the kitchen, noting the empty mug in Atkinson's right hand. He probably shouldn't have been sarcastic with his boss earlier and considered making Atkinson a brew. "Go on?"

"And DC Scott and DC Blackburn are on their way back from the post-mortem," Atkinson advised.

Shit.

He'd forgotten all about it.

"If you need more time off, George, all you have to do is ask. I personally think you've come back too soon."

"I'm fine, Alistair, but thank you for your concern. We didn't get in until late, as I said before."

"Suit yourself," the DCI replied with a shrug. "Anyway, customs' found another lorry potentially linked to Schmidt."

"How? Where?" George's full attention was now on the DCI.

DCI Atkinson pushed open the kitchen door and crossed to the kettle. "Hull."

As George followed Atkinson in, the smell of takeaway from the night shift assaulted his nostrils. He knew for a fact the culprit would have been DS Luke Mason. He could eat whatever he wanted, whenever he wanted, without any fear of his wife, whilst working the night shift. He made a mental note to wind the older DS up when he next saw him.

The DI grabbed a mug from the cupboard to begin preparing his own brew, then winced as a pain shot through his shoulder.

DCI Atkinson looked at him, his brow raised. George knew his superior would love nothing more than to send George home, having advocated for him to have more sick leave. So, George said nothing, hoping the DCI would elaborate on Schmidt.

"Schmidt's getting craftier by the day, George, so for all we know, this shipment could be a decoy." Atkinson's mouth pursed. Apparently, Atkinson was as cool as a cucumber, a complete contradiction to George with his fiery temperament. But even George could see Atkinson's displeasure at Schmidt's constant evasion of the law. "It could also be something he shouldn't be importing into the country, something we could use against him."

The kettle bubbled and rattled before clicking off, and Alistair popped a PG Tips into his mug before adding boiling water.

George needed something more robust. Something bitter. So scooped a large spoon of Columbian into his mug and added a dash of cold water to it before, with a shaking hand, pouring hot water into his cup.

"We've arrested somebody on the take in Hull. Benny Ludlum."

George raised both his brows. "Excellent."

"Yeah, whilst you've been off, I've managed to get security measures tightened in Hull, which is why we caught him."

Obviously, the DCI wanted a smack on the back. Or a medal.

CHAPTER FIVE

George wasn't going to give him anything.

"We're now looking at CMRs to see where the road haulage companies are taking the goods, who send them, and who they were sent to."

"I suggest you tread carefully, sir," George warned. "If we know, then Schmidt does."

During his sick leave, especially towards the end when he felt better, George had spent a lot of time looking through the paperwork Isabella had brought for him. She shouldn't have done it and would have been sacked if anybody found out, but he needed to get his mind working again. All the paperwork did, however, was convince him Schmidt had somebody working at HMET.

The DCI nodded whilst extracting the teabag from his mug. George watched him pour in three sugars and a precarious amount of milk, turning the dark water lily white. The colour of the tea made George shudder, and he made a mental note never to allow the DCI to make him a cuppa.

"If we get anything else, I'll obviously keep you in the loop, George."

"Thank you, sir. Any idea what Schmidt is shipping in?"

"We think he's working with a guy from Scunthorpe. A Russian. They're using shell companies as expected."

"So what's the plan?"

"I'm preparing a team to intercept the lorry."

"I want in."

The DCI took a sip of his tea, then continued, "I'll be directing the interception in Hull docks. DC Reza Malik is ready to liaise with Customs, Humberside Police's Major Investigation Team, and their uniforms. DC Sutcliffe is supporting him."

George knew Jack Sutcliffe very well. More than most, truth

be told. And whilst George liked Jack, not many other people did. Sutcliffe was a forty-year-old, embittered, twice-married detective who smoked and drank way too much. "When's the lorry coming?"

Atkinson scowled. "We're not sure."

"So, interrogate Ludlum."

"We are."

"Want me to take a crack at him?"

"No." The DCI drained his tea, which was clearly only lukewarm from the copious amount of milk he added, then said, "Ludlum says it'll be here within the next week and that he just doesn't know when."

George's shoulders sank. Needle in a haystack sprung to mind. It wasn't good news. "Can't you set up some ANPR cameras around Hull so you can track it?"

"Already thought of that. Sutcliffe is in Hull as we speak."

Atkinson turned on his heel and headed towards the kitchen door.

George asked, "Has anything come in overnight about the Lickiss case?"

But Atkinson was already gone, the back of his grey suit jacket flapping as the door swung closed behind him.

The DCI was probably heading to Smith's office to tell him how George had already fucked up that morning. "Bollocks." He took a deep breath, pulled out his phone and rang Tashan.

When Tashan didn't answer, he called Jay.

"Morning, boss, you OK?"

"Fine, Jay. Where are you?"

"Tashan's just parking up in the car park, boss."

"OK, come straight to the Incident Room and brief me on the post-mortem."

CHAPTER FIVE

* * *

Tashan and Jay stood up at the front of the Incident Room and talked through what they'd witnessed during the post mortem.

Two hours ago

The rain that had fallen last night had evaporated from the scorching August sun that battered Leeds that morning. Tashan pulled the squad car into the St James' Hospital car park before both detectives got out and headed into the labyrinth.

Luckily, they knew where to go, so they headed down the muggy corridors to where pathology was located.

They were buzzed in, and the smell of antiseptic assaulted their noses. It was better than the pungent scent of death, though.

Dr Christian Ross had already started the post-mortem when the junior detectives arrived and was walking around the steel table that held the fifteen-year-old body of Hope Lickiss.

Without looking up, Christian said, "Good morning, Detective Inspector." The pathologist's voice was sharp and professional. "I'll continue if you don't mind."

"Go ahead," Jay said, suiting up and settling on a high stool beside a stainless-steel counter. Tashan did the same, nodding to the pathologist when he looked up, noticing the voice wasn't that of George Beaumont.

"Hello, lads, George, not coming?"

"No, Doc," Jay said. "The DCI sent us two."

The elderly pathologist nodded and continued with his work whilst the two young detectives watched the efficient team in awe.

After about half an hour, Jay was starting to feel impatient, so he asked, "Cause of death, Doc?"

"It's clearly murder, Jay," Tashan added.

Jay grinned but raised his brows at the pathologist.

Christian Ross turned and stared. "I'm not finished yet, son. If you need to get off, then get off, I can email your boss my findings." The pathologist turned back and continued his examination.

"DI Beaumont said something about blunt-force trauma?" Tashan offered. "That's what he advised you said last night."

With a sigh, Christian walked over. "That's correct, lads." He shook his head. "I understand how busy you all are, but this cannot be rushed. As it stands, I've prioritised Miss Lickiss' PM so that your boss had something to work with."

"And we're so appreciative, Doc," said Jay, "but we need to be out there, investigating. And so far, we got nothing—"

"Cause of death will most likely be blunt-force trauma to the head, OK. Satisfied?"

"Thank you, Doc," said Jay. "Any idea what type of weapon was used?"

"As I surmised to George last night, something hard and rounded. Whatever it was, it was applied with great force. One strike to the head. Multiple to other parts of the body. In fact, the bruising suggests a frenzied attack. I currently don't know what killed her, but I will know later."

"Could it be the metal baseball bat CSI found at the scene?"

Dr Ross stared. "Could be, yes. I assume it's with the lab?" the pathologist asked, and Jay and Tashan both nodded. "Then once they know, you'll know."

"Thank you," Jay said and made for the door. "One last thing. Any signs of sexual assault?" He was thinking about Geoff Lickiss, who was currently their prime suspect.

"I'll take swabs, but it's hard to tell because of the bruising.

CHAPTER FIVE

DI Beaumont will have my preliminary report this afternoon."

With a final glance at the young Hope Lickiss, Tashan rushed from the autopsy room. His little sister was fifteen, and seeing that young woman on the slab affected him more than he thought possible.

* * *

"So we don't really know anything from the PM yet," said George.

"That's right, boss, sorry," said Jay.

The DI looked at the death-mask photograph of Hope Lickiss, a social media picture of Faith Lickiss, and an image from the DVLA of the missing Martha Lickiss, then turned to Isabella. "Any update on door-to-door?" He'd asked her to liaise with PS Greenwood and his uniforms.

"It happened quite late, and only seven houses are near the farmhouse. No CCTV, no doorbell cams, no nothing."

"Shite. Any results back from the lab yet?"

"Be later today at least," Wood said. "Lindsey and her team are still on site this morning, though. They think they've figured out how the intruder entered and exited the grounds."

"Go on."

There was a knock on the door, and DS Yolanda Williams entered. "Sorry I'm late, sir, but the DCI wanted me to print these off."

George smiled at the plucky detective sergeant, who had recently got engaged to her girlfriend, and nodded for her to pin them to the board. They were of the Lickiss farm kitchen.

"Lindsey's team found tracks through the hedgerows in the back garden. The rain softened the ground just enough last night to create prints which they took casts of last night. This morning's intense sun has also hardened the ground, so the route is quite clear. She's going to send some photos in soon."

"From first glance, are we looking at a male or female?"

"Size seven, so it could be any gender," she explained.

Jay pointed at the kitchen. "Proper mess is that, boss. It looks like a right fight happened."

George nodded. "It was worse in real-life, Jay." He pointed to Hope. "Any theories?"

Jay said, "Mother and daughter had a row. Mother battered her daughter to death and fled."

"OK, what about Faith?"

Jay grimaced, then shrugged. "Out with friends?"

George considered it but moved on. "Anything else?"

Tashan looked up from his notes. "I think it's Geoff Lickiss. Probably a case of mistaken identity. When he realised he'd killed his daughter, he fled."

"Interesting." George turned to Wood. "Did CSI find Hope's phone?"

Wood shook her head. "Luke's ordered Hope's, Faith's, and Martha's phone records. Geoff's too. We have Hope's aunt, Jean Lickiss, and her partner, Taylor Corbyn, coming in soon, too. I'll ask them if we can look through their phones."

"Good; anything else?"

Tashan explained, "Luke's report suggests they still haven't found Geoff yet, nor has his reg pinged any ANPR cameras. We don't have an address for him, either. He thinks we should put out an appeal."

"I think an appeal is necessary," George said. "Local and national press. Put out his mugshot." George scratched his beard, and then his fingers reached for his skull, but he managed to stop himself in time. "I'll speak with the DCI and see if he wants to lead a press conference, too."

"What did Lickiss and Corbyn have to say last night, boss?" asked Jay.

"They didn't give us much to tell you the truth, Jay," Wood said. "You can come in with me and take statements when they arrive."

George nodded at his team. "FLO Cathy Hoskins is with them." He turned and looked Jay in the eyes. "Taylor Corbyn said something about how Martha hasn't been well recently, but she wouldn't elaborate. I want you to push her, OK?"

"OK, boss."

The door to the incident room burst open, and the tall, lanky DCI entered. "Go ahead, Detective Inspector Beaumont. Don't let me interrupt you." He leaned against the wall and folded his arms across his narrow torso.

"Thank you, sir," George said, trying to remember what he wanted to talk about next. All eyes were on George, and he started sweating.

Atkinson narrowed his eyes, then pointed at the pictures of the kitchen. "Looks like a domestic to me."

"Those pictures don't tell the full story," said George, who immediately winced. He needed to be a role model for his team, and even though the DCI didn't really deserve George's respect, it was irrelevant. "It was much worse at the scene, sir."

The DCI nodded.

"Until forensics are complete, we're not in a position to speculate, sir," he said. "Dr Ross is still finishing the post-mortem as we speak but confirmed that blunt-force trauma to the head is the most likely contributor to Miss Lickiss' death."

Unfolding his arms and marching through the room towards

George, the DCI asked, "Blunt-force trauma? With what?"

"CSI found a potential weapon outside in the garden, sir." George pointed to a grainy night-time photograph that showed nothing. "It's being forensically examined at Calder Park."

"Is that a baseball bat?"

George nodded.

"Who owns one of those these days?"

George knew of one man who kept a baseball bat by his front door but said nothing. "We haven't determined who owned the bat yet, sir."

"Where's Martha Lickiss?"

"We don't know."

"And Geoff Lickiss?"

George shook his head.

"So you currently have nothing?"

"We're working flat out, sir."

"Clearly not flat out enough, DI Beaumont." The DCI stepped towards the Big Board and looked at the photo of Hope Lickiss. "I have a fifteen-year-old daughter myself." He turned to the room. "One of the parents has just lost their daughter, and the other was probably the one who murdered her. I can't imagine how that must feel."

"We're doing everything we can."

"Well, do more, OK. I want both parents found and in cells before the day is out, OK?"

George nodded.

The DCI turned and eyed the team. "Is that clear?"

A round of "Yes, sir," rang out around the room.

"Good, now get back to work!" With a smug grin, he straightened his narrow shoulders and marched out of the door.

"Prick," George said under his breath.

Jay grinned, and George narrowed his eyes at the young DC. "My thoughts exactly, boss."

George's mobile rang. He looked down at the screen to find an internal number. "DI Beaumont."

It was the desk sergeant.

"A Jean Lickiss and a Taylor Corbyn are waiting for you, sir. I've placed them in separate interview rooms. They've been there for nearly half an hour. Did you forget about them?"

Were they early? He looked down at his watch, only then remembering he didn't wear one any more, so he pulled his mobile away from his ear. Shit. The time had run away with them. "Sorry, Sarge, we'll be down in a minute."

George explained the call to his team, and they all filed out of the incident room and into the shared office space. "DS Wood and DS Scott, are you both ready?"

The two detectives nodded and followed George downstairs.

He wasn't going to be part of the interviews, so he sat in a separate room, watching via a live feed.

Chapter Six

"I'm so sorry for keeping you, Miss Corbyn," DS Wood said as she pulled out a chair and sat facing a stern-faced Taylor Corbyn. She looked different to last night, with hastily applied foundation and jagged eyebrows pencilled in. "This morning has been hectic."

Jay nodded at the woman as he sat down.

The older woman, who appeared to be in her late forties, folded her arms across her chest. "I'm really not happy, Detective. We've been here for over half an hour already. I've got places to be and stuff to do!"

Taylor's short hair was starting to grey at the ends. She ran a manicured hand through them, though the manicure needed refreshing. The paint was chipped and scratched.

"As I said, I'm very sorry for keeping you, but please understand we're at the beginning of a murder investigation which is a bit chaotic."

With her professional smile in place, Wood switched on the recording equipment and then introduced herself for the tape. Jay did likewise. Then he asked Taylor to identify herself for the recording.

"Why the hell am I being recorded?" Taylor nodded toward the machine. "I'm not a suspect, am I? You said I wasn't last night." She gestured rapidly with her hands as she spoke. "Do I need a solicitor? I only came in because you asked me."

"Usual procedure, that's all." Wood didn't like the look on Taylor's face. "Please identify yourself for the recording, and then tell me what you know about Martha Lickiss."

"Taylor Corbyn," she said, folding her arms across her chest again, "and there's not much to tell."

Wood eyed Jay from the corner of her eye. It was going to be one of those interviews where they had to extract a statement word by word.

"Not much to tell? That means there's something," said Jay. "So tell us." Taylor was about to speak when Jay added. "I specifically want to know what you meant when you told my boss you didn't think Martha had been too well."

"You know," Taylor said and pointed to her temple. "Up here."

"What does that gesture mean?" asked Jay. He knew exactly what she meant but wanted his revenge.

Taylor sighed and shook her head. "Since kicking Geoff out, she hasn't been the same. Jean's noticed prescription painkillers and anti-depressants lying around the kitchen when she's been there, too. Plus, Hope was spending more and more time with us."

Wood noticed she didn't wince at the dead girl's name. She wondered why.

"I know for a fact she's on benefits. And PIP, too, because of her mental health."

"How do you know that?" Wood asked.

"Jean saw a bank statement with money going in. It said DWP and PIP. I'm sure that's what she said."

"Mental illness is a legitimate disability, so what's the

problem?" Jay asked.

Taylor held up her hands defensively. "I didn't say I had a problem. Martha is the one with the problem."

"Did Hope ever mention it to you?"

"She didn't like that Geoff was kicked out. Hope was always a daddy's girl."

"You keep saying Geoff was kicked out, but the courts decided that," Wood explained.

"Yes, I know that."

"So why do you keep saying Martha kicked him out?" Wood asked.

"Because he did nothing wrong."

"I've read the files, and there's evidence there that Geoff beat Martha black and blue," said Jay.

"Well, I never saw the bruises with my own eyes."

"So what are you suggesting?" asked Jay.

"That Martha Lickiss is a liar!"

Jay frowned. The night Martha Lickiss'd had enough and called the police, a uniformed officer had attended the farmhouse to find her curled up in a ball beside the oven, beaten black and blue. She never changed her story, though Geoff denied it, of course. Finally, he said, "What evidence do you have that suggests she's a liar?"

"Just the stuff Hope told me."

"What kind of stuff?" asked Wood.

"That Martha would gaslight Geoff. Manipulate him into losing his temper. That kind of stuff."

They could only take Taylor's word at face value because Hope wasn't alive to confirm or deny Taylor's claims. They could speak with Geoff if they found him, of course, but he probably would say anything to get back at his ex-wife.

CHAPTER SIX

Jay asked, "What does Jean think of all this?"

"You'll have to ask her."

"I'm asking you," said Jay.

"Jean's one of those old-fashioned people who believed in 'for better, for worse, and in sickness and in health'. You married once and stayed that way." Taylor shrugged. "She doesn't believe in divorce."

"Even when the worse was so bad you had to go to court to get your husband out?" asked Wood.

"It's not my place. You'll have to ask Jean."

"We will," said Jay. "Can you recall any domestic violence in the Lickiss farmhouse?"

"Nope."

"Did Hope ever share any stories of any domestic violence?"

"Nope. As far as Hope was concerned, her dad was a lovely dad and a lovely husband."

"How did Hope feel about Martha?"

"That's not my place to say, either."

"Anything you say is confidential," explained Wood.

"Whatever. I know how you guys roll. It'll end up online or in a paper. Or on a TV show on Amazon Prime one day."

"You're here to help us, Miss Corbyn, and we need to find Faith and Martha," he said. "Whether she's a suspect or a victim, something you say may help us locate her."

With another sigh, Taylor said, "I think Martha used to beat Hope and Faith."

Wood exchanged a glance with Jay. "Why do you say that?" she asked.

"It's just something Hope told Jean once. It was terrible how the courts treated her dad when Geoff was like a puppy compared to Martha."

"And that's all?"

"What do you mean, is that all? Ask Jean, and she'll confirm it."

"Can anybody else confirm it?"

"Other than Geoff?" Taylor asked, and both detectives nodded. "Probably not. But after what happened last night, I think I can believe it."

"You think Martha attacked her daughter and left her dead on the kitchen floor?" Jay asked.

"From where I'm sitting, it seems like it."

"What about Faith?"

Taylor shrugged. "She fled with Martha."

"You don't think Geoff attacked Hope and abducted Martha and Faith?" Jay asked.

"No, that's ridiculous." Then it dawned on her. "Is that what you think?"

"We're investigating many lines of investigation at the moment, and it's not something we can share with you."

"Typical police explanation, eh?" Taylor taunted.

"Is there anything else you'd like to add?" Wood asked.

"No. I want to go home." Taylor Corbyn stood up.

"Of course," Wood said, standing up. "But I'd like you to stay where you are so I can get forensics in here to take DNA and prints from you." When Taylor's cheeks flared red, Wood explained, "To exclude you from the investigation, remember?"

* * *

Guns N' Roses blared from George's pocket, and he pulled it out, his eye on Taylor Corbyn as she left the interview room, followed by Jay, who escorted her back to reception.

DS Wood and DC Scott were supposed to interview Jean Lickiss, next, but the person on the other end of the phone changed all that.

It was DS Williams. "Sir, we have an address for Geoff Lickiss. He's been staying at a Bed and Breakfast in Carlton. I spoke with the landlady. He's there at the moment."

"Thank you, Yolanda. Wood and I'll go and have a word with him. Can you interview Jean Lickiss with Jay, please?"

"Of course, sir. Is there anything you need me to concentrate on?"

"I'll get Wood to pass the notes and focus to Jay, so you two can have a strategy meeting before interviewing her."

"She's not going to like that, sir. She's been here for over an hour already."

"It's tough, Detective Sergeant," George said.

Wood entered the room where George was, and he explained what Yolanda told him.

"It's unlikely he had anything to do with the attack," she said.

"Why not?"

"If he did it, surely he'd be long gone by now."

George considered that for a moment, then shrugged. "True, but he could also think he got away with it. It wouldn't be the first time a killer hid in plain sight."

"I guess the least we can do is check where he was last night," Wood said.

George nodded. "Aye, and then we can look at means, motive and opportunity."

Chapter Seven

Geoff Lickiss was on his bed, headphones on, screaming at somebody through the microphone. "He's to your left, you fucking dickhead!"

"No, not that left; the other left."

"Oh, for fuck's sake! Do I have to do everything by myself?"

Geoff was so ingrained in the video game he was playing that he didn't notice the two people standing before him.

He pulled off the headphones, scratched the skin on his shaved head, and said, "How the hell did you get in here? And what do you want?"

"Mr Lickiss? Geoff Lickiss?" said the beautiful brunette woman with cascading curls.

He looked down at her swelling stomach and then at the ring on her left hand.

Somebody had done well.

Unlike him, anyway, who had married a fucking psycho.

Though at least he had his twins.

"Who's asking?" He placed the controller on the bed and stood up.

"Detective Inspector George Beaumont," the man said. He had long blond hair and a scruffy beard. He was bent over as if he had a constant bend in his spine. The detective did not

CHAPTER SEVEN

offer Geoff his hand to shake.

Which Geoff thought was rude. Men always offered to shake. And the women were at it recently, too.

"I'm Detective Sergeant Wood," said the beautiful brunette.

He liked the sound of her voice. And the curve of her breasts through her blouse. In his early fifties, she was far too young for him. Then again, age was just a number.

"How the fuck did you get in?"

"Your landlady. Nice place," the detective inspector said.

It really was a nice place.

George had always wanted to live in the small village of Carlton with its listed buildings and farmhouses.

"What do you want? I haven't done anything."

"Breach of an occupation order Mr Lickiss," the man said.

"What fucking breach? I haven't been to that house since that fucker kicked me out. Ask her!"

"We will," he said. "When was the last time you saw your ex-wife?"

"Why does she want more dosh from me?" Geoff raised his brows. "She's shit outa luck because I'm fucking skint!"

The female detective pointed at the PlayStation 5. "Skint, you say?"

Geoff met her eyes, avoiding the games console. "Aye."

The detective inspector repeated his question. "When was the last time you saw your ex-wife?"

"In court when she got me kicked out of my family home." Geoff said, enunciating the word, 'my', then shrugged. "Ask her!"

The inspector said, "We would if we could find her."

"Well, I'm told she barely leaves the house. Have you tried there?"

The detective inspector nodded. "When was the last time you saw your daughters?"

Geoff narrowed his eyes. "What's this about?"

The DI stepped closer. "Answer the question."

"No, I won't answer the fucking question! Now fuck off before I call a solicitor." Geoff stepped towards the inspector, who also stood his ground.

The female detective said, "It's in your best interests to answer our questions."

"In my best interests, is it?" Geoff shook his head and started to laugh. He clenched his fists and ground his teeth. "Fuck off."

"Why are you so angry, Mr Lickiss?" asked the detective sergeant. The DI took another step into his personal space. One more step, and I'll fucking flatten you, he thought. So the DI got the point, he snarled.

But it didn't have the intended effect. Instead, the inspector grinned, then asked, "Where were you last night between six and eleven?"

"Do I need a solicitor?"

"That's up to you, Geoff," he said. "Have you something to hide?"

Geoff shook his head and then cricked his neck. "You already think I do, so I may as well pretend like I do."

"Then prove to us that you don't," the woman said.

"Otherwise, we'll take you to the station to make a statement," the DI said.

"Is that a threat?"

The tall, broad man stepped closer. "No, it's a promise."

But the detective sergeant, the inspector's junior colleague, grabbed hold of the man's wrist, who then stopped in his tracks. Geoff was sure an inspector was superior to a sergeant, so he wondered what was going on between the two.

"What am I supposed to have done?" Geoff asked.

"You tell us," said the male detective. "Last night, where were you?"

Lickiss sat down, picked up his controller, and switched the games console off. "I was at work until six, got home and showered. The landlady called me down for some tea, which I ate with her, and then I came back upstairs."

"Where do you work, and what did you do when you came back upstairs?" asked the male detective.

"Do I really need to tell you that?" asked Geoff. Pricks were always wanting to know your business.

The woman slowly nodded her head.

"Fine, McDonald's in Hunslet. I got the bus home. And before you ask, I don't have my ticket, and I paid with cash."

The two detectives looked at each other. Were they deciding what to do? Arseholes, Geoff thought and shook his head.

"And after your tea?" the male asked.

"I was playing on the PlayStation, OK?"

"All night?"

"Until I went to sleep, yer."

"Do you have anybody who can vouch for you?" the woman asked.

Geoff shrugged. "Just the people I played online with," he explained.

He saw the pair look at each other again. They looked like they were scheming. Just like his ex-wife used to. Fucking bitch!

"Then we're going to have to take the games console with us," the DI said with a grin.

* * *

Geoff Lickiss was one of the most unpleasant individuals DI George Beaumont had ever met. And, given he dealt with criminals and killers most days, this was really saying something.

Wood agreed. She said, "He's a proper piece of work."

George ended the call with PS Greenwood and looked at his fiancée. "The skinhead and long, mangy beard is fashionable, is it not?"

"Maybe, but the gut sticking out beneath a tight t-shirt is not."

"How did you find the smell?"

Wood shuddered. "I wanted to gip but knew I'd best not." She took in a gulp of air, which tasted like manure. "It's not much better out here."

George nodded. "Carlton always smells like this in the summer."

The pair went to give their thanks to the landlady and ask for Geoff's alibi. Mrs Grantham confirmed Geoff joined her for tea at seven last night, which lasted about thirty minutes, but that didn't even slightly alibi the thug.

DS Wood fired up the Merc, and George placed the PS5 in the boot. Lickiss had kicked the fuck off about losing his console for a few days, and whilst George milked every second of it, that console was the only way they could verify his alibi.

As they headed down Westfield Road, Wood said, "Maybe we should've told him about his dead daughter and his missing wife."

"I think we were right not to," said George. "I want to see what Geoff does next."

CHAPTER SEVEN

PS Greenwood had agreed to spare some of his uniforms to keep an eye out on the Bed and Breakfast.

When they reached Leeds Road, Wood asked, "Do you think Martha killed her own daughter?" referring to what Taylor Corbyn had said earlier.

"I guess all we can do is ask her that when we find her," George said.

* * *

After personally dropping off the PS5 to DS Josh Fry and the tech team back at Elland Road, George and Wood headed to the Lickiss farmhouse in Rothwell.

After suiting and booting up, the pair joined Lindsey Yardley and a couple of members of her SOC team upstairs.

They searched the property at the DCI's request, hoping they could find something to move the case along.

Stepping into the living room, George felt around the wall for a light switch and flicked it on. Weathered curtains were drawn across the large bay window. A two and a three-seater sofa made an L shape, the three-seater against the back wall, the two-seater in front of the bay window. To the left of them was a large TV atop an old, brown unit.

Below them was a flowery deep-pile carpet. Probably an Axminster.

With gloved hands, the pair started looking through the living room cabinets.

"What are we looking for?" Wood asked.

"Dunno," offered George. "But we need something. Anything. And if it's hidden, then it's worthwhile."

CSI had already swept most of the ground floor and was

currently upstairs.

The two detectives joined them. They were searching the bathroom.

When asked about the prescription painkillers and anti-depressants, Lindsey said, "No signs of any prescription medicines, no, but we've found a packet of paracetamol."

George nodded and looked around. There were bottles of shampoo and liquid soaps, razors and shaving gel, hair spray and deodorants—nothing out of the ordinary.

"How many more rooms do you have left to search?" George asked.

Lindsey explained there was only the master bedroom left to search and that Hope's and Faith's rooms didn't provide much. She did explain, though, that they'd taken samples from her hairbrush to match against the corpse. They'd also found what looked like a men's leather jacket on the newel post they'd sent off to the lab for testing.

From the décor of the farmhouse, Mrs Lickiss' bedroom was what Isabella had expected. An old four-poster bed made up with an ancient duvet sat proudly against the feature wall and a painted picture of what looked like a fox hunt hung above it.

George gingerly got down on his knees, scrabbling beneath the double bed. Decades worth of dust assaulted him, and he sneezed, the jerk reaction sending pain down his neck. He heard Wood searching drawers and cabinets as he shone a torch around.

That's how he found a cardboard box—a shoebox, actually. As he dragged it out, another cloud of dust rose up.

Wood pointed to the mattress. "I'll get Lindsey's team to check under that. Neither of us is in any condition to lift it."

She looked at her fiancé to see if she'd insulted him, but he nodded like it was a good idea. Which it was.

"What's in the box?" Wood hovered over George.

George shook it. "Dunno."

"Are you going to open it or bag it?"

George called Lindsey in and asked her to photograph each stage of the unpacking of the shoebox.

Unfortunately for DI Beaumont, she sent in Hayden Wyatt, who was overly excited about the reveal.

Lifting the lid, George peered into the rectangular space that had once, according to the label, once held size seven Sketchers to find a bundle of letters held together with a rubber band.

"Looks like she hadn't touched those in years," Wood said.

"What do you think they are?" asked Wyatt.

"No idea," said George. "Bag, please."

Wyatt produced an evidence bag, within which George placed the letters. "I'll leave it to you, Hayden."

"Not going to have a sneaky look?" the American asked.

"No, we need to get it logged," George said whilst he rooted through the wardrobe. It was filled with dresses, blouses, trousers and coats. He looked at the shoes on the floor, all sized seven. Same size as the prints they'd done casts of outside. He got Hayden to bag them up, too.

No sign of any Sketchers, though.

Wood was searching through a bedside cabinet when George had finished with the wardrobe.

She opened the bottom drawer, which held knickers and thongs. The middle contained socks and tights. When she opened the top drawer, they found the prescription medicine Taylor Corbyn had mentioned—strong painkillers and anti-depressants.

But that wasn't all.

She pulled out a rather long, thick vibrator, which Wood instantly let fall back into the drawer.

Hayden Wyatt started pissing himself laughing, and George couldn't help but grin. But Isabella had turned scarlet.

"I bet we'd get some decent DNA from that," Wyatt joked. Or at least it looked like he was joking. George could never really tell with the Yank.

Both detectives shook their heads and headed back downstairs.

"Time to go back to the station?" Wood asked.

"Yeah, I think we've had enough excitement for one day," George grinned.

Wood turned scarlet once again, but one look at George's face made her laugh. Since the accident, George hadn't cracked as many jokes as he used to.

Chapter Eight

"Remember when we used to come here after work?" asked Isabella.

"The amount of junk food we used to eat whilst working cases was ridiculous," George said with a smile. "I'm getting too old now, though. Every time I eat something from here, I gain a stone."

"You do not," she said.

"How do you explain this, then?" He grabbed his gut and laughed.

"You're just not as conditioned as you used to be," Isabella said with a wink. "A bit of extra weight doesn't look bad on you at all, George."

"Did I tell you how beautiful you are today?" he asked.

"Nope. Nor have you told me how much you love me."

"I'll tell you later."

George and Wood were sat in a booth at the McDonald's in Hunslet, waiting for the manager to come out and speak with them. They apparently weren't allowed to use a backroom for hygiene reasons, but they were only here for an alibi.

The smell of oil and animal fat made his stomach grumble. He did love a burger, and when the fries were fresh, Maccie's were the best.

But they'd both behaved and accepted only a hot beverage instead.

A spotty, squat teenager wearing a McDonald's uniform appeared and slid onto the bench opposite the detectives.

"Hi, I'm Jordan, the manager." He offered his hand, which both George and Wood shook. "How can I help?"

After both detectives introduced themselves and showed their warrant cards, Wood asked, "Do you know Geoff Lickiss?"

"Well yeah, he works here. I thought you knew that. Why are you asking?"

"Just something we're following up on. Was Geoff working yesterday?"

"He was. But he's off today."

"What time did his shift end?"

"Yesterday? Let me think." Then he pulled out his mobile. "Rota's on here." The teenager swiped through until he found what he was looking for. "He started at eight and finished at six."

"Did he leave straight away?"

"I dunno." The young man shrugged. "Sometimes he has a meal before he goes. Why?"

George ground his teeth. The teenager was like a young child, always asking why. "Can you find out for me?"

"Can't you ask him yourself?"

"I'm asking you," said George.

The teenager nodded and struggled to get his girth from out of the padded bench. Eventually, he succeeded, and George watched as he went and spoke with a woman behind the counter bagging up food.

Both came over. "I'm Denise," the woman said. "Gee went

straight home last night. I got on the bus with 'im."

"Gee?"

"Yeh, Gee. Geoff."

"OK, thanks," said George. He turned to the spotty teenager. "I'm going to need a copy of the rota sent to me." He handed over a business card with an email address on it.

"OK."

"I need you to email it across now."

"I need to clear it with the franchisee."

"Why?"

"Because of data protection."

"You've just told me he started at eight and finished at six. I just want proof of that."

"But this has employee names and shifts on it."

"So redact it."

The teenager looked confused.

George rubbed his eyes and ground his teeth. Teenagers were infuriating. "Black out the other data."

"I'll have to do that on the PC in the back."

"Go on then."

* * *

The office was suffering from a mixture of bad moods, the smell of sweat, and the suffocating heat. George's hair was stuck to his scalp when they arrived back at Elland Road. Dampness lined the neck of his shirt, and his trousers were stuck to his legs.

DS Mason was sat in the shared office, a grin on his face. "Now then, son, how ya doing?"

"I'm OK, Luke, and you?"

"Grand."

"Aye, I bet. I could smell what you had for tea last night. I'm guessing the wife doesn't know?" George grinned.

Luke tapped his nose. "Happy wife, happy life, and what the wife doesn't know doesn't hurt her."

"Giving my fiancée marriage advice, DS Mason?" Wood asked, a coy grin on her face.

She was headed towards the kitchen when Luke said. "Oh, I wouldn't dare, Sarge."

Luke stood up and handed over a bundle of what looked like letters. "These are copies of what you found under Martha Lickiss' bed."

George sat down at Wood's desk and flicked through them. They weren't dated, nor were they signed. Anybody could have written them and at any point in time.

He started to read the first one, which appeared to be a love letter. The poetry was clean and sharp. The message short and sweet.

Wood appeared but without any mugs in her hands. George frowned. "PS Greenwood has arrived with Geoff Lickiss."

George nodded, put the letters into a folder, and slipped it into Wood's drawer.

* * *

Geoff Lickiss sat across the table from George and Wood, rolling his tongue around and around in his teeth like he was trying to remove some food that was stuck. He had his arms folded across his chest and his head tilted back so he was peering at the ceiling, clearly wanting to give the impression that he wasn't impressed by being dragged to the station.

"Just to reiterate, Mr Lickiss, you've declined legal representation," Wood said.

"Don't need it, do I? I ain't done anything wrong."

"My growing pile of evidence would beg to differ," George lied.

"I doubt that, or you'd have charged me already," Geoff spat back. The rotund man grinned, exposing his nicotine-stained teeth. "I know how to play the game, detective."

"Given the number of run-ins you've had with the police over the years, it's no great surprise," Wood said.

"Then you'll know I've never been charged with anything."

"Correct, but the PNC shows your colourful history, Geoff," said George. "Your history suggests you're a violent man. Is that right, Geoff?"

"I'm a hard man if that's what you mean."

"If by hard you mean abusing women and children, then yes, you're bang on, Geoff."

"I never fucking touched them."

"That's not what the evidence—"

"I said I never fucking touched them, alright?"

George grinned. "How did you feel when your wife kicked you out?"

Wood asked, "Did it make you angry?"

Geoff licked his lips, unfolded his arms, and met George's eyes but said nothing.

"Oh, I bet it pissed you off," George said. "The Lickiss family farmhouse going to somebody only related by marriage."

"How did the family take it?" Wood added.

"It was none of their fucking business."

Wood said, "But surely, they weren't happy? I did my research, and your family has had it for over two-hundred years."

"I know what you're trying to do," Geoff sneered. "You're trying to get me riled up, so I'll say something incriminating."

"What sized shoe are you?" George asked.

"What the fuck does that have to do with owt?"

"Answer the question."

"A size seven."

The two detectives shared a knowing look.

Geoff frowned.

"Let's talk about Martha," George said. Hopefully, he'd trip himself up if they kept repeating questions in different ways. He'd declined a solicitor, so they pretty much could lead the conversation in whichever direction they wanted. "When was the last time you spoke with her?" George asked.

"I already told you. At the court."

"You didn't much care for her, did you?"

"Hated her. Doesn't mean I killed her."

"Who said she's dead."

"A journalist told me. She called the landlady, who passed the phone to me. Paige something. She wanted a quote from me and mentioned the police presence at the farm and how a body had been taken out."

"Paige McGuiness?" asked Wood, and Geoff nodded. "What did you say to her?"

"She asked me if I was involved, and I told her what I told you. But with worse language. Told her if she ever called me again, she'd regret it. I've been trying to call the girls to see if they're OK, but I can't get in touch with either of them. That's why I'm here, right? Because you think I killed Martha?"

George glanced over at Wood, who shrugged. He said, "OK, Geoff, I need you to tell me where you were between six and eleven last night."

"Fucking told you this morning when you interrupted my gaming."

"For the tape, please tell us again."

"I didn't kill the old twat, OK."

"We didn't say you did; we're just gathering evidence."

Lickiss rubbed his shaved head with one hand and twirled his fingers through his beard with the other. Worry lines deepened around his eyes. The reality of his situation was sinking in, George thought. Good. "What evidence? I told you, I didn't do anything."

"Do you own a baseball bat, Mr Lickiss?" George asked quickly. He was truly fed up with Geoff's antics.

Geoff's eyes darted around the room, and then he said, "Yeah. I do." Uncertainty flickered in his eyes. "Not a crime that, is it?"

"Not when it's used for sport, no. Though there's not much scope for playing baseball in Leeds, is there?"

"I bought it for one of the girls about five years ago when we were in the States. Proper popular is baseball over there. It's been in the shed at home ever since. I haven't touched it since buying it. Doubt any of the girls have either."

"Interesting." It would explain any DNA and prints they found. Unfortunately, forensics weren't yet so technically advanced that you could tell when the prints and DNA were left behind.

"Did Martha's killer use the bat to kill her?"

"Why would you ask that?" asked Wood.

Geoff shrugged.

"Is that what you wanted to do, Geoff? Batter Martha with the bat?"

"I already told you I didn't kill Martha."

"We never said you did."

"So what the hell are you getting at?"

"Martha Lickiss wasn't the person who was murdered in the farmhouse."

Chapter Nine

A blink. A frown. Another seed of doubt was sown. Geoff didn't know that his daughter was dead. The bastard didn't know.

"What do you mean?" Geoff asked George. Then, when no reply came, he tried Wood. "What's he on about? What's he saying? Whose body did you find?"

When neither detective said nothing, Geoff thumped the table and jumped up, crashing his chair back against the wall. "Stop fucking playing games with me!"

Wood said, "We're not playing games. Your ex-wife is missing. Know anything about that?"

Lickiss slammed his fist on the table again. "No, I don't. Whose body did you find?"

"We'll get to that later," said George. "Do you know where Martha is?"

Geoff said, "No," and Wood scoffed. "What the fuck's your problem?" Geoff asked her.

Ignoring him, George said, "Last night, I believe you went to Martha's house, where a fight happened and you abducted her."

Lickiss jumped up for the second time. "What the fuck?"

"Sit down. Now," George said, lacing his voice with grit. "Tell me about your relationship with Martha."

Leaning forward, Geoff Lickiss lowered his head and spoke to the table. "Volatile, that's how I'd describe it. We got married too quickly. She resented me because she gave up her career. But when we had the twins, even the explosive rows were worth it. Those girls are the light of my life. Martha is a bitch. I mean that. A full-on fucking bitch."

George frowned. "What career?"

"She was trained as a nursery nurse but wanted to go into full-time teaching. Martha got accepted on the course but found out about the twins, and she had to give it up."

"I need you to confirm for the tape where you were last night," said Wood.

"Why are we going over the same questions over and over?"

"Because you refused to answer them, Geoff."

"I wasn't anywhere near the farmhouse. And I didn't kill anybody or abduct anybody, either."

George nodded. "I need a detailed statement from you."

"I got up at six, had a shower, shit and shave." He pointed at his head. "Got on the bus and arrived about half-seven. Had a coffee whilst I waited for my shift to start at eight."

"That's at McDonald's in Hunslet, right?"

"Right." He pulled at his beard. "I finished at six, and I got the bus home. Had tea with the landlady, which she will confirm. Then I played on my PS5 until I went to bed."

"For the tape, what time did you go to bed?"

"Not sure. Probably around one or two."

"So no one can corroborate your whereabouts once you'd finished your tea?"

"You have my console. I thought you were looking into it?"

"We are."

"What did you do after we left you this morning?"

"Stayed inside and fucked about on my phone. All day. Then some of your lot arrived again and forced me 'ere."

"Can anybody confirm that?" Wood asked.

"No."

A ping interrupted the flow of the interview. George read the message and smiled. He pulled a print from out of his folder. "Do you know whose car this is?"

"Mine."

"You're sure?"

"Positive." Geoff ground his teeth. "Stop fucking about."

George said, "I've just got a text."

"This isn't fucking Love Island, Detective," said Geoff.

Wood grinned. The joke had been pretty funny, but George looked fired up, so she said nothing and let him continue.

"It's from a colleague of mine. She's been running your car's reg through our systems, looking for any ANPR hits."

Geoff narrowed his eyes as if he knew what was coming. "And?"

"And you told us, repeatedly, that you were home all night last night playing video games." George turned to Wood. "That's correct, isn't it, DS Wood?"

"That's right, DI Beaumont."

"So why was your car in Rothwell last night?"

"I went to the shop."

"Which shop?" Wood asked.

"Aldi."

"Why did you turn right out of Aldi and then right up Royds Lane?" The camera had pinged at the traffic lights on the A654.

"Because I wanted to clear my head. I miss the house. But I can also get home if I head up Wakefield Road and cut up Castle

Gate."

"That puts you near the house last night at the right time," George said.

"I don't really fucking care because I didn't do anything."

"Why lie about it earlier?" George asked.

His scowl returning, Geoff sat back. "Because I knew this would happen, didn't I? Soon as you started questioning me about that bitch, I knew something had happened. I knew you lot would put two and two together and come up with five like you always fucking do."

"As we told you earlier, the PNC has a list of your transgressions which is about a mile long. You're also on the DNA and IDENT1 databases on which we store DNA profiles and fingerprints, respectively."

"And?"

"If you're innocent, I'm just wondering why your prints were all over the murder weapon."

"What murder weapon?"

When neither detective said anything, Geoff added, "You still haven't told me who died!"

"Want to know my theory?"

"I don't really give a fuck."

George said, "Well, I do, Geoff, because as a father myself, I can't figure out why you'd kill your daughter with a baseball bat."

"What."

"I said, what I can't figure out is why you'd kill your daughter, Hope."

"Kill my daughter? What? Why? I don't know anything about..."

But neither detective said anything.

CHAPTER NINE

Lickiss shook his head vigorously and said, "No! Where the fuck are my daughters?"

"You haven't asked how it happened. Is that because you already know?"

"I don't like your tone," Lickiss said. "Why the hell would I kill Hope?"

The oppressive atmosphere in the small room was grating on George's nerves. "You tell us."

"Where's Faith."

When neither detective said anything, Geoff said, "I think..." he began, then he swallowed hard. He pawed moisture from his eyes. "I think I want that solicitor, after all."

Another text message arrived, this time from DCI Alexander, who was watching via live link.

'Make the arrest.'

George passed his phone across the table to Wood, who gave a brief nod.

"Geoff Lickiss, I'm arresting you on suspicion of the murder of your daughter, Hope. You do not have to say anything. But, it may harm your defence if you do not mention when questioned something which you later rely on in court. Anything you do say may be given in evidence."

* * *

Back upstairs in the shared office, George was talking to the team, telling them about the arrest.

"Congratulations, George." Alistair smiled at them as he walked past. "I've spoken to the super, and he's overjoyed." At the looks on the team's faces, the DCI stopped. "What's wrong with you all?"

He glanced at them each in turn. "Why do you all look so miserable? You all did a cracking job. You followed the evidence and made an arrest. Even the CPS agreed there was more than enough to charge him."

"Something feels wrong." George wiped a bead of sweat off his forehead. He didn't like it when he didn't have all the answers. "He was a piss-poor liar. One of the worst I've ever seen. And the look on his face, once he found out Hope had been murdered wasn't one you could make up."

"Maybe he's just a good actor?" the DCI said. "He has form, George, and a motive. His prints were on the baseball bat, and he's a size seven, so he clearly had the means. And from the ANPR, the opportunity, too."

"We need to check CCTV from Aldi, sir," George said. He turned to Tashan, who nodded. "And he explained the prints on the baseball bat."

"I've ordered a search of the Bed and Breakfast, George. They'll find size seven shoes they can match to the casts, which will be a clean sweep. Anything else will come to light in court."

Alistair was undeterred.

George gave a low grunt.

All the DCI cared about was the crime stats. Another case was closed, and the 'killer' was put away.

And the papers would vilify Geoff, too. The occupation order would come out. And no doubt, people would come out of the woodwork and give statements to the press about how they knew Geoff used to beat Martha, Faith, and Hope.

But ultimately, it was all about politics. Which always got in the way of police work. Lickiss' anguish had seemed real; his confusion was palpable.

And he was a terrible liar.

CHAPTER NINE

Still, there was a chance he was playing them. Geoff could pretend to be a lousy liar if he were a good enough actor.

And certainly, what the DCI said was true. Geoff Lickiss had the motive, means and opportunity to abduct Martha Lickiss, but why would he kill his daughter?

That's what made no sense to George.

"I just hope we're not sending an innocent man to prison, sir," George muttered as the DCI sauntered back to his office.

"I'll keep digging," Luke said. "And the DCI has ordered CSI to search the B&B and Geoff's car." His voice sounded hopeful when he added, "They might find something there."

"Let me know if they find anything," George asked, and Luke nodded. Then he turned to the rest of the team. "Don't stay too late. Lickiss is not going anywhere, so we can pick this up tomorrow." Geoff would be held in the cells until the following day when he'd be transferred to court and officially charged. After that, he'd be remanded in Armley to await trial. Geoff's entire life was about to collapse. He would lose his freedom, his room at the B&B, and his job.

But all George could think about was what if Geoff was innocent.

It didn't bear thinking about, but if Geoff Lickiss was innocent, then a huge miscarriage of justice had been done.

Chapter Ten

The doorbell rang, a key turned, and the door opened.

His mother. Marie Beaumont. At sixty-five, she was unusually vigorous and energetic.

Whilst George was recovering in hospital, Marie had decided to move back to Leeds from Scotland to be closer to him and Jack. And my was she surprised when she found out about Isabella and the baby.

"Hello, Mother," George said. She hated being called 'Mother', and he grinned. He was being vindictive on purpose because he still didn't fully trust her. "Are you OK?"

"I'm fine, love. And you?" Marie headed straight into the kitchen and flicked the kettle on.

"That's good." George didn't want to talk. After the day he'd had, he needed five minutes to himself.

"So it's true then, love?"

"What's true?"

"That Hope Lickiss was murdered, and both Martha and Faith are missing?"

"How did you find out about that?" They hadn't put out a press release regarding Faith and Martha yet because of Geoff Lickiss' arrest. They would in the morning, though.

"I know Geoff's landlady," Marie explained.

"I had no idea," George said, scratching his beard. "Did you know the Lickiss family?"

"Sure." Marie plopped three teabags into mugs and poured in boiling water. She let them stew whilst she said, "Well, it was your father who knew them."

George grimaced, and Marie saw. "Sorry, son, I shouldn't have said that."

Taking a deep breath, George said, "It's fine. How did he know them?"

"You really could do with employing a cleaner, son," Marie said. She started rinsing mugs under the running tap.

"We both work silly hours, Mother. And it's not as if the place is filthy." It wasn't. It was actually very clean, except for the clothes in the washing machine and the dishes in the sink.

"I'll come and do the washing in the morning, love. I noticed it's full." She pointed, and George frowned. "I'm only trying to help, love," she added. "With your accident and Izzy's condition, I can help you."

"We don't need any help."

Marie cocked an eyebrow. "Fine." She added sweetener to each cuppa, then small dashes of Milk to George's and Isabella's, and a large glug in hers. Then she went and sat at the kitchen counter. She heaved a deep sigh, and George shook his head. As she got older, his mother was turning more and more into a teenager.

George joined her and sipped his tea. Eventually, he said, "Tell me about the Lickiss family."

"I only know Geoff and Martha. They're younger than me, obviously, but because your father grew up in Rothwell, he knew the entire family."

"They have many farms, right?"

Marie shrugged. "They used to." Marie fidgeted with the handle of the mug. "They used to own a big one on Leeds Road, but I think it's abandoned now."

"How would you describe Geoff?"

"It's not really my place."

George frowned. "Mother."

Marie looked around the kitchen before letting her eyes drop back to her mug of tea. "I heard terrible rumours."

George raised a quizzical eyebrow. "Was he violent?"

"Apparently."

"You're not being very helpful, Mother."

"I didn't know them that well. Perhaps if you rang your—"

"Don't say it," George warned.

"But—"

"Don't fucking say it, Mother!"

She stood up, a scowl on her face. She still had to look up at her son. "You can't speak to me that way, George Beaumont!"

"I'm sorry, Mum. But you know how I feel."

"It's been eighteen years since you've seen him, George. Don't they say time heals wounds."

"That's a wound that will never heal, Mother. So leave it."

Marie shrugged and sat back down. "How's the investigation going?"

George wondered how much he could say and decided the less his mother knew, the better. "You know more than most. I can't tell you much else."

"And you think Geoff is involved."

"Why do you say that?"

"Because you asked if he was violent. I'm quite confident I can add two and two together to get four, son."

George grinned. "How bad were the rumours?"

CHAPTER TEN

"The worst you could imagine, and more." Marie stared vacantly at her tea. "Geoff Lickiss was involved in more than just farming. Maybe something from his past returned to haunt his family."

"What..." George stopped and momentarily thought about what his mother had just said. "What sort of things was he involved in?"

"Women and children trafficking, drugs, firearms... You name it, and Geoff Lickiss could supply it. Or so the rumours said."

Jesus Christ. He'd had no idea. George knew the man had been involved in crimes that made a list about a mile long, but he'd barely been charged for anything. And none of them were considered as serious as his mother had described. He wondered whether anybody at the station knew. Detective Superintendent Jim Smith would probably know, but their relationship felt fractured of late.

Marie got up, washed her mug and dried it. Then she put it in the cupboard. Without turning around, she said, "He was always scrapping in the pub, too. A proper hard man."

"What about Martha?"

Marie folded the tea towel repeatedly until she had one neat square. "I believe she was forced to marry Geoff." She placed it on the counter. "If I remember right, she was adopted." She shrugged. "She's also younger than him by about a decade, I think."

"Interesting. Was she ever violent towards Geoff?"

"Not that I'm aware of, son, but I knew them twenty years ago. Before they had the twins."

"Did you know she wanted to be a teacher?"

Marie's eyes darkened for a split second, but George caught

it. He was about to question his mother when she picked her jacket up from the back of the chair and headed for the front door. "I'm tired," she said.

"But you haven't seen Isabella yet. Or Rex."

"I'll see Rex in the morning. He deserves a nice big walk."

Marie had been given a key so she could feed, water, and let Rex out when they were busy working long hours.

"Mother," he began, but when he looked up, Marie had gone.

George went to the counter, picked up the tea towel and scrunched it into a ball. Then with a deep breath, he slammed it against the back door and tightly clenched his fists. Somehow, she always managed to grate upon his last nerve.

***

Outside, somebody walked to their car at the end of the road, a phone to their ear.

"The mother just left the house. The other two are now alone."

The person listened, nodding as further instructions were relayed.

"To be clear, you want me to leave my post here and follow the old woman home?"

"Correct."

"And then come back here to continue my surveillance?"

"Yes."

Ending the call on their burner phone, the person slipped it into their inside pocket and took out a set of car keys. Climbing behind the wheel, they fired up the engine, then shifted the car into gear and headed after Marie Beaumont.

CHAPTER TEN

* * *

Jean curled up against the wall, her back to Taylor, who was sparko. What was this nightmare all about? Who could have done that to her niece? And where was Martha?

Her stomach hurt, and her eyes stung. She wanted to see her brother, Geoff, too. But that wasn't possible. It wouldn't surprise her if Martha killed Hope, then staged her own abduction. That stupid bitch had destroyed Geoff's life. Again.

She heard the front door open and chatter in the hallway. Then the door closed. Maybe the family liaison officer had left. She slid down the bed and crept out of her room, looking down the stairs. Coming towards her was a young man in a police uniform.

"Who are you?" Jean asked.

"Hi, Jean; I'm here for your protection." He smiled and offered his hand, which Jean didn't take. "I'll be standing guard outside. DS Cathy Hoskins has just left."

"You can go. I've got Taylor. We can look after ourselves." Jean turned back into her bedroom.

"No can do, I'm afraid. I have orders from way above. You're stuck with me for the night." The uniform hovered on the landing. "I'll be downstairs by the front door. My colleagues are outside in a squad car."

"Fine, just leave me alone."

Lying on the bed, Jean spooned Taylor, listening to her soft, gentle breathing.

Without Taylor, life would be shite. Her niece was dead, her sister-in-law was probably dying, and her brother was going to be falsely convicted as a murderer.

Or so she hoped it would be a miscarriage of justice.
She knew all about his temper.
It made it imperative that she spoke with Geoff.
There was something he needed to know.

* * *

As Marie Beaumont entered her house through the back door and into the kitchen, she noticed it was pitch dark. She flicked the light switch. Nothing. She opened the drawer, her fingers finding the small torch, which she clicked on.

The fuse box was in the cupboard by the front door, so she walked through the house slowly, listening.

Hope Lickiss' death, and Martha Lickiss' assault, terrified the woman. And Faith was still missing. What if a madman or woman was out there, preying on people in the dark? What if the Lickiss farmhouse had been involved in a house invasion, and the murder and assault were a burglary gone wrong?

Heart hammering, she eventually made it to the front door and inspected the fuse box. The one for the lights was down. She flicked it up, and the hall light flashed on immediately.

Heading back into the kitchen, and after throwing the torch back into the drawer, she closed the back door and then stopped. She was sure she'd shut it. So why was it still open?

She was getting old, and the fatigue was setting in earlier and earlier these days. That morning she'd made a large pot of Cullen Skink, her husband's favourite. The thick and creamy soup made by cooking the smoked haddock in milk alongside leeks or onions and potatoes was also George's favourite, though he'd never admit it.

Turning on the gas and lighting the flame with a match,

CHAPTER TEN

Marie stirred the creamy soup, gently warming it through. There were enough for three generous portions, and she decided she'd decant two portions for George and Izzy and leave it at the house tomorrow when she went to see to Rex.

But that meant she'd need something for dinner tomorrow.

Marie headed to the fridge and looked inside. She had mince, chicken breasts, and some pork chops. She had intended to make Balmoral Chicken, but at her age, cooking took too much time and played havoc with her arthritis.

So she pulled out the pork chops and a jar of curry sauce from the cupboard. She'd sear the chops in the oven first, then braise them in the sauce. Then the sauce would develop overnight.

Already she was salivating. Marie knew she had a couple of packets of microwave rice in the cupboard, and all she'd have to do tomorrow was reheat the curry and microwave the rice.

So easy.

The heat from outside, and the heat from the flame, meant Marie struggled to breathe. Then she realised she'd left her jacket on. "Silly old fool!"

Marie headed towards the cupboard by the front door to hang up her jacket when she realised the fuse box was open. Why? Had somebody been in her home?

From her left, she caught car headlights outside, streaming in through the small semi-circle of glass atop the front door.

The lights outside disappeared, and fuse box forgotten; she headed back to the kitchen, thinking about Geoff and Martha Lickiss. She hadn't lied to her son; it was her husband who knew Geoff rather than her. And the rumours she'd mentioned had been rife at the time. But they'd seemed cordial whenever the couples met at the pub or bumped into each other at differing events.

The more she thought about it, the more she realised Geoff and her husband had spent more time together than she'd ever realised. It was a shame her son was so stubborn. Her husband had changed in old age. She wished George would give him another chance.

Marie filled the plastic containers with soup and ladled her own portion into a bowl. Then she buttered a couple of slices of bread to go with it, remembering she'd put chops into the oven to sear.

Opening the oven door, she stared at the raw meat. She'd forgotten to turn on the oven. "Yer aff yer heid, Auld Yin."

Not for the first time, Marie Beaumont wondered whether she was losing her mind.

* * *

"What's worrying you, my love?" Isabella asked George. "Is it your mum?"

"No, it's Geoff Lickiss," he said. They were making tea together. "I'm not absolutely certain he's guilty."

She leaned over and kissed him. "That's why I love you," she crooned. "You care."

But did he care enough? He smiled at her. She was just being supportive, but the thought of Geoff Lickiss sitting in a cell right now, not only dealing with the loss of his daughter but the loss of his freedom, played heavily on him.

She said, "People like the DCI, the DCS, and the DSU don't. They just want convictions and quick."

"What if he's innocent, Isabella?"

"Then it'll come out in court," she said. "You know how the

CHAPTER TEN

justice system works. We have to follow the evidence, and in this case, everything you have is pointing to Geoff Lickiss."

But waiting until a trial meant the man could be remanded for a year or more which was a heavy price to pay if the guy was innocent. "I feel as if the DCI has picked and chosen the evidence to suit a specific narrative." The visit of his mother, and the mention of his bastard father, had left him out of sorts. "I just feel like we have to consider everything, and there are some things that don't add up."

"But the justice system doesn't always work like that, George," Isabella reminded him. "It's up to you to disprove that because he can't."

George met her loving gaze and smiled. "I intend to do just that."

She returned his grin. "I know you do."

Chapter Eleven

A low growl jolted George awake. He sat up, groggy. What time was it?

Glancing at his phone, he saw it was just after four in the morning.

More growling, low and continuous like an idling engine.

Rex. He was supposed to be in the kitchen in his crate. Had he forgotten to put him away for the night?

George slid off the bed.

"Rex?" The dog was outside on the landing.

If there was an intruder, he didn't want to alert them to his presence, so George poked his head cautiously around the door. "Rex, what's wrong, boy?" he whispered.

Rex was arched low, glaring at something downstairs, growling softly. The hair on his back bristled, his lithe body tense.

George took each step lightly, placing his feet at the edges to try to reduce the amount of noise he was making.

The kitchen door was open, and the living room door was closed.

Funny, he remembered doing the complete opposite before heading to bed. Could someone be in the living room?

A loud creak confirmed it.

Shit. Had Schmidt sent someone for him?

CHAPTER ELEVEN

More rustling. Whoever it was, they were still in there.

Heart pounding, George looked around for anything heavy that he could use to protect himself. There was nothing.

So he darted into the kitchen and pulled a knife from the block.

Rex was still growling at the living room door, but oddly, he wasn't reacting as violently as George would have anticipated if there had been an intruder who intended to hurt them. He took a few slow, deep breaths to control his heart rate. It may not have been a planned hit. Maybe a mouse got in there or something.

You're a dead man.

Schmidt's words were still fresh in his mind.

He could visualise the criminal's cynical smirk and unfriendly gaze.

George opened the door carefully just an inch, and Rex shoved his nose through first. The growling became more menacing.

"Who's there?" George called.

Then he opened it another inch.

Then another.

As soon as the door was wide enough, Rex bolted through. George followed, holding the knife out in front of him.

He felt the chill first and then smelled the distinctive nighttime smell. The door to the foyer was open and quite clearly was the front door. But surprisingly, Rex hadn't switched to attack mode. Still emitting a low, quiet growl, the pup was watching someone in the darkened room.

George flicked the light on, bracing himself. A voice from the sofa said, "Hello, son."

"Jesus, Mother!" George placed the knife on the bookcase to

his left and then put both hands on his knees to calm himself. "What on earth are you doing here? And at this time!"

Seeing it was Marie, Rex wandered over to his bowl with a wagging tail and sniffed, checking to see if any scran had miraculously appeared since his tea.

George collapsed on the three-seater sofa, feeling weak and shaky now the adrenalin was wearing off—and rather stupid.

Of course, it wasn't a hired hitman. Schmidt was full of shit. His threat was nothing but an attempt to intimidate the man who'd wanted to arrest him and lock him away.

The problem was it was working.

Chapter Twelve

The jog must have worn George out as the next thing he knew; his phone was ringing. He checked the time. 7.15 am.

"DI Beaumont."

"George, it's DCI Atkinson. Where are you?"

"At home in bed, sir."

"Where's DS Wood? I tried her first, but she's not answering her phone."

George looked over and saw Isabella sound asleep.

"Why do you need DS Wood and not me, sir?"

"I want her to head up a murder inquiry. Tell her she's SIO and to get to Holy Trinity Church in Rothwell as soon as possible."

George sat up sharply, causing Isabella to stir. "What shall I do, sir?"

"You being there would undermine her authority, George," the DCI said. "I want you here at Elland Road."

"Right."

"Good. Wake her up and tell her to get over there as quickly as she can. They've found a dead body in the grounds of the church."

* * *

George arrived at the shared office space to find no other members of his team.

Hanging up his jacket in his office, he quickly looked around. The three DCs and the two other teams weren't around, either. Had he missed something?

He understood why Luke wasn't here, considering he was working lates. Yolanda worked on CCTV for all three Homicide and Major Enquiry Teams.

But his two detective constables were usually there, raring to go.

Or Tashan usually was.

During the last case, George was SIO on, and Jay had started showing up late and was getting seriously sloppy with his work. But then it turned out he'd been drugged with scopolamine, a drug with hallucinogenic properties that could even cause psychosis.

Writing his report on yesterday's activities, George couldn't concentrate. He hadn't slept well last night. Rex's howls and growls had kept him up, but that wasn't the only reason. Geoff Lickiss was on his mind.

It still wasn't adding up.

And only Wood was taking his doubts seriously.

And then his mum showing up at silly o'clock didn't help, either. She'd spent the rest of the night in the spare room.

Taking a quick break, he called Jay and listened to the call go to voicemail. He tried Tashan and got no answer. When they were together, Jay usually drove, so it was understandable why he wasn't answering, but Tashan always answered his phone.

* * *

CHAPTER TWELVE

DS Wood left her house in Morley and headed towards Rothwell. It was just after 8 am, and the sun was already relentless.

She turned left onto Butcher Lane, and where it met Church Street, Wood could see police officers had blocked off the road at the roundabout in front of the church, but a flash of her warrant card allowed her entry, and she parked up in the pub's car park.

They'd lose out on business today but knew over the next few days, with police officers, journalists and sightseers, they'd make a killing. She grimaced at the pun.

It was cooler in Rothwell than in Morley, being slightly nearer to sea level than Morley was. It always surprised her how different parts of Leeds got drastically different weather, especially Morley and Middleton. It was even worse up Yeadon near the airport.

As a teen growing up in Middleton, it always amazed her how they got snow, whilst many other areas of Leeds didn't. It made it awkward at school because Lofthouse wouldn't get the same amount of snow as Miggy.

As Wood left her vehicle, her mind was racing. There were so many questions, and currently, all of them were unanswered. The only thing she could be reasonably sure about was that anyone leaving a body in a graveyard intended for it to be found.

The church stood tall and proud, looking glorious in the summer sun. The Cross of St George fluttered from the flagpole on the top of the church tower. She passed by two marked CSI vans and walked through the lychgate, flashing her warrant card at PC Candy Nichols, who manned the cordon.

"Morning, DS Wood. Shall I sign you in?"

"Please, Candy," she said.

"No DI Beaumont today?"

She shook her head. "I'm SIO on this one."

"Ooh, very nice; good luck."

"Thank you, Candy."

DS Wood waddled up the stone path towards the open wooden doors of the church. She knew the graveyard was to the north-west and would make her way around soon enough, but she wanted to see if the reverend was around. She most likely would be, considering it was a Sunday morning.

An older woman with smoky-grey hair approached her, each step leaden and lethargic. She wore a black cassock, and the woman's smile met blood-flecked eyes that looked sorrowful. With careful patience, time had chiselled away at her wizened face, the chapters of her life there for all to see. "Reverend Suzanne Priestley," she said, offering her hand.

"Detective Sergeant Isabella Wood," Izzy said, lightly shaking the reverend's hand. She didn't really want to break the news that the church service would need to be cancelled, but it was part of the job. "Unfortunately, you'll need to cancel the service this morning."

"Completely understandable, Sergeant," Suzanne said. "Is that all events for today?"

Wood nodded. "Thank you for understanding."

"Of course. Can I help in any way?"

She thanked her for her concern and politely explained that she could not be of assistance currently, but Wood explained, "I may need your help later, Reverend Priestley."

"You mean to see if the person belonged to my congregation?"

Wood nodded.

"I'll be here. The door will be left open, and I'll be in my office."

Isabella turned to her left and continued across the grass, noticing a line of something dark. She immediately gave the stain a large berth and headed towards the inner cordon, keeping her eye on the trail of dark stains.

Sergeant Greenwood was at the inner cordon with a male PC she didn't recognise.

"Morning, Detective Sergeant," said Greenwood.

"Morning, Sergeant," she said. "I need your man here to cordon off the area of grass to the left of the church door, as it looks like a trail of blood starts from somewhere over there and ends by the door."

Greenwood said, "You heard the detective," and was met with a, 'Yes, sir!'

Once suited and booted in a Tyvek suit, mask, gloves and shoe covers, Wood entered the inner cordon and immediately picked up the trail of dark stains. She followed it around to the back of the church. This sort of area was a nightmare for the police. She knew beyond the overgrown graveyard she was looking at was a short wall surrounding it. It could easily be jumped.

She continued and met with a PC and a man wearing green overalls.

"Good morning, Constable." She pulled out her warrant card. "DS Wood, SIO."

"Good morning, ma'am, I'm PC Mazur. This is Michał Dudek, one of the cemetery workers here. He found the body."

"Good morning, Mr Dudek."

Behind them was a tent CSI had erected over the body. Part of her job as SIO was to look at the body and see if she could understand how and why the person was killed. She wasn't particularly squeamish, and usually, the sight of blood didn't upset her, but the changes to her body because of the pregnancy meant she struggled with the strong, coppery odour that came with death.

The trail of blood was easily identifiable now in the long grass, as was a significant pool of blood with its own cordon erected around it. Isabella hypothesised that the murderer killed their victim where the pool of blood was, then placed the body where it now lay under the tent before walking towards the front of the church, causing the trail of blood on the grass. It made sense, but she wondered why the killer chose to head towards the front of the church instead of escaping over the back wall.

Isabella took a deep breath, placed her mask over her mouth, and headed inside the tent.

The first thing she noticed was eyes which were wide and bulging, and a wide open mouth with its tongue sticking out. It was something out of a horror movie, the look on the face one of complete surprise, shock and horror rolled into one. It would stay with Isabella for life.

The killer had looked the victim in the eye as they murdered them.

No, her. The victim was a woman with short, grey hair, aged between sixty-five and seventy-five, who was posed as sitting on the ground, her back resting against a gravestone. Beneath her bum was a large patch of dark, blood-stained grass.

She left the tent and removed the mask, panting. The smell of blood had been overwhelming. She turned to PC Mazur. "Where has CSI gone?"

"They're taking pictures of another bloodstain over there," he explained.

Wood nodded, then turned to the cemetery worker. "When did you find the body?"

"About seven-ish," he said, his words heavily accented. "I was out tending to the graves." He held out his arms. "As you can see, it's starting to get overgrown." He scratched his beard. "It's Sunday, so I better get back to the church and let them know they need to cancel the service," said Dudek.

"Please stay where you are, Mr Dudek," Wood said. "I've already spoken with the reverend, and we'll need a formal statement from you before you go anywhere."

PC Mazur's radio crackled into life. "Lindsey Yardley would like to see you, ma'am," he explained.

DS Wood nodded and headed to where the PC pointed. When she turned the corner, she could see the senior Scenes of Crime Officer, Lindsey Yardley, directing the Yank, Hayden Wyatt. She could hear the sounds of clicking as photographers did their job. The smell of blood was overwhelming.

Lindsey Yardley walked over to her. "Did you take a look, DS Wood?"

She nodded gravely.

"Not nice, is it?"

"The look on that poor woman's face will probably live with me forever."

Lindsey shuddered. "I was thinking the same."

Wood pointed to two uniformed officers. "Who are they?"

"Officers from the West Yorkshire Police Drone Unit," Lindsey explained. "I've asked them for help photographing the area, though I think this is the kill site." Lindsey pointed northwest. "Her body was then dragged that way and then south towards the grave."

"So that specific grave was chosen?" Wood asked.

Lindsey nodded. "I think so." She held out her hands, gesturing to the graveyard. "Have a look around. What do you see?"

"Overgrown bushes."

"Exactly. And dense undergrowth. If you wanted to hide a body, that's where you'd hide it, right?

"Right," Wood said. "But, she wasn't hidden, was she? She was left for us to find."

Isabella made a mental note to speak with the reverend again, hoping the church would have records. It would be a while before the body was removed and even longer until she could inspect the gravestone. But if it had significance, which it must have, she needed to know.

Chapter Thirteen

DCs Blackburn and Scott were dressed in SOC suits and outside the tent by the time DS Wood returned. She pointed to Michał Dudek. "DC Blackburn, that's the cemetery worker, Mr Dudek. He found the body this morning. Get a detailed statement from him, OK? Take him inside the church and take the statement there."

"Will do, Sarge," Tashan said.

She turned to Jay. "Jay, I need you to take pictures of the graves surrounding the tent on your phone and go speak with Reverend Suzanne Priestley. She was killed around the back of the church, and the culprit dragged her body here."

"So, the grave's important then, boss?"

"Correct, Jay."

"What a name for a Reverend," Jay said, grinning. He didn't wait for Wood to reply and followed after Tashan.

Before Isabella could reprimand the young DC and talk to him about respect, PC Mazur shouted across to her.

"DCI Atkinson has arrived, ma'am. He's on his way up."

"That's all I need," she mumbled. She took a deep breath and met her boss.

"Dr Ross arrived yet?"

"Not yet, sir," Wood explained.

He turned to PC Mazur. "Find out where the pathologist is, will you?"

"Yes, sir."

Atkinson then turned to Wood. "What have we got then, Wood?"

"The dead body of a woman, sir." Wood pointed towards where Lindsey Yardley and her team were. "CSI are around the back of the church as that was where the woman was killed before being dragged and placed here."

He furrowed his brows. "Placed?"

"Correct, sir. I believe the gravestone is significant, so I have DC Scott looking into that as we speak.

"Good."

"I also have DC Blackburn interviewing the cemetery worker who found the body."

Atkinson nodded.

"I also found a blood trail on my way around the church."

The DCI nodded again. "Looks like it's been cordoned off now."

"Ah, good. I believe the culprit left the scene that way."

"Interesting," said the DCI. "Why would he leave that way and not through the back?"

"'He', sir?"

"Habit, Wood, I'm afraid." He smiled. "I call all murderers' he' until I'm proved otherwise. Any ID on the woman?"

"No, not yet, sir," Wood explained. "We've used a lantern device, but it appears the victim isn't on any of our databases."

"No phone or purse? No bag? Anything like that?"

"Nothing, sir."

"Damn." He pointed to the tent. "Mind if I take a look?"

"It's not a pretty sight, sir."

CHAPTER THIRTEEN

"Don't worry, Wood; I'm used to it."

Whilst DCI Alistair Atkinson was inside the tent, pathologist Dr Christian Ross walked around the corner and greeted DS Wood. "Hello, dear, how are you?" He eyed her swollen stomach.

"About to burst, Dr Ross," she said with a grin.

"Indeed. I'm so sorry we have to keep meeting like this."

"Part of the job."

"Indeed it is, my dear." He ran a hand through his salt-and-pepper hair. "So what have we got today on this fine Sunday morning?

"An elderly woman. Possibly strangled and definitely stabbed. But I'm sure you'll find out more than me," she said.

"After you then."

Isabella walked back towards the tent, with Dr Ross in tow, and bumped into DCI Atkinson, who left the tent looking a bit green. Dr Ross nodded his head at the DCI, then disappeared inside the tent to begin his examination.

"We're going to have the press all over this Wood," Atkinson said. "I'll speak with Juliette Thompson, the press officer. She can organise liaison. The vultures are going to have a field day."

Isabella frowned. "Don't they always, sir?"

"We'll sort out the details of exactly what we release later when you're back at Elland Road, OK?"

"Yes, sir."

Dr Ross reappeared five minutes later.

"I've finished my preliminary examination, Isabella," he said. "Elderly IC1 female approximately seventy years of age. There are what appear to be ligature marks on the neck. She was then stabbed in the heart repeatedly.

"Time of death?" Wood asked.

"Last night or the early hours of this morning."

"Anything else?" DCI Atkinson asked.

"No, DCI Atkinson," Dr Ross said. "PM will be tonight. Whom shall I send the report?"

"To DS Wood," the DCI said.

"Thank you, Dr Ross," Isabella said. The pathologist nodded his head at each detective in turn, then turned on his heel and headed back to his car.

"Is there anything else you need, Wood?" asked Alistair.

"I need PS Greenwood's uniforms so we can start a house-to-house in the local area, please, sir. I think it might also be worth getting a sniffer dog to follow that trail and see where it goes. I might need Yolanda on CCTV, too. I'll ring Jay now and see if the church has any."

"OK, I'll organise that straight away and see you back at Elland Road later."

"Thank you, sir."

Alistair was about to leave, and then a tone shattered the silence of the graveyard. Wood watched him nodding along to whoever was speaking on the other end.

After hanging up, DCI Atkinson shouted across to Wood. "I've spoken to Juliette. She's had journalists calling up already, so she's going to organise a press conference at 6 pm tonight, OK?"

"OK, sir."

* * *

An hour later, Jay was back at the station, and George called a meeting in the incident room.

"Where have you been?" asked George. "I've been trying to ring you."

"Crime scene, boss," said Jay. "Dispatch called, and as we've arrested Geoff Lickiss, the DCI cleared Tashan and me to attend. DS Wood's SIO. Tashan's stayed with her."

George nodded. It all made sense. "How are we getting on tracing Martha's last movements?"

"I thought we weren't doing that now, boss?" asked Jay.

"Who said that?"

Jay frowned. "The DCI."

George mirrored his young colleague's frown. "I'm not convinced Geoff Lickiss killed his daughter and abducted his ex-wife." He scratched his beard. "We need to figure out where Martha Lickiss is."

Jay nodded. "I'll get on it now, boss."

"Good."

* * *

Isabella turned to see DC Tashan Blackburn running towards her, phone at his ear. He arrived slightly out of breath. Eventually, he managed to say, "Dispatch is on the phone. They received a triple nine call advising there's a burnt-out car in Springhead Park."

Izzy frowned. "Why am I only just hearing about this now?"

"Two reasons, Sarge," Tashan said. "One, because the firefighters have only managed to control it. And two, they've only just got the information back from the DVLA."

Isabella frowned again.

"The registered keeper is a Rita Holdsworth of 2 Maple Rise,

Rothwell." He handed his phone over. "This is a picture of her driving license."

"Shit," she said.

"Yep."

"Anybody reported her missing?"

"Not as yet, Sarge, no," he said. Tashan returned the phone by his ear, nodding as the person on the other end relayed instructions. "I'll ask," he eventually said and turned to DS Wood. "They want to know whether to send a uniform to the house, Sarge."

"Tell them we'll visit once we've looked at the car." She paused. "Is there a body in the car?"

Tashan relayed both messages and then waited for a reply. "There's no body in the car, Sarge."

Wood turned to PC Mazur. "Has Lindsey Yardley left yet?"

He spoke into his radio and received a quick reply. "No," he told Wood. "Nor has Dr Ross or DCI Atkinson. They're in the car park discussing the body."

Isabella and Tashan raced down to the car park. Or Tashan did. Isabella waddled behind him as quickly as she could. PC Mazur had radioed an officer in the car park to stop DCI Atkinson and Lindsey Yardley from leaving and to instead head for Springhead Park car park.

At the car park, Isabella jumped into her car, with Tashan plonking his arse onto the passenger seat. Lindsey and DCI Atkinson followed them in their own vehicles. There was no body, so they sent Dr Ross back to the mortuary so he could prep to receive the body.

She drove out of the car park and turned left onto Ingram Parade, going straight ahead at the roundabout until she reached another roundabout. She turned right onto Gillet

Lane, then left onto the A654, where they were greeted at the entrance to the car park by a police constable who removed the blue tape allowing the fleet of vehicles through.

They parked to the left of the entrance, facing the main road, the burnt-out vehicle to the north, by two large, yellow skips, still smouldering in a disabled bay.

Wood surveyed the crime scene. The cordon was just one section of ground that had been taped off, large enough for a reasonable sweep of the immediate area, but nothing more. She got a horrible sense of déjà vu. She'd been here before, eighteen months ago, taking in the red Fiat. Though at least this time, a body wasn't inside the car.

"Any witnesses?" she asked the PC guarding the inner cordon, not keeping her eyes from the grey Kia Venga.

"No, ma'am," she said.

"Who found the car?"

"A Mrs Nicole Baker. She was walking her dog in the park when she noticed the smoke. I've got her address."

"You let her go?"

"Yes, ma'am. I'm afraid her dog was very distressed, so I let her go home. She lives locally, though, and I ensured she will be available to speak to you when required."

"Thank you."

She and Tashan suited, gloved, and booted up, waiting until they were signed in before donning their masks. She hated wearing the suits at the best of times, but twice in one day was too much. Isabella turned to the young DC. "Stay here and ring the station, Tashan. I want as much info as we've got about Rita Holdsworth."

Isabella circled the Kia, noticing the ground at the back of the car had been churned into a muddy pulp by the firefighters' hoses.

"Wait a second, DS Wood," Lindsey Yardley said. "I want to put some stepping plates down."

"Sure." Wood swept the area for CCTV, wondering whether the council had decided to put any up during the last year and a half, but it didn't look that way. She'd get uniforms scouring the area later and get them on door-to-door.

It was eerily quiet that Sunday morning; the only noise was dripping water that fell from the car's chassis.

After Lindsey was done, Isabella risked the stepping plates to get a closer look at the car, recoiling at the damage the fire had done to the inside of the vehicle. The fabric seats had burnt down to the springs, and the dashboard had bubbled like chocolate that was left out in the summer sun.

The pungent odour of petrol meant to Isabella that this was an act of arson.

When Wood looked away, holding back those awful memories, Tashan was making his way over. "What have we got?"

"Rita Holdsworth. Eighty-seven years old. Widowed. The electoral roll shows she lives alone. She's not known to us."

Chapter Fourteen

DS Williams was standing inside the Lickiss farmhouse kitchen, looking through the window. "It's stunning outside during the day."

CSI was still outside, looking for evidence. They were mulling around what looked like a giant coal bunker.

Yolanda asked, "What's that they're looking at?"

DI Beaumont shrugged. "Looks like a giant coal bunker to me. Wonder what's inside."

Stuart Kent was shining a torch inside. He turned to George and beckoned him over. "We've found something interesting."

"What?"

Once George was nearby, Stuart handed him his torch and said, "Take a look."

George swept the light down and around the cavernous space. It was like a greenhouse down there. "Jesus, there are plants growing down there." There was also a strong, pleasing fragrance, and George had to stand back. He was sure he recognised those plants, though. But from where?

"I've got SOCOs checking the sheds over there, too," Kent said, pointing.

The trio headed over towards Hayden Wyatt, who was

signalling for them. "The boss sent me here from Rothwell, boss," he said to Kent.

Inside one of the sheds were hundreds of spare pots that could be used to house the same plants they'd found in the coal bunker. But they could only see half the shed because logs were stacked atop each other to the ceiling.

Had Martha Lickiss got a little sideline going here? Or were these remnants of Geoff Lickiss?

He thought back to what his mother had said. *Women and children trafficking, drugs, firearms... You name it, and Geoff Lickiss could supply it. Or so the rumours said.*

But who'd know about this? Martha would, definitely, but she was gone. And he doubted Geoff would admit to it.

But it would give them a motive they hadn't explored yet. It made George think about the cottage in Oulton and the possibility of a grow house.

It was very interesting.

"I want those logs moved," he told Kent. "There might be something behind them."

George turned on his heel, and Stuart said, "Where are you going?"

"We'll be back soon, Stuart," George said. "I want to speak to Jean Lickiss."

* * *

After strolling into the living room, Jean slumped down on a chair. The clothes she was wearing appeared to be too big for her, and her hair was a complete mess.

"Found Hope's killer yet?"

George shook his head and said, "And you've no idea who

would do something like that to her? Or why?" Jean bit her lip, then shook her head. "The night of Hope's death, are you sure you didn't see anything unusual around the house?"

"No, nothing. Sorry."

"Why were you out so late?" he asked.

Jean shrugged. "Hope was acting weird that night, and it kept bugging me, so after I cooked tea for Taylor and me, I decided to go and see Martha. I knew she wouldn't go straight home, so I went to Nikki Malin's."

Jay and Tashan had already visited Nikki and found out Hope hadn't gone there after leaving Jean's, so Jean's judgement had been wrong. "Then what?" George asked.

"I went to see Martha, saw a body, and rang you lot."

Her story hadn't changed, George was glad to hear. But it worried him that Jean could have been in the area when Hope was murdered. But what would be Jean's motive?

"Look, I need to ask you about something I found at the farmhouse," said George.

"Go on."

"Are you aware of the farmhouse and its grounds being used as a grow house?"

Jean hesitated, eyes searching out the corners of the room rather than meeting George's. "A grow house?"

George watched her closely. "Correct. Was Martha growing cannabis?"

"What?"

"Was Martha growing cannabis?"

Jean shrugged. "I wouldn't know anything about that."

"So, to be clear, you're telling us you don't know anything about any drugs-related activity going on at the farmhouse?"

"Correct."

George studied the woman carefully; he was sure her eyes flickered, indicating a lie. "You're sure of that?"

"Yes."

"Do you know where Faith Lickiss is?"

"I don't, I'm sorry."

"Do you know who Martha was close to?"

Jean shrugged. "She was a bit of a recluse, as I said before. She didn't really have any friends. It was just her and the twins at the farm. I think she did go to a family tree group, though."

George wanted to press on, but Wood's hand on his back warned him to relent. They needed to build trust with Jean, and hopefully, she'd then explain the plants growing in the coal bunker.

* * *

By mid-afternoon, the forensic examination of the church and the car park was essentially complete. The burnt-out car had been recovered, and the evidence from the church entered into exhibits. A fingertip search of the church grounds and the park car park was now underway and would continue until the summer light faded into darkness. House-to-house enquiries were also taking place in the local area, including Maple Rise, where Rita lived.

Rita Holdsworth was now in the St James' Hospital mortuary awaiting her post-mortem.

They were still trying to trace Rita's next of kin, which was difficult considering she had no social media presence. Tomorrow was Monday, though, so they'd get in touch with Rita's GP and request access to her medical records, which would give them next of kin details.

CHAPTER FOURTEEN

* * *

Sitting down heavily on the steel chair, Geoff Lickiss faced the two detectives, listening as they went through the formalities and fiddled with the recording equipment.

"Did they offer you something to eat, Mr Lickiss?" George asked once the tape had been started. "HMP Leeds treating you OK?"

"Not really," Geoff said. "Food's shit. And cold. It's fucking noisy 'ere." He gestured to the notepad of the grey-haired, rotund solicitor Armley Nick had provided. "When they let me out of here, I'm suing. So make sure you write that down, yeah?"

When the solicitor did nothing, Geoff tapped the table. "Come on, man. The food was cold. And shit." He looked at George. "I'm fucking suing."

The solicitor wrote down Geoff's comments, looking extremely disinterested. It was probably due to the amount of evidence they had.

"This shouldn't take long," George said. "We just have a few more questions, and then you can go back to your cell."

"Oh, how fucking brilliant."

"Any chance of a decent cup of tea?" he asked. "That's what I'm missing in this shithole!"

DS Williams stood up and banged on the door, and a prison guard entered. He nodded at the request, and five minutes later, a cuppa in a paper cup was handed to him. It was hot and sweet, and Lickiss savoured it. "Well, come on, detectives. Let's have it."

George said, "I've heard a rumour that you used to be involved in all sorts of sordid affairs?"

"Sordid. What the fuck?"

"Drugs, firearms, child and woman trafficking," George said.

"Why the fuck would I be involved in any of that?" Lickiss shook his head. "I'm a farmer."

"You did it on the side, maybe?"

Geoff sighed. "It's not enough that you have me locked up in here for nothing, but now you're trying to pin other fucking crimes on me. Do one, prick!"

"So, to be clear, you're saying you weren't involved in drugs, firearms, or trafficking?"

"Yeah," Geoff sneered. "That's what I'm saying."

"Do you have any idea where Faith is?" Yolanda asked.

He hadn't been expecting this. "I already told you I've no clue." He looked at his solicitor. "I'm innocent. Make sure that gets written down."

The solicitor said, "This interview is being recorded, Mr Lickiss, so say whatever you need. I don't need to keep writing notes down."

Hyperventilating now, Geoff tried to get the words out of his mouth. "You should be out there looking for Faith, not in 'ere, trying to frame me for things I didn't do!"

"Does Faith have any friends she could have visited? Or a boyfriend, perhaps?" asked Yolanda.

Geoff shook his head. "Faith doesn't have a boyfriend."

"You sure?"

Running his hand furiously across his scalped head, he tried to think. "No, but Faith never mentioned anyone. And she'd have told me."

"We found this at the farmhouse," DS Williams said, changing tact. "Is it yours?"

CHAPTER FOURTEEN

George placed a black leather jacket in a plastic bag on the table.

The man shrugged. "Who hasn't got a leather jacket?" Geoff said.

"But is this yours?" asked George.

"Nah."

"You're sure?"

"Positive."

"Then how do you explain this?" asked George. He slid an A4 page across the table.

Geoff could see it was a copy of a bus ticket.

Williams said, "Do you want to change your story about what you did the night your daughter was murdered, and your ex-wife disappeared?"

Lickiss pushed the A4 page away and said, "Why would I change my story when it's the truth."

"You said you got straight on the bus after leaving your shift, Geoff. This tells us you didn't," George said, pointing at the ticket.

Lickiss tugged at his beard. "Who says it's my ticket?"

Yolanda slid across another A4 page. "Can you identify the person in this picture?" It was a CCTV still of Geoff getting on the bus.

"Fine, so I left work later than I told you. So what?"

"It makes me wonder what else you lied about, that's all," said George. And it would make jurors wonder why he lied, too. The evidence was mounting, and George didn't like it. "And you're forgetting we found this jacket in the farmhouse."

"Your prints are on the murder weapon, too," added Yolanda.

"So, explain!" demanded George.

"Murder weapon?"

"The baseball bat you bought in America."

Grinning and shaking his head, Lickiss said, "So what if my fingerprints are on the baseball bat? I already told you it's because I bought the fucking thing!"

"And the jacket?"

"Not mine."

"Your bus ticket was in the pocket."

"I said it's not fucking mine."

"The ticket?"

"Not the ticket, you knobhead, the jacket."

"Explain why you're wearing the jacket in this picture, then?" George said, stabbing his finger at the CCTV print.

"Mine's at home, dickhead. Search the place, and you'll see."

"We already searched it."

"And?"

George slid across yet another A4 page. "This is an inventory of everything in your room at the B and B." George saw the man's lips move as he skimmed the list. "As you can see, there's no jacket."

"That's a load of fucking bollocks."

"No," said Wood, "it's a fact."

"I fucking knew you were all the same." Lickiss folded his arms and sat back in his chair. "I may have hated Martha, but it didn't mean I abducted her, OK. And why would I kill Hope? She's my girl."

Yolanda said, "You tell us."

George added, "And tell us where Faith is."

"No comment."

George looked at Geoff's solicitor, who shrugged. Then he

said, "No comment isn't going to look good in court, Geoff. This is your chance to tell us your side of the story."

"You're not listening to me, so what's the point."

"Because you're lying to us," said George. "Where is Martha? Did you hurt her?"

"I've no idea," Geoff said. "I didn't hurt Martha. I never have."

George thought about Jean Lickiss and Taylor Corbyn, specifically about what they'd said regarding Martha. "Tell me about the assaults at the farmhouse, Geoff," George eventually said.

"What assaults?"

"Well, was anybody ever assaulted at the farmhouse?"

"Anybody?"

George nodded. "Anybody."

Chapter Fifteen

Wood returned to Elland Road Police Station for a meeting with DCI Atkinson and the Press Liaison Officer, Juliette Thompson. The press conference was scheduled for 6 pm, which gave them less than half an hour.

It was rare that Wood took a dislike to somebody, usually waiting until they had given her good reason to dislike them, but Juliette had always been frosty with her. She was in her mid-thirties with curly, auburn hair that framed her round face. Thompson wore a black skirt and a white blouse; everything about her screaming efficiency. Isabella thought it was something to do with George, remembering how flirty she always was around him.

She grinned and rubbed her swollen stomach as she sat, not breaking eye contact.

"So, what can we tell the vultures, Juliette?" asked DCI Atkinson.

"We can tell them that the victim was strangled and then stabbed. The press probably knows that already, though." Juliette turned to Wood. "Has the victim been formally identified?"

Isabella shook her head. "We're struggling to find next of kin, so we will be seeking her medical records tomorrow."

CHAPTER FIFTEEN

Juliette nodded her round face, her auburn ringlets bouncing. "We can tell the press there's been no formal identification yet, and family are in the process of being identified." She paused. "Who is the victim?"

"Eighty-seven-year-old Rita Holdsworth of 2 Maple Rise, Rothwell, though we obviously can't tell them that."

Juliette frowned. "What can we tell them?"

"A detailed search of both scenes will go into a second day, and house-to-house enquiries are continuing."

The DCI nodded. "What did you learn from Dr Ross?" asked Atkinson.

Wood said, "Time of death not conclusive as of yet, but Dr Ross said last night or the early hours of this morning. He'll know more once he does the PM."

"Do we need to appeal for information about the burn-out grey Kia Venga?" asked Juliette.

"I think we do, yes," said Wood. "As you know, a dog walker found the car in Rothwell's Springfield Park car park this morning. So far, house-to-house has come up with nothing, and we could really do with identifying any witnesses who saw anything unusual in both the vicinity of Holy Trinity Church and Springfield Park car park."

Atkinson and Thompson were taking notes; then, the DCI met eyes with Wood. "Are you going to attend?"

"Do I have to?"

"As SIO, I think it's necessary," said Juliette Thompson.

Of course, it is, Isabella thought.

She was about to protest when her phone began ringing in her pocket. She looked at the caller ID. "It's the pathologist," Wood explained, getting up and leaving the DCI's office. "Hello, Dr Ross."

"Isabella, I'm just about to start the PM. Can you get here?"

She chewed the inside of her cheek as she considered the lesser evil. A PM or a press conference? Isabella weighed up her options. Ideally, she'd attend neither, but she couldn't be arsed dealing with the ice queen.

"OK, I'm on my way."

She knocked on the door to Atkinson's office and entered. She smiled at Alistair. "Dr Ross is about to start the PM and thinks it would be a good idea if I were there."

"That's rather convenient," said Juliette Thompson.

"Convenient but essential," Wood said with a smirk. She turned to DCI Atkinson. "I'll be back later for the briefing."

* * *

At his desk, George quickly typed up a statement of their conversation with Jean Lickiss, then started typing up Geoff's. He'd left his door open, and the shared office was unusually quiet, and none of his detectives were around. Out searching for Martha and Faith Lickiss, he hoped.

Nobody had seen either of them.

Even the calls from well-meaning members of the public had dackered off.

As usual, they'd had hundreds of calls from across the country, but not one of them had paid off.

What was he missing?

Mr Lickiss had confided in them that Martha had often beaten the girls black and blue when they were growing up. Geoff told George he'd even considered kicking Martha out at one point, but the girls had convinced him not to.

He headed towards Yolanda's desk, remembering he needed

to go through Martha's letters. Opening Yolanda's drawer, he found the copies.

Would they give him a clue as to why the Lickiss family had been targeted?

"I've looked through those," Yolanda said, coming in with two cups of tea. She sat down and patted the office chair next to her.

"Find owt?"

"Nope." She took a sip of her tea. "Love letters by the look of it."

"From Geoff?"

"No clue," she said. "The letters are undated and unsigned, remember."

"Shite, I wish we could ask her." George scratched his beard, then took a sip of his tea. "Maybe they were from another guy?"

Yolanda nodded. "Maybe. It'd make sense why they weren't signed."

"Any news on Faith?" George asked.

"I've arranged for us to go to Rothwell Academy in the morning and interview the twins' classmates. They may know something."

"Why didn't we do this sooner?"

"I guess we were so focussed on Geoff Lickiss that we thought he'd tell us where she was."

"Yeah, I suppose." His head was hurting, and he wanted to call it a day. But they still had a missing girl and mother out there, and Hope in the morgue.

Just as George was about to take a sip of tea, his mobile rang. "DI Beaumont."

"Hi George, it's Lindsey. I've got something for you."

"DS Yolanda is here. I'm putting you on speaker." He placed the phone down on Yolanda's desk. "Go on."

"After finishing up in Martha's room, we conducted further searches of the twins' bedrooms."

"How come?" asked Yolanda.

"Because we find all sorts of hidey-holes. It's an old house, so we assumed the other bedrooms would have similar hiding places."

"And did they?" George asked.

"They did. We found money in Faith's bedroom."

"Money? How much."

"Over a grand, George. All notes. Rolled up and stuffed in a sock."

"Holy shit," he said.

"How does a fifteen-year-old get a grand in cash?" asked Yolanda.

"I don't know," said Lindsey. "It's at the lab as we speak to see if they can pull any profiles or prints, but I'll be honest with you, the material these new notes are made of makes it difficult to get anything from them."

Thinking about the rumours and what Jean and Taylor told them, George asked, "Could she have been saving that money to run away?"

The question was aimed at Yolanda, but Lindsey answered, "That's your job, not mine."

"Did you find anything else, Lindsey?"

"A laptop. That's been sent to digital forensics."

"Thank you."

Lindsey hung up, and both detectives turned to each other.

"Think it's a running-away fund?" George asked.

"She's already gone." Yolanda shrugged. "Why would she

do it without this money, though?"

Thinking about the plants, George asked, "Could it be drug money?" He didn't think they were cannabis plants but was sure he'd seen something like them before. He'd forgotten to ask Lindsey for an update.

* * *

The post-mortem was well underway by the time DS Wood arrived at St James' Hospital. She had driven slowly in the hope that Dr Ross would start without her, and her plan seemed to have worked. Isabella had been let in by one of the technicians and was shown through to a room adjacent to the lab where Wood could see Dr Ross hard at work through viewing windows.

She could also see Rita Holdsworth laid out on the slab.

With Dictaphone in hand, she watched Dr Ross measuring and recording before he was interrupted by the technician who had let her in. The next thing he knew, the intercom crackled into life.

"Come in, dear, and have a look. You won't find out much from there."

Wood considered using her pregnancy as an excuse but took a deep breath and walked into the lab. The technician handed Wood a paper mask, which she put across her nose and mouth and hooked the elastic over her ears. "Anything interesting?"

"Yes," replied Ross, "take a look at this."

Ross pointed to Rita Holdsworth's neck. Wood stepped forward. The sight that greeted her took her breath away. She swallowed a tiny bit of puke.

Dr Ross smiled but said nothing.

Rita Holdsworth's eyes and mouth were now closed, but all she could think about were the bulging eyes and tongue she'd witnessed earlier.

"Can you see the bruising on the neck?"

Wood nodded. "Yes."

"It's uniform in width. See that?"

Wood nodded. "What could have caused it?"

"A collar of some kind or a belt."

Wood's eyes bulged. "Oh my god."

"Indeed."

"I also want you to look at this," Ross said. He pointed to her knees and then her hands. "What does that look like to you?" asked Ross.

"That she was dragged along the ground."

"That's right. I imagine this poor woman was dragged towards where she was killed, wearing a collar or belt around her neck."

"Like a dog on a lead?"

Dr Ross nodded gravely.

"Christ."

"Indeed."

"So, what's the official cause of death?" asked Wood.

"She was stabbed in the chest with a blade that penetrated her heart, causing tremendous blood loss."

Wood nodded. "Exsanguination?"

"Correct."

"Any guess as to what kind of blade?"

"The wound measures ten inches long and two inches wide. The blade was extremely sharp. That's all I can tell you." He shrugged. "If you find a weapon, though, we can test the profile against the wound."

CHAPTER FIFTEEN

"Thank you." CSI hadn't found anything yet, but the churchyard was vast, and the search would definitely continue into tomorrow.

"Any defensive wounds?"

Dr Ross shook his head. "I've taken blood samples and sent them to toxicology already," he explained. "It appears she was subdued by a chemical before being collared."

Wood asked, "What sort of chemical would do that?"

"There are many that would work. GHB, ketamine, or Rohypnol would work. As would the scopolamine you had to deal with earlier in the year."

"And you're testing for all of those?"

"Correct," said Ross.

"How long before they come back?"

"A few days, Isabella."

"Have you found anything we can tie to the killer?" Wood asked.

"I've found some fibres. Once the lab has processed them, they'll let you know. And it'll all be in my report. I've still got a few hours of work ahead of me."

Isabella nodded. "Found any foreign DNA or prints?"

He shook his head. "She wasn't sexually assaulted either before you ask."

"Thank you, Dr Ross," she said. "I'll leave you to it, then." She removed her mask, and the technician showed her out.

Chapter Sixteen

The Incident Room at Elland Road Police Station was a hive of activity when DS Wood arrived for the briefing just after 7 pm. DC Tashan Blackburn was staring intently at the Big Board, and various other officers, who had been drafted in to assist the investigation, were answering telephones. It appeared the press conference had gone well.

DS Yolanda Williams was reviewing CCTV footage on her computer. Isabella stood up at the front of the room, next to the whiteboard, and called the briefing to order.

"Good evening, everyone. As you know, we're looking into the death of Rita Holdsworth. I've just returned from the PM and I'm awaiting Dr Ross' formal report, but the cause of death was exsanguination caused by a sharp blade to the heart." She explained the dimensions of the blade to the team, then explained the ligature marks around Rita's neck and the theory Dr Ross had.

After the noises of shock and disgust had died down, Wood looked at Tashan. "What have you got for us?"

"Rita lived alone, her husband having passed away a decade ago. She has no social media presence, but officers taking statements from neighbours mentioned a daughter named Elizabeth. I've searched for Elizabeth Holdsworth on the

PNC but found nothing. I also checked with the DWP but got nothing, Sarge."

"Good job, DC Blackburn. Keep looking." She explained how she would visit Rita's GP in the morning to retrieve the next of kin details. "Did any of the neighbours say anything about other friends or family?"

DC Blackburn checked his notes. "Only that she was really into genealogy, and she was part of a club in Rothwell. They meet at Blackburn Hall every second Monday of the month."

"That's tomorrow, right?" asked Wood.

"Right."

"OK, call the group in the morning. I want to attend."

"Yes, Sarge," said Tashan.

"Anything else?"

"I've checked for CCTV coverage, Sarge," said Yolanda, "but it's minimal at best. The pub next to the church does, however, have a camera in the car park, but it belongs to the council. In between working with DI Beaumont, I've been trying all day to contact them without much luck."

"Visit Merrion House in the morning, Yolanda, and demand the CCTV. The killer must have transported Rita to the church in a vehicle, especially if she was drugged as Dr Ross suggested."

"I agree, Sarge."

"Right, you lot, head home, and I'll see you all bright and early in the morning."

* * *

Rex, the Jack Russel Terrier, jumped up, dotting George with licks, his tail wagging so fast it made George's eyes go funny.

Wincing, George dropped to a knee and started to fuss with the dog. "Now then, boy, I missed you too." He patted the dog and scratched his chin.

George threw on his orange Dragon Ball hoodie and grabbed Rex's lead and harness, the metal clasp of the leash clinking against the shoe cabinet they had by the front door. Before he could call the dog, Rex barrelled out, sliding on the rug by the front door as he quickly came to a halt. "Walkies?" he asked the dog as he bent down to put Rex into his red harness. Then he clipped Rex's lead to it, sending him into another frenzy of excitement.

George tested the pavement with his hand before committing to the walk. It was still bright outside on that summer night, but the heat had started to dissipate. He'd left Isabella in the bath. Her entire body was aching from the pregnancy now, and whilst he desperately wanted to be home with her, washing her back and holding her hand, he knew the pup needed some attention too.

With his tongue sticking out, Rex yammered as he pulled George up the garden path. George's stomach growled as they headed towards Lewisham Park, where Rex could have a run out on the field for a bit. George was tired from work, but he'd made a commitment to Rex when they'd got him.

He unclipped Rex from the lead and let the dog race off towards a tree to their left, standing to watch the dog run loops around the trunk as he chased his tail.

His phone buzzed in his pocket. "DI Beaumont?"

"George, it's DCI Alexander. Were you aware Jean Lickiss visited her brother Geoff in prison this evening?"

The DI scratched his chin. "No, sir."

The silence was awkward, but George didn't want to break it.

CHAPTER SIXTEEN

The DCI rarely called him, especially when he was home. He looked up at the sky; it was getting darker as the day progressed into the night. He hoped for rain but knew there wasn't any forecast. A hosepipe ban was currently in place.

"It's suspicious," the DCI eventually said.

Sweating, George walked after the pup, who was sniffing a different trunk. "I agree, sir. What do you want me to do about it?" When Rex saw his master, he sprinted over. "Sit," George said, gingerly kneeling and placing the mobile between his ear and shoulder. And the pup did. "Paw." The pup offered his paw. George pulled a treat from his hoodie pocket and offered it to the dog, who took it from George and greedily inhaled it. "Good boy."

"I want you to bring her in and interview her. I want to know why she went to visit Geoff."

"I can tell you that now, sir," the DI said, forging after Rex, who had sprinted towards the basketball court, tail wagging. "Rex, here, boy!"

The dog stopped in his tracks and turned towards George, who, again, gingerly kneeled. "Here!" George commanded.

"You out with the dog, George?" the DCI asked.

'Whatever gave you that bloody idea, Sherlock?' he wanted to ask. Instead, he said, "Yes." The DI took a deep breath, then said, "I'll sort Jean Lickiss for you tomorrow, sir."

Looping back and forth, Rex barked happily, delighted he was allowed to continue towards the kids playing in the park. The pup loved children, but welcoming a baby into the family did worry George. He hung up his mobile and put it away.

Half an hour later, George kicked his shoes off by the door and took off his jacket, making a mental note to put the shoes away in the cabinet later; otherwise, Isabella would moan at him. He chucked his hoodie into the cupboard next to it, and after removing Rex's harness and lead, he scooped up the post from atop the shoe cabinet.

Rex trotted ahead, tail wagging.

Then he sat on the sofa, Rex curled into his side, with the TV on, but George wasn't paying attention to it in the slightest. The letters were all bills, but it was the case distracting him from the TV, as usual, taking over all of his mental space.

Isabella had chucked together a stir fry—noodles, bean sprouts, chicken, and some soy sauce—and handed him a plate filled to the brim before leaving him with the dog and sitting down on the two-seater opposite.

"Thanks, babe," he said, smiling at Isabella.

"Are you OK?"

"I'm not sure."

"The case getting to you?"

George shrugged. "Always does, you know that."

"Indeed I do." She took a mouthful, chewed slowly, and then swallowed. "You still thinking about Geoff Lickiss?"

George nodded. "The DCI called me when I was out with Rex. Apparently, Jean Lickiss went to visit him at Armley. He wants me to bring her in and question her."

She cocked her brow. "Can't a sister visit her brother in prison without it being suspicious?"

"Apparently not." He ran a hand through his blond hair and scratched behind his ear. "I think interviewing her is a waste of time. All she'll say is she thinks Geoff is innocent, and I think I'm starting to agree." He shrugged and took a bite of his tea.

"But if Geoff isn't involved, then who is?" she asked.

Again, George shrugged. He'd put it to the team tomorrow

and see what questions and answers got thrown about. He couldn't do this alone, and he knew it. He needed the team. "I really don't know."

* * *

Sobbing, Faith Lickiss shivered beneath the rough blanket. Everything that had happened was all her fault. She should never have listened to him. Some people were just bad news. But the money had been impossible to resist. Things had gone too far. Liberties had been taken. And now her family had paid the ultimate price.

She was next; she just knew it. There was no reason to keep her alive any more. She was a witness he wouldn't want alive.

She picked up her phone and debated putting in the SIM and switching it on. Faith knew if she did that, then it could be traced.

That or she could call them—the police. Explain the situation.

But then, they'd hear her, surely. The walls were thin.

They'd been too trusting and hadn't searched her, but she was done if they found the mobile on her. It would be the end for her.

But Faith knew she had to tell someone about what she'd overheard, what she'd seen. Could she wait another day? Or was she killing more people by waiting?

What should she do?

Pulling the musty blanket over her head, she lay in the darkness and listened to the birds singing outside.

She missed her mother.

She missed her twin.

She wanted her father.

Faith Lickiss was terrified, not of death, but of what might happen next.

Chapter Seventeen

Back at the station that morning, George stood in the middle of the Incident Room, wondering which direction to lead the investigation.

Bursting through the door, Detective Chief Inspector Atkinson said, "Inspector Beaumont, my office."

"Fuck me," George muttered as the DCI turned on his heel and left the Incident Room door.

George strolled down the hall after the DCI and into his office. A mixture of scents assaulted George's nose. Lynx Africa mixed with sweat and something spicy and garlicky. A curry? Or a kebab? Was DCI Alexander working late last night? Is that why he called George whilst he was out with the dog?

"Sit."

"Everything OK?" George asked, then added, "Sir?"

"I thought I asked you to bring Jean Lickiss into the station this morning?"

George nodded. "I did." The DI frowned. "Well, I asked PS Greenwood to get his uniforms to bring her in."

"Why wasn't I informed?"

"I didn't realise you wanted to be informed, sir."

"I specifically asked you to bring her in, Beaumont. That means I want to be in the know."

"Oh, right. Sorry, sir."

The DCI hadn't sat down yet and towered over George. If he was trying to be intimidating, then he was failing.

George sat there, unfazed.

"What did she tell you?"

'What I thought she'd tell me,' George wanted to say. Instead, he gritted his teeth momentarily, then said, "Geoff is Jean's brother. She doesn't think for one minute he's guilty, so she wanted to visit him and remind him he wasn't alone during all of this."

"That's it?"

George nodded. "Correct, sir."

"Did you push her for information?"

George began to stand, but the DCI held out his hand. "Sit down and answer the question."

"I did not, no."

"Why not?"

"Because it seemed pointless." George scratched his beard. "Why don't you review the tape, sir? And then, if you're unhappy with what I did, bring her back in and question her yourself?"

The DCI stood up straight, and his face flashed crimson. "I'm going to take that in the way I hope it was meant, Beaumont, and not how it sounded. OK?"

George shifted in his seat. It was uncomfortable, and he was in a lot of pain today. "OK."

Atkinson continued. "Any other updates for me?"

The DI shook his head. "No, sir. We're still looking for Faith and Martha Lickiss, but there's no sign of them."

"Then piss off, and get some bloody work done!"

George nodded and left as fast as he could. Outside he took

a deep breath, getting rid of the stink of the DCI's office as quickly as possible.

* * *

Standing in front of the Big Board in the incident room, George said, "We need to find Martha, thirty-nine, and Faith Lickiss, fifteen, and put all of this to bed! Now!"

He was met with nods from his team. They looked unmotivated, and he couldn't blame them. They'd already arrested somebody, yet George asked them to look through all the evidence in case they missed something.

"As you know, fifteen-year-old Hope Lickiss was murdered in her home in Rothwell. We believe the culprit was her father, Geoff Lickiss." George outlined the details of the assault, concluding with, "Death was via blunt-force trauma to the back of the skull, causing a fatal brain aneurysm. His prints are on the murder weapon, which he says he bought as a gift in America."

"Any other prints, boss?"

"What you'd expect, Jay," George said. "We've found Hope's and another two sets we assume belong to Martha and Faith." Despite the girls being identical twins, fingerprints were always unique. "There's another set of unique prints on the back window of the farmhouse."

"Those prints could be the killers, though, boss."

"They could be," said George. "Whoever they belong to isn't on the system."

"Geoff Lickiss also wears a size seven shoe, and we found a leather jacket at the farmhouse with his bus ticket in it. We also have evidence he was threatening his ex-wife most nights leading up to her disappearance. So far, he denies everything."

"What's Geoff's motive?" Jay asked.

George said, "You tell me."

"Martha had an occupational order against him, effectively kicking him out of his family home. The Lickiss twins look like younger versions of their mother, so I suspect he attacked Hope thinking it was Martha. Then he abducted Martha and Faith."

It sounded solid, but the man was an incredibly bad liar.

When nobody said anything, Yolanda said, "I think we need to start from scratch because it's looking increasingly like Geoff Lickiss is innocent."

"But still a liar," George pointed out.

"Oh, I agree, I think he's hiding something, but I don't think he killed his daughter and then abducted his other daughter and ex-wife."

"Speaking of the ex-wife, what do we know about her?"

Rustling through a file on his knee, Jay extracted a printout. "I spoke with the neighbours, and there are no reports of a partner in her life, boss. One did say she was addicted to a genealogy website, and another mentioned Martha was doing a university course."

"What was she studying?" George asked.

"Teaching. The hard drive is corrupt from the beating the laptop received, but we've sent it off to see if anything can be salvaged."

"Contact whoever is running the course."

"I did, sir. All the secretary did was confirm Martha had completed year one and was to start year two in October."

George nodded. "What else do we know about her?"

"She was adopted, and as far as I could tell, didn't have

CHAPTER SEVENTEEN

anything to do with her birth family." He looked down at the printouts. "Adopted parents are now deceased. Her mother, Mavis Mook, got terminal cancer and died first, and then her father, Ted Mook, died on the operating table after falling and breaking a hip."

"It's interesting that Martha was addicted to genealogy when she was adopted. Look into that, Jay. And get Martha's adoption records. The killer could be somebody from her birth family."

"Will do, boss."

He looked around the room. "Anything else?"

DS Yolanda Williams said, "Luke left a note on my desk saying he'd received more calls from the appeal regarding Faith Lickiss. Of the ten calls he thought were genuine, only one appeared to be sound. But by the time uniform arrived, whoever the public had seen was gone."

"Did you check the Aldi CCTV, Yolanda?" George asked.

"I did, sir. Geoff definitely went inside the supermarket. He had his leather jacket on, too. He bought cider and crisps. And as we already know, he turned right."

George nodded. "OK, did you all read the email I sent last night?"

Each detective nodded.

What did we all think of the money found in Faith's bedroom."

"Same as you, boss," said Jay. "Gotta be drug money, right?"

Yolanda was also nodding.

"There's no other explanation, is there?" said George.

"Did she have a rich boyfriend? Or girlfriend?" Jay offered.

"We asked Geoff whether Faith had a boyfriend, but he said he thought not. DS Wood and I are going to Rothwell Academy shortly to interview the twins' friends and peers."

Despite it being the holidays, the staff, parents, and pupils of the year 11 class who had finished their GCSEs in June had agreed to come in and chat with them.

"I still think it's drug-related. Have the plants found in the coal bunker been identified yet?" He looked at his team, who looked clueless. "Jay, email Lindsey and get her to follow it up, please."

The young DC nodded his head and blinked his blue eyes, then looked down at his computer and started clacking away.

George took a deep breath. "Are you all clear on what you've got to do?"

He was met with nods of the head and thumbs up.

"Then off you go."

Chapter Eighteen

Despite being born in Oldham and growing up in Middleton, Isabella Wood had actually attended Rothwell Academy, though it had been called something different back then. The sight and smells of the place, even devoid of any pupils, immediately carried her back to her own teenage years.

The crumbling corridors were still the same, bringing back memories, both good and bad.

She held up her warrant card so the elderly woman behind the front desk could see and was met with a warm smile. Isabella was sure the woman had worked there when she'd attended. In fact, she was positive. But back then, she wouldn't have received a smile. No, she'd have received a scowl and a bollocking.

After a quick chat, the receptionist took Wood to an empty classroom near the hall and advised she would get Faith's form tutor.

She couldn't remember whether she'd had any classes in this particular room back in the day, but then they all looked the same.

A slim, female teacher in her late fifties or early sixties with short greying hair entered after knocking and sat opposite the detective. She was dressed conservatively, with only minimum makeup, a bit like Wood herself, really, wearing black trousers and a lilac blouse.

"I'm Detective Sergeant Wood," Isabella said, holding out her warrant card. "Have you been told why I'm here?"

"To talk about the Lickiss twins?" the teacher asked, and Wood nodded. "I'm Liz Brearley." She held out a hand which Wood shook. "It's awful what's happened," Liz said, showing her teeth. Her smile was wide and toothy, revealing a set of dimples. "That poor family."

"So, what have you heard?" Wood pressed.

A look of panic spread across Liz's face, though that didn't mean anything. Most people panicked when questioned by the police. She took a sip of water from the bottle she'd brought with her. "Just what everybody else knows, that Faith's missing."

"That's all you know?" Wood asked. She had no reason to believe Faith's form tutor had abducted her, but stranger things had happened.

"Well, other than what happened to poor Hope. And their mother." Liz looked down at the ground, blinking. Her concern for herself gave way to worry about the family.

"How well did you know Faith?"

"As well as any form tutor who has another thirty children in her form could," Liz said. "I have them for fifteen minutes in the morning and fifteen minutes at the end of school. Take that as you will."

Not very well then, Wood thought. "When was the last time you saw her?"

"In June, I think," said Liz. "Year eleven get to leave after their GCSEs."

Isabella took a breath. She was eyeing up the water bottle.

She'd left hers in the Merc. "Thanks. We're hoping one of her friends might be able to tell us something."

"Sure," Liz said. "You'll want to talk to Zara, Skye, and Kenzie. They're nice girls, just like Faith is."

Liz grimaced, and Wood decided to move on. "If you could send them in, that would be perfect."

"Together?"

"Yes."

"Without their parents."

Wood nodded.

"I'm not sure Mr Gentle will be too happy about that."

"What, Mental Gentle, Jesus Christ. Looks like a vicious version of Professor Snape?"

Liz giggled at that. "Aye, that's right. Mental Gentle."

"He was my chemistry teacher when I was here, and he was no spring chicken then," Wood said. He was a tall, slender man she remembered had worked at Lofthouse Academy, too. "I'm amazed he's still alive. Is he going for the world record or something? World's Oldest Teacher?"

Liz's smile widened. "I mean, he's already got the Oldest Teacher With The Greasiest Hair award and the Oldest Teacher Who Wears Sandals With Socks medal, so he might as well go for the treble."

Wood chuckled at that. "What a legend."

Liz stood up. "Shall I get those girls for you then?"

* * *

Wood took pleasure in the relative quiet as she sat on a hard plastic seat and softly massaged her temples with the tips of her fingers. She had forgotten how demanding teenage girls could be, especially when there was a hint of drama to whip themselves up over. She ought to have brought them in one at a time. They would have been easier to handle on their own. Trying to get serious answers from them all at once was like herding kittens, kittens who were overly animated and didn't hesitate to talk a lot of rubbish. They had said a lot, but Wood had taken in very little.

Faith, it seemed, had many best friends in her year group. That, or many girls in the year group, considered Faith, their best friend. Wood couldn't quite figure the excitable cherubs out. What they did do, however, was reaffirm Faith's reputation as a kind girl, repeating what the teacher had said about her. Then again, they all were. The group of friends Faith belonged to didn't do drugs, nor did they drink or smoke. Zara, Skye, and Faith all lacked a boyfriend, whilst Kenzie had been in a casual relationship with a 'fit' boy named Callum, who was in the sixth form. Kenzie was apparently breaking up with the fit boy because all he wanted from her was naked selfies. That, and despite being a year older than her, Callum lacked maturity.

Plus, even if Kenzie wanted to send Callum nudes, she knew half the school would see them. And she wasn't that stupid. Just last year, Callum's mate received a nude selfie from eighteen-year-old Suzie in year thirteen, and they had quickly spread around Rothwell and Oulton.

"And they even got as far as Belle Isle, Armley, and Morley!" Kenzie was quick to point out. "God, if my tits ever got leaked, I'd have to move to Wakefield." She'd gestured emphatically. "Wakefield, can you imagine?"

Wood had tried to move the subject back to Faith Lickiss, but Kenzie wasn't finished there. She told Wood how Callum's brother hadn't even felt guilty about it; in fact, he still apparently took the piss out of Suzie even now. "Then again, Suzie was flat-chested. I'm not. Maybe Callum wouldn't have taken the piss out of them?"

A pain had started intensifying behind Wood's left eye, and she was struggling to get comfy on the hard plastic seat. It was at this point she'd regretted bringing the group in together.

Isabella tried to bring the conversation back to Faith after advising the girls not to do anything as bloody stupid as sending sexual images of themselves to anyone.

Kenzie had seen Faith the day before she disappeared. They'd met at Morrisons in Rothwell and messed about in the trolley bays.

Zara hadn't seen much of Faith because her mother had forced her to attend summer school. At first, Zara had looked annoyed, but as Wood probed, she found out that Zara was a bit of a genius, especially in maths, something that Faith, Kenzie and Skye all hated. Alongside the summer school, Zara participated in events. And two months ago, she represented the school in a national competition and won second place. Zara scowled as she mentioned second place. She should have come first, but she was robbed.

Wood puffed out her cheeks as Zara continued, explaining she wasn't a fan of English because it was all about interpretation rather than facts, like science.

Clear answers were her favourite. So was right and wrong.

Isabella had brought up their missing friend a final time during the course of the conversation.

"Are you sure Faith didn't have a boyfriend?" Wood asked.

Various phrases that meant, "If she did, I didn't know about it," came out of the girls' mouths.

"When was the last time you saw Faith, Skye?" Wood asked.

Skye indicated it had been the day she'd gone missing. They'd gone into Leeds together to look around the shops because Faith's sixteenth birthday was coming up. But they'd gotten on separate buses home because of the different parts of Rothwell they lived in.

"Tell me about money, girls. Faith was still fifteen, so she didn't have a job, right?"

"Right," said Zara.

"Did she ever have money?"

Kenzie said, "Faith always had money." She shrugged. "Faith would always buy us stuff. You know, food at Morrisons or drinks in town. She'd even pay for bus fare if we couldn't go out. She was kind like that."

"OK, talk to me about texts, girls," Wood then said. "I'm always messaging my girlfriends on WhatsApp and other social media sites."

"We do that too," said Kenzie.

After ten or so minutes, and Wood taking a gander through the girls' phones, Faith had stopped messaging them around 6 pm the night she'd gone missing and hadn't messaged them since, which of course, they'd all thought was a bit weird, since they usually messaged each other all evening, right into the small hours.

The girls hadn't been able to offer much more. Wood had to ask them to return to their parents, who were waiting in the hall, because she couldn't cope with one more minute of unrelated anecdotes, even if it were about two year seven kids who organised a scrap on the bus on the last day of school.

But then, as the girls got up to leave, one more question came to Wood's mind. "Has Faith had a falling out with anyone

CHAPTER EIGHTEEN

recently, girls?"

They all shook their heads. Faith hadn't.

And that question meant Wood had a follow-up. She'd asked if Faith had been upset, or depressed, or was acting differently.

Again, they all shook their heads. Faith wasn't.

More and more questions occurred to Wood, so she apologised and asked the girls to sit back down. Then she asked about Martha and Geoff.

"We all argue with our parents, Detective," Zara said. "Faith did, too, though I think she argued more with her mum because of the divorce."

"What do you mean."

"I meant because her dad wasn't living with her."

Wood nodded. "Did she get on well with her dad?"

Zara had said, "Yes, she loved the man. She always talked about how she would live with him when she was eighteen."

"Did she say why?"

"No, never," Kenzie added. "She was quiet like that. Withdrawn. She kept things close to her chest."

"Did she ever talk about any other family members?"

"Just about her uncle, Nigel," Skye said.

Wood narrowed her eyes. She knew a Nigel Lickiss existed, but he wasn't on their radar. She raised her brows at Skye, who got the point and added, "He's a paedo, isn't he?"

If Nigel was, then Isabella wasn't aware. In fact, he was sure the man wasn't a convicted paedophile; otherwise, HOLMES would have flagged that up instantly. "Can you elaborate for me, please, Skye?"

"Wasn't he arrested for child abuse?" Skye asked.

"Why would you think that?" asked Wood.

"That's what Faith told us," offered Zara. "Kiddie porn on

his laptop. Disgusting bastard."

She placed a hand over her mouth at the curse, and Wood smiled. "Don't worry; I won't tell your mum."

"Thank you," Zara mouthed.

Isabella made a note to check up on Nigel Lickiss. He could have taken Faith. Did that mean he was one of the people in the Fiesta? It made sense; paedophile rings meant people worked in groups. And if Hope had been mistaken for Martha, then it could mean somebody intended to traffic the twins.

Finally, she asked about Hope. It seemed the two twins weren't joined at the hip at school and had separate circles of friends. It meant Zara, Kenzie, and Sky didn't know Hope very well.

Wood let the girls go back to their parents. If she needed more from them, she could get it one-on-one and save herself the headache of dealing with them as a trio.

She held her bump and wondered whether she was growing a boy or a girl. She also considered whether she'd been that annoying growing up.

Scribbling down some of the things the girls had said before she could forget them, Isabella got up to check in with Sergeant Greenwood and his uniforms, who were taking statements from members of staff and the twins' peers.

Just as her bum left the seat, there was a knock on the classroom door.

"Come in," Wood called.

A young lad entered after the door was opened. He was short and had dark hair that had been graded drastically close to the boy's scalp.

The girls who had just left had all worn various fashionable outfits, whilst the boy was wearing his school uniform.

CHAPTER EIGHTEEN

Wood thought that was weird, considering it was the six-week holidays.

The lad, wearing a pair of thick-framed glasses that hung from a string around his neck, ambled towards Isabella, appearing to be a short-sighted gentleman in his seventies.

Wood smiled at how cute the lad was.

And he blushed in return.

Isabella raised her brows and gave the boy her best smile. "Can I help you?" the DS asked.

"No. But... But maybe I can help you," the lad replied.

Chapter Nineteen

"I'm Detective Sergeant Wood," Isabella said. "What's your name?"

With intense eye contact, the lad said, "Harry."

"How can I help you, Harry?"

"Like I said. I can help you."

"Go on."

"Sit down, please. This may take a while, and someone in your condition should be sat."

Isabella frowned and lowered herself back onto the hard plastic seat. "Go on."

"I have some information to share with you about Faith Lickiss."

"The floor's yours, kid," she said, grinning. She rested her elbows on the table and held her chin in her hands.

The young lad still didn't break eye contact.

"She's missing, right?"

"Right."

"I've seen the posts and the appeals."

"OK."

"My theory is that Faith's run off to be with her boyfriend."

Wood raised her brows. "I'm told she doesn't have a boyfriend."

CHAPTER NINETEEN

"Yet I know for a fact that she does," Harry insisted.

"That's not what her friends told me. Nor her father."

"Well, I know differently."

Isabella asked, "What do you know?"

"That she has a boyfriend."

"Are you a friend of hers?"

Harry shook his head. "No."

Wood frowned. "Then how do you know?"

Harry looked down at the floor and said nothing.

"Come on, Harry, spit it out."

Beetroot, Harry said. "I followed her."

The desk creaked as Wood got up and stared at Harry. "You followed her?"

"That's right."

"Why?"

"She's cute."

Wood rubbed her right eye. The exhaustion was getting to her. She only had five weeks left until she dropped.

"Plus, I live down the road from her, so I see her often."

"When was the last time you followed her?"

"The day she went missing."

Wood leaned forward and pulled out her phone. "You happy if I record this?"

"Will my voice appear anywhere?"

"No, it's just for my notes."

"Fine."

"Thank you."

"You're welcome."

"Continue, please."

"So, she got off the bus and walked past my house. I was in the living room and noticed her walking by. She stopped and answered her phone. I couldn't resist, so I snuck outside and listened in." He shrugged. "Then she turned around and walked the other way."

Wood nodded, trying to process what the lad was saying. "So you followed her, and you saw what, exactly?"

"Faith with her boyfriend. He's not from the school, though; he's older."

"How do you know he was her boyfriend? What if he was just a friend? Or a family member?"

Harry turned beetroot again, asking, "Do you let your friends or family stick their tongues down your throat? Do you let them grab your breasts as they do that?"

The DS shook her head. "No."

"Didn't think so."

"OK, boyfriend then?"

"As I said."

She was starting to get fed up with the sassy young lad, but he clearly had information nobody else had. "Do you know who he is?"

Harry shook his head.

"Can you describe him for me?"

Harry closed his eyes and then nodded. "A black man of over six foot with cornrows and a beard."

"Anything else?"

"He was wearing an oversized grey shirt with matching trousers, black dress shoes, and an absolutely massive silver chain around his neck."

"You've got a good memory," Wood remarked.

"No, my memory is awful." Harry pulled his phone out of his pocket, one of those Samsung ones that flipped in half, and held it out for Wood to have a look at.

CHAPTER NINETEEN

It showed a man matching the description Harry had just given, with one arm draped possessively over the shoulder of Faith Lickiss.

"Can you send me this?" Wood asked. "And any others you have?"

Harry nodded and accepted the business card Wood held out. It had her email address on there.

A staccato set of pings a moment later meant she'd received five images.

"Thank you."

"My pleasure." He stood quickly, then sat back down. He pointed towards the pocket where her phone was. "You recognise him." It wasn't a question but a statement.

"What makes you say that?" she asked as her phone pinged. She smiled at Harry and pulled out her phone. It was from George. The DCI had asked him to return to the station ASAP, so he'd left her the Merc and called a taxi. "Sorry about that, Harry. What makes you think I recognise him?"

"Because you didn't ask me for his name," said Harry. "I've seen how this works on TV, and detectives always ask for a name." Then he shrugged. "Well, unless the detective already knows. Which you quite clearly do."

Wood said nothing, not taking her eyes from the lad. She wondered whether he was autistic and was about to ask him when she figured it was none of her business.

"Your silence means I'm correct." Again, another statement.

"Perhaps," Wood said with a smile. "I'll ask the team and see if they know him."

* * *

DC Tashan Blackburn's name flashed up on DS Wood's phone a minute or two after she'd excused Harry. She was waiting for Liz Brearley to come and collect her, wanting to have a more in-depth chat about the twins as the teacher escorted her out of the premises.

"DS Wood," she said.

"Sarge, it's Tashan."

"What have you got for me, Constable?"

"Rita's next of kin is her daughter, Elizabeth."

"Well, we already knew that from the house-to-house, Tashan. Tell me something I don't know."

"Her full name is Elizabeth Brearley," he said, "a married teacher at Rothwell Academy."

"Which is where I am now."

"Exactly."

"Shit." She wasn't prepared to give out bad news. "Thanks, Tashan, much appreciated." She paused. "Any other family members?"

"Not that I can see from the medical records, Sarge, but I'll keep looking."

"Cheers." She hung up the phone just as Liz Brearley entered the classroom and plonked her bum on a chair.

"It really is awful what's happened," Liz said, still attempting to smile. She'd removed her jacket since Isabella last saw her, and her hair fell in curls behind her ears instead of being tied atop her head in a tight bun.

"I need to talk to you about something sensitive, Liz," said Wood. "Something that has just come to my attention."

Another look of panic spread across Liz's face. "Is everything OK?"

"I'm afraid it's not, no. This is about your mother, Rita."

CHAPTER NINETEEN

* * *

After looking at the images Isabella had emailed to the shared inbox, DC Jason Scott said, "I know him. Tyrell Grant. He used to hang around with Colby Raggett."

George asked, "One of Jürgen Schmidt's lads?"

"That's right, boss, or he was, anyway." The young DC shrugged. "I haven't heard much about him for a while. To be fair, I assumed he'd gotten clean. Or left the business, anyway."

George nodded. He knew addiction was challenging to overcome. He also knew once the underworld got its hooks into you, even if you thought you were swimming away, they could easily reel you back in.

"I've got his address," Tashan piped up. The DI had noticed the young DC clacking away at his keyboard while discussing Raggett.

"He's on the PNC, then?"

Tashan nodded. "Not quite as long as Geoff Lickiss', but his list is pretty extensive."

Beaumont stood up. "Jay, I want you with me." He turned to the rest of the team. "Meanwhile, I want you all to look into Schmidt and his known associates. If he's involved in this, it could be an opportunity to finally get the fucker!"

Chapter Twenty

DI Beaumont learned a lot about Tyrell Grant on the way, specifically that he was a thief, a scallywag, and an ex-drug dealer if there was such a thing. He was twenty-three, and while the fact that he appeared to be shagging a fifteen-year-old was depressingly shocking, George didn't have him pegged as a kidnapper.

But he'd been wrong before and would be wrong again.

Hopefully, Faith had taken it upon herself to move in with him.

Tyrell, for all intents and purposes, was a good-looking lad. Isabella had called him 'easy on the eye' and said she could understand why a teenage girl could be drawn to a guy like that.

He'd raised his brow at her, and she'd winked back at him. George wasn't the jealous type, but since nearly falling to his death and the resulting change in his appearance and physique, he'd started feeling insecure.

Both detectives stood outside Tyrell's last known address, a terraced house on Third Avenue, holding down the buzzer.

On the way over, Jay had warned the DI about Tyrell's grandmother, a feisty woman with a short temper who had no love for the police. Her son, Tyrell's father, had been shot dead by armed police. During the investigation, the police watchdog looked into the shooting. Due to Grant being unarmed, they classified the death as a homicide. The Independent Office for Police Conduct (IOPC) charged the offending officer.

So George didn't exactly blame her.

Still, if Faith was with Tyrell, then it was in everyone's best interests that she surrender herself into protective custody straight away.

George rang the buzzer again, then looked over his shoulder at the young DC, who shrugged.

Soon, a shadow darkened the peephole, and George offered his best smile.

"What do you pigs want?" a female voice muttered from behind the door, very slurred and sounding as if she had chain-smoked for decades.

"Mrs Grant, I'm DI Beaumont and my colleague here is DC Scott."

"What do yer want?" Her voice sounded like she had a mouth full of gravel.

"Can we come in?" George asked.

"Have you got a warrant?"

George shook his head and bit the inside of his cheek. "No," he admitted.

"Then no, you fucking can't! What a stupid bloody question," the old woman rasped. "After what you lot did to my boy, you can get fucked!"

"It's about Tyrell." George scratched his beard. "We think he's in trouble," he lied.

"The boy's not 'ere, an' even if he wa', I wouldn't tell you, bastards."

"He's not in trouble with us, Mrs Grant," George said. "Is

Faith Lickiss with you?"

There was a long pause, and the DI was sure he could smell cigarette smoke. Eventually, she said, "Who?" and then erupted into a coughing fit that went on for several seconds.

"Faith Lickiss, Mrs Grant. Tyrell's girlfriend. She's missing. So is her mother."

The silence was deafening as George listened. A sudden wheeze broke it. "Tyrell doesn't have a girlfriend."

"Faith's fifteen, Mrs Grant. Her sister's been murdered, and her mother's missing." George paused for dramatic effect. "Please help us."

Another silence.

Then the sound of a chain jangling.

Mrs Grant opened the door, cigarette in one hand, a bottle of vodka in the other, her face scrunched up with fury. Her shoulders were stiff, her entire body like a spring, ready to explode. After taking in both detectives, she eventually said, "He's not 'ere. Hasn't been 'ere for four or five days."

That would mean he hadn't been home since Hope Lickiss was murdered, George thought.

"And he's not shagging a fifteen-year-old, trust me."

George grinned. "I agree with you, Mrs Grant. I think it's all just a misunderstanding," he said. "That's why I want to find him. Sort this all out before he gets accused of doing something he didn't do." Or somebody he didn't do, George wanted to say but held back.

When the reply came, she toned down the venom. "Sorry, love, not seen him." She shrugged, and her hand twitched, spilling ash everywhere. "I don't even know where he's gone."

Bollocks. That wasn't what George had been hoping for.

"You're sure?"

CHAPTER TWENTY

"Calling me a liar, boy?" Mrs Grant spat, her anger swelling again. "If I say I don't know where he's gone, then I dunno where he's gone, OK?"

"Right. OK. Well, thank you, Mrs Grant." He paused, wondering how best to frame his following sentence. "As I'm sure you realise, it's crucial that I talk to him. I'm sure you don't want your grandson being nicked by police for something he didn't do. You understand?"

"How fucking dare you use my boy against me?"

"I'm not using your son against you; I'm just saying I'm sure you don't want—"

Behind Mrs Grant, a shadow caught George's eye. The DI stepped closer, nearing the pungent scent of Mrs Grant, and squinted.

There, framed by the backdoor in the kitchen, was Tyrell Grant, his hands in the pockets of his trackie bottoms, his hood up, staring straight at George.

"Tyrell, we need to talk to you," George said, taking another step but being blocked by the older woman.

Tyrell's eyes widened, his jaw tightened, and George could see precisely what was about to happen. The DI raised a hand and called out to him, trying to stop him. "Tyrell, stop!"

But, like a startled rabbit, Tyrell spun around and pulled open the back door. Then Tyrell ran with a turn of speed, befitting somebody of his profession.

"I'll head around the back, boss," Jay said, spinning around and heading up Third Avenue.

George was conflicted. Did he also turn and head down Third Avenue? He knew from experience that the terraced housing had a ginnel that ran behind the back of the gardens, which could be accessed to the north on Temple Avenue, where Jay was racing towards, or Crescent Avenue, where George himself considered heading.

But if the DI didn't chase the scallywag, Grant could easily double back through his grandma's house, and then they'd have no chance of catching him.

So, he sidestepped Mrs Grant and launched himself through the house and into the back garden, seeing a flash of green—Tyrell's tracksuit—as he launched himself over the fence and into the ginnel.

"Stop, Tyrell; we just want to talk to you about Faith Lickiss! She's gone missing, and we need to find her!" George shouted.

But by the time George got to the fence and hoisted himself up to look over it, the scally was gone. He was fast. Way too fast. There was no way George could vault the fence like Grant had, not with the pain he was in. His lack of conditioning didn't help, either.

So he pulled out his mobile and jogged past Mrs Grant, who was Effing and Blinding, and headed towards Crescent Avenue when Jay picked up.

"Boss."

"He's in the ginnel, but I don't know which way he went," George explained. "I'm heading towards Crescent Ave as we speak, so I'll meet you in the middle. Hopefully, we can pincer him in."

But George wasn't convinced. All he could hope was that Tyrell tired quickly, but considering the lad's age and physique, he doubted it.

"It's too hot for this bullshit, boss," Jay said.

George powered on, hoping the man was still in the ginnel and not back at his grandma's, laughing his tits off as the two detectives chased a ghost. "Any sign, Jay?"

CHAPTER TWENTY

"Not yet, boss," Jay panted.

Then suddenly Jay shouted, "Tyrell, we just want to talk!" and the phone call disconnected.

In the distance, George saw a junction to his left, and then a flash of green appeared. He hadn't remembered that there were another two exits, one further north-west that would take the scally straight back onto Temple Avenue or another that would take him west towards Second Avenue.

"For fuck's sake!" George spat, forcing his legs to move faster, the scar on his back hurting as he moved his arms to gain more speed.

Another flash of colour caused George to slide to a stop, but it was only Jay.

"I saw him head that way, Boss," the lad said.

"OK, you head west towards Second Ave, and I'll take the path splitting north." He pulled out his phone and called Jay. "Keep the call connected."

The DC took a deep breath and sprinted. George took a few breaths of his own and then jogged after him.

By the time the DI got to the junction, he couldn't see Grant or Jay, so he headed north, keeping his eyes peeled and ears open.

As George continued north, he hoped Grant had gone west, instead, desperately pleading to whatever gods were out there that Jay would catch their man.

But the DI caught a fleeting glimpse of a hooded figure to his right, holding onto a black, metal railing for a moment before continuing towards the junction of Temple Avenue and Third Avenue, where the scally turned left.

Fuck.

George knew where Grant was heading; if he got there,

they'd lose all chance of speaking with him.

Beyond the cycle gate at the end of the road were fields that would lead Grant towards Rothwell Country Park next to the River Aire.

But as luck would have it, Grant hadn't seen George, so he placed the phone to his ear and ordered Jay to get back to George's position ASAP.

* * *

"Detective Inspector," DCI Atkinson uttered. "A word in private."

George wondered what he'd done this time. Perhaps word had filtered through that he and Jay had lost Tyrell Grant. By the time Jay had arrived at George's position, the scallywag was long gone. They'd spent an hour looking around the fields and had even knocked on doors, but they got nothing.

The DCI's office was dark when they arrived, the blinds drawn, the light fighting through the slats. It was muggy, too. There was no air. Atkinson sat down and sharply gestured for him to take the chair opposite the moment he shut the door.

Alistair Atkinson was dressed in a dark grey suit and navy tie, his hair severely cropped like a soldier. George had seen photos of Atkinson around the station taken when the DCI was younger, and it was no surprise that age and stress had pushed Alistair's hairline higher and higher.

DS Mason once told George that as you progressed the ranks, your hair got thinner and your hairline higher, which was why he'd decided to stay as a sergeant. George had grinned and raised his brow, joking with his mentor about Luke's own near-baldness, only to be told it was a 'personal choice' and not one that Mother Nature had cruelly forced upon him.

"I hear you allowed Tyrell Grant to get away?" he said, tapping a finger against the wooden desk.

"We didn't allow him to get away, sir. We had to split up, but he got away."

"You should have called for backup."

Attempting not to frown, George said, "There was no time."

"There's always time," the DCI said. "You're hardly fit for fieldwork as it is, Beaumont. In fact, I'm starting to consider you a liability."

"With respect, sir, I'm not a liability." He wanted to tell the DCI to piss off and mention how even in his shoes, the DCI wouldn't have done any better but kept his mouth shut. "I've been signed off to return, and I'm doing my best. Grant had a massive head start. He's a fit young man. Even DC Scott had no chance."

A knife could have cut the tension.

"Still, I've spoken with the DSU. He's going to speak with the DCS and see how to progress. I've asked him to put DS Wood in charge as SIO. When you were off, she did a great job."

George fought hard not to wince. "I know she did, sir, but she's about ready to pop. And for the record, replacing me would be a mistake."

Alistair shrugged, then steepled his fingers and watched George in silence for a moment. Then he said, "I respect you, George, which is why I wanted you to learn this from me." He stood up and gestured for the door. "I've got PS Greenwood and his uniforms searching for Grant. I want you to go home."

"I can put a few more hours on it," George said, but the DCI countered with a firm shake of his head.

"You don't look well, George," he told the DI. "You struggled to match my pace when following me here, and I see you wince every time you change positions in that chair." He paused for a moment. "Get home, get some rest, and hopefully, a decision will have been made by the morning."

"But I can—"

"That wasn't a request, Detective Inspector Beaumont."

His glare was laced with meaning, and George knew that arguing would get him nowhere. Exhaustion was creeping in, and it was getting late, but he needed to prove to the DCI he was fit and raring to go.

"I'm sorry, George," the DCI said, sitting back down, busying himself with a file on his desk.

Chapter Twenty-one

George knocked on Isabella's Incident Room door and let himself in. The detectives were all crowded around the smart whiteboard at the head of the room, with Yolanda operating the computer connected to it.

Wood turned to George and smiled. "You OK?"

He nodded and took a seat at the back.

Isabella frowned but turned back to the whiteboard. "Can everyone see this screen?" she asked.

Nobody complained, so she switched off the lights and then took a seat. Tashan Blackburn, other members of CID, and uniformed officers were all in attendance. Yolanda started the video.

The pub car park next to Holy Trinity Church in Rothwell appeared on the screen, completely deserted. The camera's vantage was good, meaning they could see everything.

The time stamp showed 3.01 am. DS Wood looked at Yolanda. "What am I looking at?"

Then Wood felt her pulse quicken. A figure dressed in all black, with a hood obscuring its face, appeared at the entrance to the car park, and Isabella watched as they strolled through it, a blade glinting in the streetlights.

"Stop the tape, please," said Isabella. "Is that a man or a

woman?" she asked.

Nobody said anything, so she turned to Yolanda. "Did you find any other footage?"

"No, Sarge."

"OK, continue the video, please."

Yolanda obliged, and they watched as the figure left their field of view, and the video stopped.

"Is that it?" Wood asked.

"I'm afraid so, Sarge," Yolanda said. "It appears our killer entered the church another way, which makes sense considering the lychgate is closed on a night."

"And now the bloodstains make sense, leading away from the scene," Wood said. "Whoever it is will have been covered in blood."

She was greeted with nods from the team.

"I need you lot to go out and scour Ingram Parade and the surrounding streets for CCTV," Isabella said. "It's clear from this the killer walked home. They could even have stashed their vehicle nearby so it wouldn't be seen on the car park camera." She paused. "Speak with Morrisons, too. They might have CCTV on the outside. And I know there's a funeral director on that road, so see if they have any cameras, too."

"That's a massive area to search, Sarge," Yolanda said, her concern written all over her face.

"I agree, DS Williams, but we need to find the culprit, and fast. I'll speak with DCI Alexander and see if he can provide more officers."

"Thank you," said Yolanda.

"If anyone finds anything, let me know ASAP, OK?"

The team nodded.

"Good, now crack on."

CHAPTER TWENTY-ONE

* * *

George helped Isabella navigate the steps and through the wooden doors into Blackburn Hall in Rothwell.

The night had started to cool, but Izzy felt ridiculously hot and couldn't wait to tear her clothes from her body and take a cold shower.

Inside, nobody was staffing the booth to the left, so they headed straight through to the antechamber, a wide circle of purple chairs greeting them.

Most were occupied, so George dragged two from the back, and he and Wood sat down on them next to the fire exit.

It wasn't long before an older man with salt and pepper hair walked unsteadily towards them, his milky eyes squinting at the pair. DI Beaumont stood and pulled out his warrant card. "I'm DI Beaumont, and this is DS Wood," he said. "I believe a colleague of ours let you know we were coming."

The man offered a hand that, upon closer inspection, ended with inflamed, twisted fingers. "I'm Granville Crawshaw," he said as George lightly shook his hand. "I run the group." He turned to Wood and offered her an amiable smile. "I believe you're in charge of the investigation?"

"Correct, Mr Crawshaw." She smiled back at him. "We have some questions for you regarding Rita Holdsworth," she explained.

At the mention of Rita's name, a few of the group members turned in their purple chairs and started listening to the conversation.

"We're happy to wait until the meeting's finished."

"Thank you, detectives," Granville said. "We won't be long,

Ten minutes later, a dark-haired man with a long beard

noisily dragged a purple chair over to where the two detectives were sitting and plonked it directly in front of them. He then went over to Mr Crawshaw and tapped him on the shoulder before gesturing towards them.

Granville clapped the man on the shoulder and ambled over.

"Who is that?" asked George once the elderly man sat down.

"Oh, that's Kit Holdsworth."

DS Wood caught the name immediately. "Holdsworth? Is he related to Rita?"

"I don't think so, no." He gestured for Kit to come over and join them. "Kit and Rita spent a lot of time together, looking through their family trees to see if they were related, but I believe they couldn't find a link."

"What's that?" Kit asked as he got closer, noisily dragging another chair across.

"I was telling the detectives how you and Rita share the same surname but struggled to match your family trees."

"Yeah, that's right." He shrugged. "It's not the most common of surnames, so I thought I may have bumped into a relative. But I guess I was wrong."

"When was the last time you saw Rita?" asked George.

Neither man answered, looking at the other as if waiting for the other to answer.

George's voice cut through the silence. "Either of you can answer the question. Or preferably, both of you."

"During the last meeting," both men said at the same time. Then they grinned at each other.

"So despite the relationship you built with Rita, Kit, you didn't see her outside of this setting?"

Kit said, "As a group, we sometimes go to the pub across the road or for food at the pub at the end of Commercial Street."

"And don't forget the Christmas party," Granville said.

"Yeah, and that." Kit shrugged. "No offence, but she's old enough to be my grandma, and no offence but I mostly hang with people my own age. Why the interest, anyway?"

Wood said, "Because Rita Holdsworth was murdered."

Kit opened his mouth to say something, but Granville got there first. "What?"

George nodded.

"Oh my, she was such a lovely woman." Granville wiped a stray tear from his eye.

Kit looked uncomfortable. "Wow," he eventually said. "That's a lot to take in."

"How was Rita as a person?" George asked.

Kit immediately said, "A proper lovely woman, she was. Friendly and popular." He shook his head. "Who would do something like that?"

"Well, that's why we're here," said Wood. "I'm in charge of the investigation, and anything you can tell us may help find her killer."

Kit stood up. "I don't really know her," he explained. "This has upset me a bit. Can I go home?"

The two detectives shared a look, and Isabella nodded. She handed him her card. "You can go, but I'd like you to come and make a formal statement down at Elland Road station tomorrow, please. I'd like to know what sort of person she was, so think hard and give us as much detail as possible."

"I will, thank you, detective."

George watched the man flee and didn't know whether he trusted him or not. He also wondered whether Isabella was making a mistake in allowing him to leave, but it was her case, and he was only here for company.

"What can you tell us, Mr Crawshaw?" asked Wood.

"Nothing much more than you already know," Granville said. "She has a daughter, but I don't know her name, I'm afraid."

"Do you have any of her family trees here?"

Granville shook his head. "They'll be at her home."

Wood nodded. "OK, if you kindly give me your address, I'll send a uniformed officer to take an official statement from you tomorrow."

She stood up, her feet and back aching. All she wanted was to get home.

George stood up and handed Granville his trusty police notebook and pen, watching as Granville's arthritic fingers struggled to grip the pen. "I'm so sorry, Mr Crawshaw," George said. "I'll write your address down if you tell it to me."

"Well, I live opposite Rita on Maple Rise," Granville explained. "I live in the bungalow on the left when you enter the street, and Rita lives in the bungalow opposite."

"Thank you so much for your time," said DS Wood, delicately shaking Mr Crawshaw's hand. George nodded.

But no sooner than they started towards the exit, a grating, irritating voice came from behind him.

"Did I hear you say your name was DI Beaumont, buddy?" a tall, thin man asked.

George turned on his heel and took the man in. The red-headed man, who was starting to bald, flashed a brilliant smile and held out his wide hand for George to shake.

The DI took it, and a battle of who could grip the strongest ensued.

Unfortunately for George, the Yank did. He'd lost much of his strength because of the accident, so he had to loosen his grip and step back from the imposing American, a mischievous glint appearing in the red-headed man's eyes.

"I am, and who are you?"

"Brenden Steffen," he said, "nice to meet you." Maintaining intense eye contact, Brenden stepped closer to George, invading his personal space, and George took a corresponding step backwards.

"How can I help you, Mr Steffen?" the DI asked.

"Oh, call me Brenden, buddy," the Yank replied, smacking George on the shoulder. "And it's more about how I can help you rather than helping me."

"Explain."

"Shall we head over there and take a seat?" Steffen pointed to DS Wood's stomach. "I'm sure she doesn't want to stand up whilst we chat." George nodded at the comment and gestured for Brenden to head towards the chairs, but the Yank said, "After you, detectives."

Once they were sat down, George and Wood sitting opposite the American, the DI said, "So what information do you have for us?"

"This isn't about Rita Holdsworth; it's about Martha Lickiss."

The shock must have been evident on the detectives' faces because Steffen grinned, his pearly whites reflecting the bulb above his head.

"What about her?" asked George.

"I know I should have come to you guys sooner," Brenden said, looking embarrassed, "but I wasn't really sure if it was necessary."

"Spit it out, Mr Steffen." The man was grating on his last nerve.

"Brenden, please."

George rolled his eyes. "Fine, spit it out, Brenden."

"I'm Martha's lover."

George frowned. "What?"

"I'm her lover."

They'd interviewed many people while searching for Martha Lickiss, and not one person had mentioned a lover. He said as much to the Yank.

"Well, that's because she was still shacked up with that idiot when we got together."

George asked, "What idiot?"

"Oh, I'm sure you know full what idiot I refer to," Steffen said.

"Geoff Lickiss?" asked Wood.

"Bingo." He flashed her another one of those smiles.

"So let me get this straight, Mr Steffen, you're admitting to having an affair with Martha Lickiss?" asked George.

"It's Brenden, and yes, that's what I'm saying."

The DI quickly stood up and took a step towards the American. "So why the bloody hell didn't you come down to the station before?" He shook his head furiously. "We've been appealing for information for nearly a week now!"

"Because Martha didn't want anybody to know about the affair." He grinned once again, then held out his hands placatingly. "Sit back down, buddy; we're all friends here."

George ignored the Yank. He was seething. This man could have the information they needed to find Martha, and he'd been living his life as if nothing had happened. He was about to angrily remonstrate with Steffen when Isabella grasped his wrist and gently pulled him back.

"When was the last time you saw Martha?" Wood asked.

CHAPTER TWENTY-ONE

"Not last Sunday, but the Sunday before," he explained. "A few days before she went missing."

"Where were you the night she went missing?" George asked.

"I was at home."

"Alone?" asked Wood.

The Yank shook his head. "No. I share my house with three of my fellow Americans. We watched baseball on the TV. I'm a Yankees fan, and they were playing the Braves. It was a great game."

"So you have two people who can alibi you?" asked George.

"Correct."

"Until what time?"

"Well, the Red Sox played the Mets, and we watched that game, too. That started around midnight."

"And how long do baseball games take?"

"Anywhere between two and four hours.

"And when did the Yankees start?"

Brenden considered this for a moment. "It was one of the 7 pm games; that's all I can really remember. But you can ask my pals; they'll tell you I was with them all night."

If he was telling the truth, then there's no way he was involved in Hope's murder and Martha's abduction.

"I'll need your address and the names of your housemates, Mr Steffen," George said, handing over his notebook and pen.

George saw the Yank attempt to say something, but he shut his mouth and did as was instructed. Most likely, he was going to ask George to call him Brenden, which the DI had no intention of doing.

"Thank you for that, Mr Steffen," George said. "Is there anything else you can tell us that may help us locate Martha?"

"No, but I can tell you she didn't kill her daughter," Brenden explained.

"How can you be so sure?" asked Wood.

"If you ask me, it's that mental ex of hers, Geoff." Brenden shrugged. "He's a proper loon."

George said nothing about Geoff, wanting to move the conversation along. "Can you tell us anything else?"

"Only that she was adopted and had made a promise to herself that she wouldn't try and find her birth parents until her adoptive parents died. Which, as you probably know, did pass away."

"Is this where you met her?" asked Wood.

Steffen shook his head. "No, I come here to see Martha, to help her find her birth family. I, too, was adopted but decided at eighteen to find my birth family. I now have two sets of parents, and it was the best thing I ever did. In fact, that's why I live in England now, as my birth parents are both English."

"And your adoptive parents don't mind?" asked Wood.

"The culture in America is very different from yours over here. They're happy for me, in truth. Proud of me, even." He flashed those pearly whites again. "We're very supportive across the pond."

And fucking arrogant, George thought.

"Did she find her birth family?" asked Wood.

"No, they didn't want to be found, apparently." The Yank shrugged. "Sometimes it happens that way; not everybody is as lucky as I am."

"And does she still attend these meetings?"

"She does."

Wood asked, "Why?"

"She never said, and I never asked. But I do know she had

an interest in Rita Holdsworth's family tree."

Chapter Twenty-two

George and Isabella arrived at Elland Road just before 8 am and made their way to the floor that housed the Homicide and Major Enquiry Team. The DI made coffees for the pair whilst DS Wood turned on her computer.

Jason Scott, Tashan Blackburn, and Yolanda Williams arrived soon after. And even DCI Alistair Atkinson made his presence known.

After drinking the coffee George made, DS Wood left George and called the two DCs and DS Williams into their Incident Room.

"Don't mind me, DS Wood," said Alistair, plonking his arse on a chair by the door. "Carry on as you usually would."

Isabella pointed to an enlarged version of the photograph from Rita Holdsworth's driving licence. "The formal identification will take place later today. Her daughter, Liz Brearley, has agreed to do it." She looked at the team. "Does anybody have anything for me?"

"I spoke to the dog walker who found the car," said Tashan.

"Anything?"

"No, sarge," he explained. "Out with the dog, as usual, saw the car and noticed it was on fire. Dialled triple nine. Saw nobody, heard nothing."

"And the cemetery worker?"

"Same, sarge," Tashan said. "Saw nothing. Heard nothing. He was 'round the back cutting down the foliage when he smelled the blood. He followed the trail towards the graves and found the body."

"Did you go and see Brenden Steffen this morning, Jay?"

"I did, boss. And his alibi checks out. As he said, he was watching baseball with his housemates, so he couldn't have killed Hope and abducted Martha."

"Why are we discussing the Lickiss case, DS Wood?" asked DCI Atkinson.

"We haven't had the chance to tell you yet, sir, but last night, DI Beaumont and I went to the genealogy meeting in Rothwell and asked questions about Rita Holdsworth. Anyway, to cut the story short, as we were leaving, an American named Brenden Steffen introduced himself as Martha Lickiss' lover."

Alistair frowned. "Lover?"

"Correct, sir. He didn't come forward before because Martha had always wanted them to be a secret."

"Is he a suspect?" asked the DCI.

"No, sir. There's no way he's involved."

"Is that all you got from the meeting?"

Wood shook her head. "No, sir. We spoke with the organiser of the group, Granville Crawshaw, and a man named Kit Holdsworth," she said. "Both knew Rita pretty well."

"Is Kit related to Rita?"

Again, she shook her head. "No, sir. He became friends with Rita because he hoped they were related, but apparently, they couldn't find a familial connection whilst researching their family trees." She looked at Tashan. "Has Kit come in and provided a statement?"

He shook his head. "Not yet, Sarge."

"Give him until this evening, and then visit him in person if he doesn't come."

"Yes, Sarge."

"How's the CCTV going, Yolanda?"

She was clacking away at her laptop and didn't answer.

"Yolanda?" Wood repeated.

"Sorry, Sarge, something important's just come through."

"What?"

"Some footage of the killer and Rita Holdsworth," Yolanda explained. "It's a private camera on a semi-detached house on Meynell Avenue in Rothwell. Shall I put it up on the whiteboard?"

Wood nodded.

They watched a Ford Fiesta pull outside the house at the junction of Meynell Avenue and Love Lane.

It was the exact figure they'd seen in the pub's car park by the entrance to the church, but this time, the detectives watched as the figure bundled Rita Holdsworth out of the Fiesta, dragged her across the road, through the opening in the wall and into the cemetery.

"Stop the tape."

Yolanda obliged.

"That's the same person we saw in the car park, right?" asked Wood.

Jay said, "I'd say so, boss, yeah."

"OK, continue."

Again, Yolanda obliged, and they watched as the figure forced Rita to her knees. Despite the camera being quite far away, the footage was clear enough that they could see the killer place a collar around the elderly woman and clip a lead to it before dragging her out of the footage to where the killer presumably stabbed Rita to death.

"Jesus Christ," said DCI Atkinson.

"I was thinking the same, sir," said Wood.

Yolanda clicked another video file and they watched as the exact dark-clothed figure retrieved a set of keys from their trouser pocket and opened the Fiesta. The car then reversed slowly out of view; Isabella then assumed the vehicle did a three-point-turn and down Meynell Avenue.

"We don't see the car again on this camera, Sarge," said Yolanda.

"Any luck with cameras on Ingram Parade?"

"We're still looking, sarge," DS Williams said, "but it's not looking likely."

DS Wood pondered what to do for a moment, then said, "Tashan, I'd like you to use the registration and see if you can trace where it's been travelling to and from over the past week using ANPR, OK?"

"That's a lot of work," said DCI Atkinson.

Wood said, "It is, sir, but well worth it. Tashan's hard work could break the case."

"Whilst I agree, I'd like to provide him with some help." Alistair paused. "I'll draft in a few CID, OK?"

"Thanks, sir," Isabella said. She felt deflated when asked, "What do we know about Rita's movements on Saturday night?"

"Every neighbour I spoke with, Sarge, said Rita was a bit of a recluse and only had her daughter for company," said Tashan.

Isabella nodded. "Her daughter, Liz, said the same." The teacher hadn't taken the news very well. Wood had asked a few questions, received a solid alibi, and allowed Liz home.

"I want to know why the sick bastard put a collar on her and walked her like a dog to her death," said Jay. "I know it's horrible to say aloud, but that's a really sick thing to do." He shuddered. "I wouldn't wish that on my worst enemy, which begs the question, who could hate Rita Holdsworth so much?"

"I asked Liz a similar question, naturally leaving out the abuse her mother suffered." Wood shrugged. "She answered that Rita had no enemies. She had no friends and no family apart from her."

"It's got to be something to do with this family tree stuff, then," said Yolanda.

"I completely agree," said Isabella, "which was why I went last night. I'm going to head to the house at some point, once SOCO's finished, and see if I can have a look at any genealogy work she carried out."

"Let me know when you do, Sarge," said Yolanda. "I find that so interesting."

"Speaking of SOCO, boss," said Jay, "did they find the collar and lead?"

Izzy shook her head. "No sign of it." She paused. "But we really need to find them and the murder weapon." She was met with a Mexican wave of nods. "Any information on the graves, Jay?"

"Other than being ancient?" Jay asked and winced at Wood's furious frown. "No, boss. The three graves belong to the Corbyn family. From what Reverend Priestly dug up for me, they're an old farming family who owned farms in Rothwell a century or so ago."

"I wonder whether they were related to Taylor Corbyn, Jean Lickiss' partner," Wood pondered. She made a mental note to ask George to go with her to Jean's place later.

"I'm not sure, boss, but the reverend said those three graves have been there for a long time. And when I asked if she had any Corbyns in her congregation, she said there weren't any."

Wood nodded and said, "Check the electoral roll for Corbyns who live in Rothwell and the surrounding towns and villages, Jay. Thanks."

After looking at the team she'd assembled, Wood said, "Right then, let's get on with it and meet back here at six."

* * *

Detective Inspector George Beaumont was sat in his office, looking through the statements taken from the public after the appeal, on his computer.

His phone rang.

"What can I do for you, Samantha?" George asked the office manager.

"You have a visitor," she said.

"A visitor? Unless it's our murderer who has come to hand himself in, I'm busy."

"Is that what you want me to tell them?"

"Who is it?"

"Jean Lickiss. I told her you were busy, but she's insistent."

George frowned. Jean had usually contacted him through FLO Cathy Hoskins whenever she wanted an update. "What's so urgent, Samantha?"

"She'll only speak with you, I'm afraid."

"OK, show her into an interview room, and I'll be down in two minutes."

An interview room wasn't the best place to have an informal chat. They were always too cold or too warm. And the fact they had no windows didn't help. Plus, they were highly uncomfortable. And the steel table bolted to the floor was extremely intimidating.

Dragging a chair across so he could face Jean Lickiss sitting at the table, he took the woman in. She looked gaunt, with huge bags beneath her eyes. Something was worrying her.

"If you'd have spoken with DS Hoskins, I'd have come to the house," George explained.

"This couldn't wait."

George nodded his head. "OK, how can I help you, Miss Lickiss?"

Jean raised a hand with gnawed fingernails and pushed back a loose strand of hair behind her ear. She'd aged a decade since George had last seen her, and it hadn't been that long ago, either. Those gnawed fingers were trembling as she said, "I can't find Taylor anywhere."

"Taylor Corbyn?" George asked.

"Yes, do you know any other Taylors?"

George was going to comment that he knew of two, a singer and an actor, both of whom, he was sure, had dated each other but said nothing. "What do you mean you can't find her?"

"She's gone missing."

"Since when?"

"Since Saturday night. She went out and didn't come back."

"She's a grown woman, Jean."

"I've tried calling her. Plus, it's unusual for her to go out and not come back."

"Have you reported her missing?"

Tears started to fall from Jean's eyes. Eventually, though her words were punctuated with rasping breaths and sobs, she said, "No, that's why I'm here."

CHAPTER TWENTY-TWO

"I need to get a trained officer here, Jean," George explained. "They'll fill in the paperwork with you, and then it'll get allocated to a detective."

"And will that be you?"

"Probably not because I'm still searching for Martha and Faith," he advised.

"It has to be you, DI Beaumont."

"I can't give the case the effort it needs, Jean," he said. "I'm working flat-out trying to find your niece, remember." He smiled. "But there are many decent detectives upstairs who will help you find Taylor, OK?"

Jean whispered her reply, but George didn't hear it. "Can you repeat that, please, Jean?"

"I said, I don't think there's anybody better qualified than you." She shrugged. "And what if it's linked?"

George's brows met his hairline. "Is there something you haven't told me?"

Jean was quick to say, "No."

"Then why would you believe Taylor being missing is linked to Faith and Martha being missing?"

"They're family, and so is Taylor. Perhaps somebody is targeting me?"

George thought about it for a moment. "Like who?"

"Well, I don't fucking know, do I?"

George smiled but immediately tried to hide it. She was more like her brother, Geoff than he'd initially given her credit for. He looked into her eyes. "Do you have any enemies?"

"No."

"Does Taylor."

"Not that I'm aware."

"Do Taylor, Martha, and Faith have any other common

acquaintances?" he asked.

"Other than me?"

George nodded his head.

"No."

"Right, so I'll get a trained officer in here who will go through all the paperwork with you, OK?"

She nodded. "But you'll look for Taylor, won't you?"

"Not personally, Jean, no. But whoever gets the case will give it their all."

"But why can't you do it?"

George tried to mask the impatience that was starting to show on his face. "Because I'm up to my eyeballs already looking for Faith and Martha, as I said." He shrugged. "If there's a link to Taylor, then, of course, I'll be involved, but otherwise, somebody else will be in charge, OK?"

Jean was about to argue when George narrowed his brows at the woman. Eventually, she said, "OK."

"Great." He stood up. "Stay here, and I'll go fetch someone."

Chapter Twenty-three

After enjoying dinner together in the canteen, George and Wood took a slow walk up to the HMET floor, but George's phone rang before scanning their IDs to get inside. "DI Beaumont."

Wood watched his face contort into a kaleidoscope of emotions before he said, "Thank you," and hung up.

He turned to Wood. "We need to head back out."

"Why?"

"Martha Lickiss' been found."

"What? Where? Is she OK?"

"Give me a minute, Isabella; you're asking too many questions."

She smiled and nodded, waiting until they'd got to the Merc.

When they reached it, she went to drive, but George stopped her. "I want to drive."

"Are you sure you're OK to drive?"

He nodded. "If I don't start now, then I never will."

"OK, but I'm driving back."

"Deal."

He adjusted the seat, fired up the engine, and headed out of the station car park, heading towards the Armley Gyratory.

"Where are we going?"

"Jimmy's," he explained.

"Why? Is that where Martha is?"

George nodded.

"Is she alive?"

"I'm told she was when we got the call, but I'm not so sure now."

"Christ."

"Yep, she's at A&E. They're working on her. It sounds serious."

Eventually, George pulled up outside A&E and parked in an ambulance bay. Both detectives got out and headed inside the Chancellor's Wing.

As fast as they could, both detectives headed towards the reception area. People were queuing up, but Wood cut in, holding up her warrant card to a woman who wanted to start arguing. "Where can I find Martha Lickiss?" Wood asked.

"I'll have to check. Take a seat," the nurse said.

"Please hurry," said Wood.

"I'll check, but you need to calm down." She pointed at Wood's stomach. "Stress does nothing good for babies, love."

Wood took a deep breath, and George gently gripped her wrist and led her towards a chair. "Thank you," she said to the nurse, trying to conjure a smile.

George watched as the nurse started clacking away on a keyboard. After a minute or two, which felt like a lifetime, she said, "Mrs Lickiss was taken upstairs for surgery."

"She's alive then?" questioned George.

"She was when she left here to go upstairs," the nurse said. She pointed towards a set of stairs in the corner. "Third floor."

Wood barely heard the words. She pulled George up from his chair, and they marched as quickly as possible towards the

CHAPTER TWENTY-THREE

stairs.

By the time they reached the third floor, George was struggling. Exhaustion had hit, and his body felt as if it had been hit by a truck. His head boomed, and he desperately needed a drink.

Wood was slightly out of breath, but she didn't have a hair out of place.

"Press the buzzer, please; I need a minute," George said.

Wood did as was asked, and a voice came from the intercom.

"We're here about Martha Lickiss," Wood said.

"Are you family?"

"Detectives."

The nurse buzzed them in, both detectives hearing the audible click. A nurse met them at the entrance and checked for Martha's name on the list on a clipboard in her hand.

George and Wood flashed her their warrant cards. The nurse looked flustered, but she thoroughly checked their IDs before saying, "Mrs Lickiss is currently in surgery, detectives. Leave your details, and I'll personally call you as soon as she—"

"I'm sorry," George interrupted, "but we're here about a murder investigation."

"She's not dead," the nurse said.

"I know, but one of her daughters is, and the other is missing, so we need to speak with Mrs Lickiss urgently."

The nurse's eyes narrowed. "I don't think she'll be in any state to speak to anyone, detective."

"What do you mean?" Wood asked.

The nurse pushed past George and closed the door. "I've told you too much already. Mrs Lickiss is in surgery, and I'll call you. OK?"

"No, that's not OK," said George. "What are her injuries?"

The nurse conceded. "Blunt-force trauma causing bone fractures to both her legs and left arm. There's also evidence of blunt-force trauma to the back of her head. That's all I can tell you for now. You both need to leave."

George fished a business card from his inside jacket pocket and handed it over to the nurse. Then he said, "Any idea what could have caused it?"

"I don't know what to say," the nurse said. "She's been put in an induced coma."

"Anything at all," Wood pleaded. "You may think it's inconsequential, but let us be the judge."

The nurse's eyes narrowed again. "Martha said the words 'baseball bat', 'Geoff', and 'dead' before she passed out."

* * *

Parked in the ambulance bay, George looked at Wood, who was adjusting the Merc's seat and said, "Fucking hell."

"I know what you mean," said Wood.

"First, her daughter is murdered, then she disappears and turns up at the hospital with awful injuries."

"And where was she all this time? And why?"

"I don't know," said George. "I need to speak with Tashan and Jay and get them to interview whoever found Martha."

"They can also check the CCTV to see if she was dropped off or staggered in."

"Good thinking."

Wood was nodding as she pulled out of the hospital and onto Beckett Street.

"It can't be Geoff, can it?"

Isabella said, "Why not?"

CHAPTER TWENTY-THREE

"Because he's been in custody, so unless he has an accomplice, there's no way Martha could have survived on her own in the state she's apparently in."

Of course, it couldn't be Geoff, you idiot. Think, Beaumont, think! "Who else could it be?"

"I don't know, Isabella, but I have a bad feeling about this." George pondered for a moment. "I'll call Greenwood and get him to send uniforms to the hospital to take statements and use Jay and Tashan to collect and siphon through the CCTV." He pulled out his phone and dialled. The sergeant answered almost immediately, and George reeled off his orders. Then he said, "Put a uniform on the ward, too. No one enters without clearance from me, OK?"

"What about the doctors and nurses?" Greenwood questioned.

"Get a list, Sarge. Make sure the list has ID photographs, too. We need to monitor everybody going in and out of the ICU, OK?"

"Got it, sir. Anything else?"

"See if she's got her phone on her," George said. "If so, get one of your team to bring it back to Elland Road immediately."

Wood was driving on the A61 when George finished giving Tashan and Jay orders. He and Wood needed to get back to the station and look through all the evidence they had so far.

This was now much worse than just a domestic that had gone wrong. And they only really had one suspect. Geoff Lickiss. But he was still in Armley Nick. Nothing was making any sense.

When the pair pulled up at the station, they noticed the press was gathered at the front of the building. Since the accident, it was easier for George to enter via the front entrance rather than around the back, but he knew going that way, he couldn't avoid the vultures.

As the two detectives headed for the front entrance, the questions started, and the clacking of cameras went straight through George. The flash didn't help, either, and he could feel himself losing control.

Isabella put her hand on his shoulder and guided him forward.

What would he do without her?

He hoped he'd never have to know.

They were close to the revolving door when George saw Paige McGuiness running towards them.

"Detective Inspector Beaumont, I'm glad I caught you," she panted, stopping beside him.

"No comment," said George.

"But I haven't asked you anything."

"You'll get that answer no matter the question, Miss McGuiness."

"But I'm working for Mr Duke again. Do an old friend a favour, will you?"

George turned on his heel quickly and almost lost balance. "How dare you!"

"Please, George."

"No comment."

"You're looking well, Detective Sergeant," Paige said with a grin.

"No comment, Paige," said Wood. "You need to get out of our way."

A cameraman was snapping pictures of them, the flashing lights and clacking sounds forcing George to take deep, calming breaths. He'd lose his job if he lost it, and he'd fought so hard to retain it as it was.

CHAPTER TWENTY-THREE

"I just need one minute," said Paige.

"No, Paige," said George. "I've nothing to say to you." He nodded towards the station. "You'll get a press release like everyone else. Now move."

"But I've been doing some investigative work regarding the Lickiss family. I think you might be interested in what I have to say."

George stopped in his tracks and looked Paige dead in the eye. Paige grinned and forced her Dictaphone under his chin. "Detective Inspector Beaumont, can you inform the public if you have anyone in custody regarding the hospitalisation of Martha Lickiss?"

"We are currently pursuing all lines of enquiry. Anyone with information is asked to contact me, DI Beaumont, or DS Wood, at the Leeds District Homicide and Major Enquiry Team quoting reference 13664857125 or online via live chat. We're also looking for missing Faith Lickiss. Please get in touch if you have seen her." George grinned. "I'll get the press office to send some images over to you."

"That's not what I wanted, and you know it," said Paige.

"If there's anything else, then I have to insist that you go through our press office."

Chapter Twenty-four

"How's Martha?" Jean Lickiss asked. She'd asked the FLO to contact George because she wanted to ask them some questions.

DI Beaumont said, "Still in an induced coma. How do you know about her?"

"I overheard Cathy on the phone."

"Fair enough."

"I want to see her."

"I can ask and see if they'll let you," George said, "but they wouldn't let us see her."

"I'm family; you're not."

He narrowed his brows as he said, "Fair enough."

"And my brother? How is he?"

George said, "He's fine. You know he is because you went to visit him, remember."

"Because he's innocent, he didn't do anything," Jean retorted.

"Says who?"

"Says me." She started biting her nails. "I want to see my brother again."

"I can't let you do that."

"Why are you so convinced Geoff's innocent?" Wood asked.

CHAPTER TWENTY-FOUR

Jean's eyes widened. "Because I know what Martha's like."

"Yet you're aware of Martha's injuries?" asked George.

Jean nodded, and tears loomed in her eyes. "Cathy told me." She held eye contact with George. "And anyway, if Geoff assaulted Martha before you arrested him, then Martha would be dead by now, right?" She bit the inside of her cheek. "Plus, how did Martha get to the hospital? You never said."

George took a deep breath. "I can't divulge that information," he explained.

"Of course not. But it couldn't have been Geoff who dropped her off at the hospital, could it, because he was in prison."

That was, of course, the elephant in the room.

"Have you found my Taylor, yet?" Jean asked.

"Not yet, I'm afraid, but we have uniform looking for her."

"And you'll keep me informed?"

"Of course."

* * *

"So, you haven't texted her recently?" George asked Geoff Lickiss. They were in an interview room at HMP Leeds.

"No, why the fuck would I?"

"Well, we have texts that prove you did."

"Texts? What texts? What the fuck are you on about?" Geoff demanded.

He handed Geoff and his solicitor a stack of printouts.

Sergeant Greenwood had followed through on his orders and had sent Martha's phone to digital forensics immediately. It was unlocked, so DS Josh Fry and the team downloaded all the information on it instantly.

"These texts," George said, pointing at the printouts. "Ring any bells?"

With a mix of suspicion and contempt, Geoff leaned forward and regarded the printouts. "No. What are these?"

"Don't piss us about, Geoff. They're texts you've been sending Martha every night for the past month threatening her."

"I never sent those texts! Check my phone bills. Or my phone." Geoff looked at his solicitor. "I handed in my phone and gave you the pin. Check them. You'll see. I don't text. Ever," Geoff insisted. "I always call, and to tell you the truth, if I've got something to say, I'll fucking say it face to face."

Like before, Lickiss' outrage had sprinkled more seeds of doubt. "Are you saying you didn't send them?"

"Ding, ding, ding," Geoff retorted. "Fuck me! Give the detective a medal."

"Answer the question."

"Yes, I didn't send them."

"Then who did?"

"Fucked if I know."

George scratched his nose. Nothing was making sense.

"I'm guessing," Geoff's solicitor said, "you have Martha's phone because you've found her?"

George nodded. "She is currently in intensive care."

Geoff's eyebrows met his hairline. "Intensive care? How? Why? Is she OK?"

"That's what I'd like to know, Mr Lickiss," said George. "And no, she's not OK; she's in a coma."

"Did you assault your ex-wife with a baseball bat?" DS Wood asked.

"No!"

"Then who did?"

"I don't fucking know, do I? The woman's bloody mental. Doing drugs and stuff. If you want to know the truth, it was her who started beating me. But no one believed me. It wouldn't surprise me if she did it to herself."

"The wounds don't look self-inflicted," George advised.

"We're hoping to get a statement from her when she wakes up, so you might want to get in first and give us your side," said Wood.

"Oh, thank fuck for that," Geoff said, practically laughing with relief. "She'll tell you, then, won't she? She'll tell you it wasn't me."

"She already said it was you."

"What."

"Before passing out, she said you'd attacked her with a baseball bat."

"Bullshit."

"Why is it bullshit."

"Because I didn't do it. She'll tell you. She was just confused. That's it."

"Is that because you've got her too scared?" asked George.

"No, dickhead, because it wasn't me!" Geoff spat.

"Will we find your prints and DNA on the baseball bat?" asked Wood.

Geoff sat back, his scowl returning. "Probably. I bought it for one of the girls, remember."

George's phone pinged. He read the message and then showed Wood. She nodded.

Geoff frowned. "What's that all about?" he asked, pointing at George's phone.

"Evidence," George grinned.

"Nah, I don't believe you," Geoff insisted, even less convincingly. "And this is all a waste of time. You've got nothing to tie me to Martha's assault. You're just trying to piss me off in the hope I'll say something stupid so you can find a way to pin it on me. You've got nothing." He plastered a smug look across his face. "Plus, I've been locked up in 'ere, haven't I? She'd be dead by now if I'd battered her days ago."

George shook his head. "We've got far from nothing, Geoff. We've got something very interesting indeed."

"Whatever," Geoff said, a little more wary now.

"So, in your own words, you haven't seen Martha since court?" asked Wood.

Geoff sighed. "Right."

"So how do you explain your fingerprints being on Martha's mobile phone?" asked George. Once they'd downloaded the data, Josh personally took the phone to the lab to have it tested for prints and DNA. Fingerprints didn't take anywhere near as long to come back as DNA did, which was why they'd received a result. But that wasn't all they had.

"What?"

"Your fingerprints were all over Martha's phone, Geoff," said George.

"They can't be."

"But they are." George paused momentarily, then asked, "Why would your prints be on Martha's mobile when you haven't seen her for months?" The report suggested the prints were fresh and overlaid over other prints. He couldn't explain this away like he had the bat.

"I don't fucking know, do I?"

Chapter Twenty-five

"You're free to go, Mr Lickiss," said George. The DCI had agreed that there was no way he could have been involved in Hope's murder and Martha's abduction. Plus, DS Fry had come through for them. Geoff had been playing his PlayStation 5 when he said he had, and the threatening texts Martha's phone had received had been sent from Geoff Lickiss' mobile number, but they hadn't been sent from his handset. That meant one of two things. One, Geoff had a burner handset somewhere else, which he put his SIM into to text Martha, or two, he was telling the truth, and his number had been cloned. And George knew which one was the truth. Plus, they also couldn't date fingerprints, so George had no solid evidence to keep Geoff in custody.

Geoff Lickiss looked at the DI, dumbfounded. "What?"

"Did I stutter?" asked George. "You're free to go. I'm releasing you on bail."

"I fucking told you I was innocent!" he said.

"We followed the evidence trail, Mr Lickiss." George shrugged. "It wasn't personal."

"Of course, it was fucking personal, you prick." Geoff stood up and puffed out his chest. "I'm gonna fucking sue you, all of you, you wankers!" He turned to his solicitor. "Make sure you write that down!"

* * *

They still hadn't found Tyrell Grant.

But a warrant to search his grandmother's property had been signed by a magistrate that afternoon, so George headed over to the property, hoping to get there before Lindsey Yardley and her SOCOs.

Mrs Grant barely said a word, moving to one side as George held the warrant so she could see it clearly. "Fucking pigs," she muttered as she headed for the kitchen.

Suited and booted, masked and gloved, George and Jay entered Tyrell Grant's bedroom.

"Smells a bit rank in here," Jay said, sniffing the air.

"Probably from all of that shit on the table," George said. He pointed at a small table with crooked legs that stood in the corner of the room, cluttered with empty beer cans, crisp bags, chip bags, and two half-eaten Rustlers burgers. The carpet was heavily stained in places and littered with crumbs and dirt. Another corner was piled high with pizza boxes and fast-food wrappers, a few crusts littering the floor. A bookshelf lined one of the walls but was stacked with empty cans of cider rather than books. And then there was, on the floor directly to the side of where Grant slept, a receptacle he must have stolen from a pub filled with ash and cigarette buts.

"No sign of drug paraphernalia," Jay said.

"Probably not stupid enough to leave it out on view," said George.

DC Scott shrugged. "The room is a shithole, and plus, everything else is."

"True." He grinned at Jay. "Ready to get your hands dirty?"

Jay grimaced, a shudder running through his body. "Not really, boss."

After searching for ten minutes, well, Jay searching, and George watching, the young DC headed towards his boss and said, "What's with all the talcum powder?" Jay pointed towards the wardrobe floor where tubs of a popular supermarket baby powder were packed in tightly.

"Dunno," said George. "Maybe he chafes?"

"Nah, boss, it's got to be something to do with drugs." Jay pointed towards a cupboard in one of the corners. "Airing cupboard, boss."

"Go on then, Constable."

The sour, pungent smell hit them both despite the masks they wore. "Used condoms, boss," Jay said.

"Fucking disgusting." George shook his head as he headed towards the airing cupboard. "I'll get Lindsey to bag these up. You never know; we may be able to retrieve some DNA from the inside and outside. Might tie Tyrell to the crimes."

"Good thinking, boss," Jay said, rifling through the cupboard. "I'm glad I'm wearing gloves; there's all sorts of shit in here."

"What the hell would a young, pretty girl like Faith Lickiss be interested in a tramp like Tyrell for?" George said aloud. It was a rhetorical question, but Jay answered it.

"I guess it's to do with this." A bag of white powder dangled between Jay's thumb and index finger.

"You think Faith's into drugs?" George asked.

"It's the only reason I can think why: one, she's seeing this tramp, and two, she has so much cash squirrelled away in her bedroom."

It made sense to George, and he nodded. "Reckon, it's heroin?"

"I do, boss, about ten ounces. Worth a fair bit, I reckon."

George nodded as he pulled an exhibits bag from his pocket. He held it open, and Jay deposited the drugs. Then he went back to searching the cupboard.

As Jay did that, the DI lifted the duvet from the bed, finding a pair of purple, lacy knickers. He'd get Yardley to photo and bag them once she arrived. They could be Faith's, but then, he couldn't imagine a fifteen-year-old wearing such underwear. But he'd been proven wrong before.

"Found some more, boss," Jay shouted.

"I don't have any more bags, so leave them where you found them so they can be photographed and bagged by Yardley and her team."

"The contents of one of these bags looks a little finer than the others," said Jay.

"Maybe he was cutting the heroin?" George said.

"Aye, maybe, boss." He pointed towards the wardrobe. "Can you cut heroin with talc?"

"Maybe." George shrugged. "I'll speak with the drugs unit once we're back at the station, Jay. We can ask them how much the drugs would be worth, which makes me wonder..."

"What?"

"If Tyrell Grant was a big figure in the drugs game, don't you think he would live somewhere better than this?"

"I dunno, boss; some druggies like to keep a low profile so the taxman doesn't look into them if you know what I mean."

They stopped talking as someone hammered on the front door. They heard Mrs Grant cursing and then the sound of the front door opening.

CHAPTER TWENTY-FIVE

"Do you have somewhere to go, Mrs Grant, whilst we conduct a search of your property?"

George recognised the voice. It was Police Sergeant Kerr, head of the OSU, the Operational Support Unit, who assisted CSI during their searches.

"I'm not letting you lot in 'ere on your own so you can plant shite and frame us, OK?"

"I must insist, Mrs Grant," Kerr said. "Do you have a friend you could visit and have a cup of tea with?"

"Oh, for fuck's sake."

George grinned as he heard the door slam. He headed out of the bedroom, across the landing towards the top of the stairs.

Kerr looked up at him, a similar smile plastered across his face. "Now then, DI Beaumont, you good?"

"Not bad, PS Kerr. Yourself?"

"Aye, not bad. Would have preferred a warmer welcome."

"She grows on you," said George.

"Aye, I bet she does, like a cancerous mole."

"Who's like a cancerous mole?" asked Dr Lindsey Yardley. She'd snuck in whilst Beaumont and Kerr were talking.

"We're just discussing the delightful Mrs Grant," said Kerr. "Anyway, I'd love to continue our chat, DI Beaumont, but I need to start this search."

"We've found some stuff in Tyrell's bedroom," George explained. He handed the exhibit bag to Lindsey. "There's more of this upstairs in the airing cupboard," George explained about the used condoms and the purple underwear.

"I took a photograph of the drugs before the boss bagged it, Lindsey," Jay said.

"Email it over, DC Scott, please." She turned to George. "Sorry, DI Beaumont, but I need to get this place searched and photographed."

"Yeah, no worries. Ring me with your findings, please." The two detectives eased past Dr Yardley and into the squad car.

* * *

DI Beaumont called a meeting in his Incident Room, inviting the entire team. The DCI may have split them into two teams, with Yolanda being shared by Beaumont and Wood, but he trusted their instincts and wanted to know what progress the two DCs had made at St James'.

George turned to Tashan and Jay. "How'd it go at the hospital?"

"They wouldn't let us in again, boss," said Jay.

"Typical." George frowned. "How are we getting on with St James' CCTV?"

"They did let us see that, sir," said Tashan.

"And?"

Jay said, "We reviewed it with the security team, and the car was a navy-blue Fiesta, the reg clear enough to identify it as Martha Lickiss' car."

George raised his brows. "Anyone visible in it?"

Jay shook his head. "Martha was thrown out from the back seat, and then the car raced away."

"Two people involved then?"

"Correct, sir," said Tashan. "They were both wearing dark clothes and balaclavas."

George scratched his beard. "We need to figure out who the black-cladded figures are."

Tashan said, "I'll show you the footage, sir." He turned to DS Williams, who was at the computer. "Play the file, please,

CHAPTER TWENTY-FIVE

Sarge."

They all watched as a blue Ford Fiesta raced into St James' and pulled up outside A&E. Two figures then got out of the front of the car, the driver pulling Martha Lickiss from the backseat. Then, the passenger skipped around and helped the other carry Martha towards the entrance before running back to the car and racing away.

Tashan was squinting. He turned to his mate, Jay, and whispered in his ear. The whisper was greeted with a nod.

"Something you want to share, DC Blackburn?" asked George.

"Yes, sir. That Fiesta looks like the one that Rita Holdsworth was in."

"DI Beaumont wasn't part of the meeting, Tashan," Wood said from the back. She looked at Yolanda. "Do you have the footage?"

DS Williams nodded.

"Good, play it."

They watched as a blue Ford Fiesta pulled outside a house at the junction of Meynell Avenue and Love Lane, and George's eyes narrowed as the figure bundled Rita Holdsworth out of the Fiesta, dragged her across the road, through the opening in the wall and into the cemetery.

Despite the camera being quite far away, the footage was clear enough that DI Beaumont could see the killer place a collar around the older woman and clip a lead to it before dragging her out of the footage to where the killer presumably stabbed Rita to death.

"Jesus Christ," said the DI.

"We have more footage, sir," said Yolanda as she clicked another video file, and they watched as the exact dark-clothed figure retrieved a set of keys from their trouser pocket and opened the Fiesta. The timestamp showed forty-five minutes had passed. They heard the engine fire up, and then the car reversed slowly out of view.

"We don't see the car again on this camera, sir," said Yolanda.

"Any luck with cameras on Ingram Parade, DS Williams?" Wood asked Yolanda.

"No," Yolanda said. "There's nothing there we can use."

"Shit," said George.

Tashan said, "I'm even more sure that the car in this video belongs to Martha Lickiss, sir."

George squinted at the car. "Are you sure? Because the reg is different."

"Rewind it, please, Yolanda," Tashan said, and DS Williams obliged.

They all watched as the navy-blue Ford Fiesta appeared in the footage. "Stop, Yolanda."

"What are we looking at?" asked George.

Tashan pointed. "See that tax disc?"

The team squinted at the screen.

"Most cars don't have them because they're not mandatory now, but I remember this from the hospital," Tashan explained. "I'll show you in a minute."

"But it's reasonable to assume there's another navy-blue Ford Fiesta out there with a tax disc," the DI said.

"I agree, sir. However, that's a private tax disc, if you will. If I remember correctly, it's something to do with a farm show." Tashan smiled. "And I guarantee if we find the car or further footage of it, we'll see a graphic vinyl on the back window." He pointed at the screen. "I'm 99.9 per cent sure that's Martha

CHAPTER TWENTY-FIVE

Lickiss' car."

"Then that's good enough for me, Tashan," said George. "Good work."

"Thanks, sir, but I think we should look at the hospital footage again."

George nodded at Yolanda, who changed the video file.

"The Fiesta approached the camera, and Tashan said, "Stop, Yolanda, please."

She obliged, and DC Blackburn stood up. "Look, it's the same."

George nodded. He was convinced. "Excellent work, Tashan."

"So that means the two cases are related, boss?" asked Jay.

"Looks like it." He paused. "I'll need to speak to the DCI, but in the meantime, we need to focus on the area around Meynell Avenue and Love Lane to see if we can find some more footage to further prove Tashan's hypothesis. If we can do the same for the hospital footage, see where it comes from, even the DCI cannot stop us all from working together as one team again."

Chapter Twenty-six

Go for a jog, the consultant said. See how far you can go, the nurse suggested.

Not one of them mentioned the fact that his body would disprove of the jogging. Or how much pain his legs, arms, chest, and lungs would be in.

And then there was the intense heat, which had him huffing and puffing like an elderly steam train.

George could think of numerous benefits of getting exercise, one of those, and to be honest, the main reason was that he was pretty sure he was on his way to being a bit of a fat bastard. That, and he wanted to give himself something else to focus on beyond being a police officer. Being a detective took up most of his life, his vocation meaning he couldn't switch off on a night even if he wanted to. The job was full on, and not for the first time, he'd considered leaving the profession and doing something else.

But what would he do?

Being in the police was all he knew. Other than boxing, that was. But with his accident and the resulting injuries, he could no longer do that.

Being as fat as a mountain goat, Detective Constable Jay Scott had offered to come out jogging with him and had even

CHAPTER TWENTY-SIX

helped him pick out a new pair of running trainers.

As he pounded the pavement, he imagined it was Jay's face he was running on, his size elevens, twatting the young DC as he moved.

The air was dry, burning his throat with every breath he took as he sucked it down into his lungs. He wished he were at home, sitting with Izzy in bed, eating biscuits for no particular reason other than the fact that they were there. Luckily, her weird cravings had stopped, and she was eating normal food again.

George continued his route; happy people were home suffering from the heat rather than being out on the streets. His running style wouldn't be considered graceful by any stretch of the imagination. In his twenties, he was boxing in the gym and had been fit enough to run marathons. George had fond memories of training, not because he'd particularly enjoyed the gruelling exercise but more so because it had relentlessly pushed him towards something he'd never thought he was capable of.

The DI remembered the day he'd met Mia Alexander, his ex and the mother of his son, Jack. That day, he'd run up and down Briggate, through side streets and ginnels, chasing after a thief named Paul Jenkins, who had, unfortunately for him, been involved in an altercation that had turned fatal.

It had been in early December of 2019, and the news was full of a new virus they'd named COVID-19. Nobody knew what the future would hold for them and how they'd be forced into lockdown and not see their loved ones. The world changed in March 2020, especially in England, but in December 2019, people were still out in the streets in droves, blissfully unaware of what was coming their way.

Burglaries were rife during December and January, and George knew for sure he would be working flat-out. This would be his only opportunity to enjoy himself.

On the corner of Boar Lane and Briggate, a large group of youths were mulling outside the McDonald's, no doubt having a bite to eat before heading towards one of the city's many nightclubs.

They heckled George as he walked by, but the DS kept his head down. That August, a man was stabbed to death outside the American fast-food restaurant following an altercation, resulting in officers arresting three men aged eighteen, nineteen and twenty-two.

You could never be too careful, even if you were a boxer.

George hadn't lost a fight yet, but there were no rules on the streets, and George wasn't the sort of person to take unnecessary risks.

It had been a while since the DS had even entertained the idea of heading towards a nightclub, preferring a good beer or cider in an old-fashioned, traditional pub, which was why George was making his way up Briggate and towards The Angel Inn.

Completely unaware of the skirmish brewing between a man and a woman, George headed past the Trinity Centre, his hands in his pockets.

Then a shout made him stop in his tracks.

"Get the fuck off me!"

George turned on his heel.

A short, thin male had a blonde woman pushed up against the yellow and orange doors of the Trinity Stage, his forearm above her chest, forcefully trying to press it against her throat.

"Give me the fucking bag!" the man demanded as George sprinted towards them.

His police instincts spurred him to action. "Stop!" shouted

CHAPTER TWENTY-SIX

George. But he was too far away at that moment and saw the man repeatedly crash the woman into the doors.

"Give me the fucking bag, or I'll cut you, bitch!"

George pulled the man's elbow, dragging him away from the blonde woman. As the man turned, the DS observed pinpoint pupils that did not respond to the blazing light of the street lamps. The detective knew then that the situation was even more dangerous than he'd first anticipated.

With his drooping eyelids, the man said to George, "What the fuck do you want, mush? My girlfriend here owes me money!"

'Help me,' the blonde girl mouthed at George.

But the DS didn't see her mouth move; he was, instead, concentrating on the man he had in his grasp, thief Paul Jenkins.

"Paul Jenkins?" George asked, a confused look on his face.

The thief looked like a rabbit caught in the headlights, but it suddenly occurred to George how quiet everything had become. A bustling city had been reduced to a ghost town. He could hear no people, no traffic, no planes. And, so realising the situation was getting even more dangerous, the DS reached for his warrant card.

That gave Paul Jenkins the opportunity to pull his elbow away from George and snatch the bag from the vulnerable blonde woman and scarper.

Beaumont gave chase, following the thief up Briggate towards the Angel Inn, where he was supposed to be meeting Mark Finch.

A split-second decision meant Paul turned left up Commercial Street, but he hadn't anticipated the appearance of a young couple holding hands. Jenkins clattered into the young man, knocking him to the ground before jumping over and continuing his escape.

"I'm a detective," George screamed at the young woman as he chased Paul. "Call 999 and report this, please! And ask for an ambulance for your fella!"

George saw Paul make a right before making another sharp right, entering an alley lined with commercial bins all manner of colours.

The DS followed the scallywag, dodging the brightly coloured bins, knowing it would take them past the Pack Horse, where Mark had wanted to meet initially, and back onto Briggate.

"Stop, Paul!" George demanded, but the thief did nothing but continue running, this time past the bank on Briggate, heading north towards the Headrow.

But again, at the last minute, Paul took a sharp left turn between another bank and a clothes shop, and George grinned.

The narrow ginnel was the entrance to the Angel Inn, which only had one way in and out. There was another ginnel to the back, but you couldn't exit the pub onto it unless you entered the staff area.

Finally, George had the bastard cornered and sauntered cockily towards the thief. "There's nowhere for you to go, Paul," George explained. "And my friend's in there, waiting for me." He pointed towards the entrance. "You enter that pub, and you're done for."

Then the detective was unexpectedly staring down the barrel of a gun. Where it had come from, George had no clue.

He stepped back and said, "Put the gun down, Paul."

"You should have fucking stayed out of my business. Looks like I'm going to have to sort you out now!"

"Are you really going to kill a police detective, Paul?" George asked, holding up his hands in surrender. He didn't yet want to risk a step closer.

"If I have to, aye."

"You'll have no future if you do, Paul."

"I don't have a future anyway," Paul explained. "I know you have a warrant out for my arrest. I know that dickhead is dead. But I didn't mean to kill him. It was an accident."

CHAPTER TWENTY-SIX

"I agree, Paul. I think it was manslaughter, not murder, which is a lesser sentence." George risked a step closer. *"Surrender and I'll help you."*

"Don't fucking move, mate!" said Paul. He steadied the gun momentarily, his eyes blinking rapidly.

"If you kill me, Paul, you'll be charged with murder. Put the gun down. I'll arrest you, and we'll talk about a manslaughter charge, OK?"

But Paul shook his head. The thief's hand was shaking, matching the increased tempo of his rapid breathing. George was fit. He trained three or four times a week and boxed monthly, but even he was struggling to breathe in the damp, frigid air.

"You don't have to do this. Give me the bag, and I'll let you go."

"Bullshit."

George shook his head. *"Tell me what I can do to make you trust me, Paul."*

When Paul said nothing, George risked another step. The thief was cornered, but the DS knew there was nothing more dangerous than a cornered animal.

"How about we swap places, Paul?" George asked. *"That way, you can leave like I promised?"*

"For real?"

George nodded. *"For real."*

"I step, then you step?" Paul asked.

"OK."

Paul stepped towards George, but to his left, so George mirrored his movement.

They repeated this dance for three more steps, the two men closer now than ever, and George knew he needed to strike soon.

Which was when a voice echoed from behind Paul.

"There you are, you bastard. Give me my bag back!"

It was the young blonde.

Paul turned on his heel and froze, dumbfounded.

Using the distraction, George brought his right fist upwards, catching Jenkins under the chin. It was a massive blow, and Beaumont heard the crack as both upper and lower jaw connected, reducing Paul to one knee.

Suddenly the thief raised the gun, but George had already anticipated the man's reaction, and with one long stride, the DS kicked Paul's wrist, and the weapon clattered towards the blonde woman.

"Don't touch that, love," George said as he restrained Paul Jenkins.

The blonde frowned. "What, the gun?"

"Aye."

She raised a perfectly shaped brow. "I won't; I'm not bloody stupid." She ran a manicured hand through her blonde locks and met George's emerald-green eyes with blue eyes as beautiful as the sky. "Plus, my dad was a detective, so I know everything there is to know."

George grinned and was about to ask the lady to retrieve his phone and dial triple nine when two uniformed officers burst down the ginnel.

"My warrant card is in my back pocket, officers," George said, still holding down the convict.

"Good work Detective Beaumont," PC Greenwood said. George recognised him from Elland Road. "We'll handle this if you want to take a statement from that lass?"

"Thanks," he said, watching as PC Greenwood and his colleague cuffed Jenkins and arrested him.

The DS turned to the blonde. "I'm Detective Sergeant George Beaumont," he said, offering her his hand.

With a smile and blush appearing on her cheeks, she took his hand and said, "Mia Alexander, lovely to meet you."

Chapter Twenty-seven

George continued pounding the pavement, huffing and puffing, and thinking about the case. He was trying his best to push on, swearing through gritted teeth as he tried to keep himself motivated to move. He'd initially tried the NHS Couch to 5k app on his phone, but the upbeat Geordie comedian, his so-called supportive trainer, kept pissing him off. So he uninstalled it and decided to jog as far as he could, then walk for a bit, then rinse and repeat.

When it came to Hope and Martha, Geoff Lickiss was innocent, and George was sure of that. But the plants in the bunker kept coming back to him, as did what his mother had told him the other day. The DI slowed to a walk, pulled out his phone and dialled Marie Beaumont.

"Mum, can you come to the house? I need to talk with you."

"Is everything alright, love?"

"Yeah, fine; I just want to talk to you about Martha Lickiss."

"I'll set off now."

"See you soon."

George picked up the pace. He thought about Brenden Steffen, still miffed that the American hadn't contacted them earlier, not that it really mattered when he thought about it. The Yank hadn't provided them with information other

CHAPTER TWENTY-SEVEN

than his alibi, admitting he didn't know much about Martha's personal life besides what they shared during their trysts. And he hadn't met the girls, so he couldn't give them insight into their lives.

The DI was also suspicious of Taylor Corbyn and Jean Lickiss, though they had alibis for the night Martha was abducted and Hope murdered. Yet there were two people involved. They knew that now because of the CCTV procured from the hospital. And Taylor Corbyn was still missing, so perhaps she was involved in it all. That, or she would turn up somewhere dead and make the case even more complicated than it already was.

And then there was Tyrell Grant, who was still missing. He was involved in drugs and was possibly sleeping with a minor. SOCO hadn't found anything else at the property, and when Mrs Grant was interviewed, she profusely denied knowing about the drugs and being involved in any activity around them. But that didn't explain why he would kill Hope and abduct Martha. Not unless Faith was his motive. Maybe he abducted her, too. But then why would he abduct Martha and not leave her for dead as he did Hope?

Nothing was making sense, and it was pissing George off. And what made it worse was they now knew the Lickiss case and the Holdsworth case were related because of Rita's killer using Martha's Ford Fiesta.

But what linked the Lickiss and Holdsworth families? And was the person who killed Faith, the same person who killed Rita?

Back at home, George stripped and showered, his legs like jelly as he swayed under hot water. He washed himself in the scalding water, then turned the shower to cold to cool him down.

***

"I've just had a call from a book club member, and she said Martha Lickiss is in the hospital. Beaten black and blue, is that right?"

George nodded.

"Why didn't you tell me on the phone?"

"Because I can't, Mother. You know how it works by now."

"Was she assaulted in her own home?"

"We're not sure yet."

"How come?" He saw his mother looking around the house. "Where's Izzy?"

"Upstairs having a shower. We've been pretty busy with work." George yawned. "How did the club find out about Martha?" They'd tried to keep it all hush-hush but knew the press already knew.

"The book club has all manner of people as members, son," she said. The popular book club was run out of a bar in Morley. "And gossip travels fast." She grinned. "Plus, one of the members knows a reporter named Paige McGuiness."

"Trust it to be McGuiness," George said, shaking his head. "She's an absolute menace."

"She also shared some other news."

George narrowed his brows. "What news?"

"That Rita Holdsworth's been murdered."

George nodded his head. "That's right."

"She's quite a bit older than me is, Rita," said Marie, "but I did know her. I used to mind her children for her and her late husband. They were in their teens, and you were only a wee bairn."

"Kids? As in plural?"

"Yes, love, she had a boy and a girl."

George met his mother's eyes. "You're sure about that?"

"What are you trying to say, George?"

"Nothing, Mum, just we don't know anything about a son, just a daughter. Liz." He paused. "What was the son called?"

Marie Beaumont took a sip of her tea. The tension was palpable. "I'm sorry, son, but I really can't remember." She shrugged. "My memory isn't what it was; you know that."

* * *

Outside Rothwell Leisure Centre, the clouds had darkened and finally burst, letting loose fat drops of warm rain. Brenden Steffen cursed the British weather and the wet seat of his bicycle and headed up the A639 towards his home in Rothwell, his legs burning from the session in the gym.

The rain became heavier, giant droplets of warm water, and Brenden, adopting a standing posture, rode with his head lowered, meaning that he was only vaguely aware of a blur of movement to his right.

Suddenly, Brenden was hurled into the air, flying over the handlebars and into the middle of the dual carriageway, his legs in the right lane, his torso and head in the left, near the curb.

Squinting, he tried to move his head to look for his bike but could not. The helmet restricted his neck movements, so with shaking hands and sore fingers, Brenden managed to unclip the helmet and drag it from his head.

That's better, he thought. Much better.

Brenden Steffen twisted his neck, finding his bicycle crumpled in the middle of the road behind him. Behind his bike was a blue Ford Fiesta, its front registration plate hanging off and swinging.

The final sounds he heard were a revving engine and a screaming woman.

* * *

Hollie Bircumshaw heard the pop of Brenden Steffen's skull, like the cork flying out of a champagne bottle before the crimson blood spattered across her torso. She screamed, losing her footing on the pavement and nearly falling into the road.

Several cars screeched to a halt, their drivers and passengers getting out and sprinting towards the cyclist, but not the driver of the Ford Fiesta. Whoever was driving that car sped off.

"Have you called an ambulance?" a voice asked. It was a male voice.

Hollie swayed on the spot. "What?"

"I said, have you called an ambulance?"

She looked down to ensure her hands entered her pockets, searching for her phone, when she realised she was covered in blood.

"Are you OK?" the man asked, pointing at the blood. "You're not hurt, are you?"

"It's his," was all she could manage. She pulled out the phone, her hands shaking. "I was next to him when..." She stopped speaking. She felt like she was going to be sick.

"Give it 'ere, love; I'll do it."

"He's dead," she said. "There's no way he could have

survived that."

"It's OK, love, it's OK," the man said.

She was surrounded by people now, a mixture of emotions on their faces. There were a few sick bastards filming everything on their phones.

The nausea grew, so she covered her mouth with her hand but quickly pulled it away when she felt something sticky on her lips.

More blood.

Hollie started to sway. She felt light-headed. She's about to fall when the man holding her phone to his ear grips her arm.

"It's OK, love. Stay standing. You'll be OK."

"Do I have blood on my face?" Hollie asked.

He pursed his lips, then nodded.

Hollie started to sway again, feeling the bile rise up her throat, her shaking body fighting against the man's grip. It was like fighting against the tide. It made her feel even more unsteady than before, and soon enough, puke erupted from her mouth and sprayed the pavement.

The man recoiled, letting go of Hollie, who dropped to the ground, her vision turning black.

Chapter Twenty-eight

The clock on the wall showed it was 3.30 am.

"He'll be here soon," the older man said, "so be on your best behaviour."

"Yes, boss," replied the younger man. He looked up at his boss and couldn't tell how old he was. Fifty? Sixty? Seventy? Only the pale, almost translucent skin and the blood spots gave the man's age away. "I'm a bit nervous about meeting him." The younger man yawned.

"Here, have a drag of this. But not too much; it'll send you fucking wacko!"

"Thanks." The younger man took a long drag and let the relaxing feeling flood through his veins. "This is good stuff."

"It should be; it's his," the older one said.

"Oh shit, really? Same as I took the other night?"

"Aye."

"Fuck me. I don't know why we even have to go through with this stupid meeting," the younger one said as he took another drag. "We did as we were asked."

"Killing the old woman wasn't part of the plan, though, was it? You need to explain to him why you did it."

"Shit." The young man laughed nervously and took another drag, the drugs making the guilt melt away.

CHAPTER TWENTY-EIGHT

The older one was worried, much more worried than he was putting on. The younger one had royally fucked up, which was his responsibility. The older man just hoped the boss was in a forgiving mood.

The young man felt the same. He'd signed up for this and knew that there was no backing out once he was in. He hadn't even known why he'd been so violent. It wasn't like him. It must have been the drugs. In fact, he was sure. He started laughing. Yes, the drugs were to blame, not him. That's what he'd tell the boss.

"What the fuck are you laughing at, you knob?" the older man said.

But the young man kept laughing. And after taking a long drag, his companion joined in.

The noise they were making was so loud they didn't hear the door open or see the black-cladded figure enter the building, clutching a hunting knife tightly in one hand and a jerrycan of petrol in the other.

Chapter Twenty-nine

DCs Blackburn and Scott pulled up outside the smouldering wreck of a cottage situated on Calverley Road in Oulton, just outside Rothwell. Water from fire hoses flowed down the closed road and settled in puddles on the leaf-clogged gutters.

The day was scorching again, so the puddles wouldn't take long to evaporate.

"Hot enough for you?" Jay asked, getting out of the car. He yanked open his suit jacket and yawned.

"I'm OK, actually, Jay," Tashan replied. "Late night?"

Jay grinned. "Aye."

"She forgiven you then?"

"I don't think so."

Tashan laughed. "You never learn." He tried to keep up with Jay's short, quick steps. They stopped beside a fire truck and surveyed the scene.

"You smell that?" Jay asked, sniffing the air.

Tashan sniffed the air. "I smell burning." He shrugged.

Then a gust of wind made Tashan's eyes water, and he looked at Jay.

"Do you smell cannabis?" they asked together.

Tashan scratched the dark waves atop his head. "A grow house?"

Jay agreed. "Smells like it."

They approached Sergeant Greenwood, who was coordinating his uniforms.

"What have we got, sir?" Tashan asked.

"Grade two Single-storey nineteen sixties cottage. Careful lads, the roof's about to cave in."

"How many casualties?" Jay asked.

"One male. There's another male who should be dead but is somehow still alive." Greenwood shrugged. "The body's inside, but there's not much left of him." Greenwood grimaced.

"Where's the survivor?" asked Tashan.

Greenwood pointed to an ambulance firing up its engine with a whoop-whoop of its siren. Lights flashing, it began to move, but Jay had already started running towards it.

The ambulance stopped, and Jay banged a fist against the door.

The paramedic lowered the window and leaned out. "Who are you? What do you want?"

"Detective Constable Scott. I need to speak with the victim."

"Look, I'm sorry, but he needs treatment. If I don't go now, you'll never be able to speak with him."

"Shit." He turned to Tashan, who had just caught up.

"Which hospital?" asked Tashan.

"Pinderfields is the nearest, though he might have to be airlifted to the LGI. His fingers have been chopped off, and he's badly burnt." The paramedic shifted the ambulance into gear.

"Chopped off how?" asked Jay.

"With a knife," said the other paramedic. "I think it's still inside."

With flashing lights and wailing sirens, the ambulance drove away, and Tashan turned to Jay. Sergeant Greenwood joined them.

"When can we take a look around?" Jay asked.

"The roof is about to collapse, and the structure has been deemed unsound. The fire's out, so I reckon a few hours, lads."

Eyeing the tendrils of smoke creeping up from the house, Tashan asked, "Any idea how it started, sir?"

"Doors were screwed shut, and there's evidence of an accelerant."

"Murder then?" said Jay.

Greenwood nodded. "I've got my team on house-to-house."

"Did anybody live here?"

"No, it's a listed building."

"Who called it in?"

"A couple who live over there." Greenwood pointed towards North Lane. "Number four. They saw the flames and called it in. Then calls came in like a domino effect, apparently. CSI know, but there's no point in them coming until it's safe."

Jay nodded at the PS, then turned to Tashan. "Gonna be a few hours until we can get in, so we may as well interview the couple."

Tashan nodded.

The pair headed towards number four. An older man wearing khaki cargo shorts and a black t-shirt was outside, smoking. He nodded at the pair as they opened the gate and walked down the stone-lined path.

The grass was immaculate and a vibrant green despite the scorching weather. There was a hosepipe ban, and Tashan wondered whether the gentleman was ignoring it.

Jay marched over to the man and whipped out his ID. "Detective Constable Scott," he said. "This is my colleague, Detective Constable Blackburn."

"Here about the fire, lads?" the man asked. He placed the cig in his gob and offered a work-roughened hand to shake. "I'm Arthur Grady."

Tashan thought the man looked to be in his sixties or seventies. The outfit he wore made it difficult to be sure—the bushy eyebrows with grey strands and the liver spots adorning his pale cheeks that aged Arthur.

"Aye," said Jay. "What can you tell us about it?"

"Noticed the smoke and the smell when I came out for a fag this morning. The wind changed, and the air turned pungent." Arthur grinned. "I got our lass to call it in."

Tashan said, "Did you hear anything before that? Like an explosion?"

"No. Never heard a thing." Arthur tapped his ear, and Tashan saw a tiny hearing aid.

"Wife hear anything?" Tashan asked.

"She said not," Arthur said. "You can ask her when she gets back from the bakery. She won't be long; it's just 'round the corner."

Tashan knew the place. He wasn't sure about the 'won't be long' comment. The bakery usually had long queues out of the door. "You know who lived there?" he asked, nodding towards the smouldering building.

"Rented out online. Something B&B, I think. The original owner moved away. I haven't seen him in years."

"Do you know his name?"

"No, but I know he's foreign. European, but his accent wasn't that thick as if he'd lived here a while."

"Don't suppose you know who the estate agent is?"

"Come on, lads, why would I know that?" Arthur shrugged. "Check online."

CID detectives back at Elland Road already were. They'd find the listing soon enough and trace it back to the owner so they could find out who was renting it. That, in turn, may help them find who was responsible.

Deflated, Jay sighed. "Here's my card. We'll need you and your wife to come to Elland Road to provide a formal statement. Tomorrow is fine. Or later today. But if you remember anything else in the meantime, don't hesitate to contact me."

"Told you all I know, lad." Arthur stuck his cigarette back in his mouth.

"Thanks for your time, sir," Tashan said.

Both men walked back towards the scene. "Do you smell what I smell, sir?" Tashan asked PS Greenwood.

"Cannabis?"

"Aye," said Jay. "See anything inside?"

"There's a concrete bunker you can access from the garden, but whoever torched the cottage also torched whatever was inside the bunker. The garden is a swamp because of the fire crew." Greenwood shrugged. "Once it's safe, CSI will be allowed on-site." He grinned. "I've no doubt they'll find the source of the smell."

Turning to Tashan, Jay said, "So we got nothing?"

"Nothing yet, anyway."

"Wanna wait for a bit?"

Tashan shrugged. They'd arrested Geoff Lickiss for the murder of his daughter and the assault of his ex-wife, but that didn't mean the end of the case. They'd still need to ensure the evidence was solid to secure sentencing. He said as much

CHAPTER TWENTY-NINE

to Jay.

"We could go back to the station, but I think we should go to the hospital." Jay marched back to the car. "Hopefully, that fella doesn't die on us."

* * *

More and more people were entering the shared office space, so George left his office and asked DC Sutcliffe if he'd seen either of the lads that morning.

"They might be at that house fire," he offered.

"House fire? What house fire?"

"The one in Oulton," said Jack. "The DCI is SIO on it."

"Cheers, Jack," said George, and he made his way towards Wood, who called up the incident report log on her computer.

"House fire. Oulton. Suspicion of arson." She pointed at her screen. "They're there. Dispatch called for detectives to attend. One male deceased at the house, another badly injured."

George shook his head. "Who authorised Tashan and Jay?"

"DCI Atkinson," said Wood.

"Shit." That was all he needed. They still hadn't gone through the hospital CCTV yet, so they had no idea how Martha had arrived. They were up the creek without a paddle.

Chapter Thirty

"Where have you two been?" asked DI Beaumont. "There was a hit and run in Rothwell last night that the DCI has given us the case. I've been waiting for you both."

"Cottage fire, boss," said Jay. "Dispatch called, and the DCI cleared us to attend."

George shook his head. Because Rita Holdsworth's killer was Hope Lickiss' killer, they were now back working together as a team. It pissed him off that DCI Atkinson had taken away two valuable team members.

"The chief fire officer thinks it's malicious, sir," said Tashan. "We have one dead male that was apparently burnt to a crisp. I believe we'll only identify him via dental records. The second male is in hospital, badly burned and minus his fingers and thumbs."

"Minus his fingers and thumbs? Explain?"

"That's all we were told, boss," said Jay. "Paramedic reckons they were cut off via a knife.

"How strange. CSI say anything?"

Jay shook his head. "It's a grade two listed building, so it was pretty old. The fire caused so much damage we weren't allowed inside."

Tashan added, "We suspect it might have been a grow house.

CHAPTER THIRTY

Above the stench of the house burning was a pungent smell of cannabis. It's why the DCI cleared us to attend."

"What, because of Tyrell Grant?" asked George and Tashan nodded. "OK. Any theories?"

"Could be gang-related," offered Wood. "There are about forty gangs in Leeds."

"Unusual for it to kick off in Oulton, though." The main four gangs were Schmidt's gang from out of Middleton, plus gangs in Armley, Harehills and the city centre. "Maybe they were skimming off the top? Or selling on somebody else's territory."

"Call Greenwood and get uniforms on the door, just in case." He'd get the DCI to clear it with Wakefield, as Pinderfields was their jurisdiction.

* * *

"Why has the DCI given us a hit-and-run case, boss?" asked DC Jason Scott.

"I'll show you why," said George. He nodded at DS Yolanda Williams, who darkened the lights and sat down at the computer by the whiteboard. She clicked her mouse, and a video showed up on the screen. She clicked play.

After they'd finished watching, the room was silent. Nobody quite knew what to say.

Eventually, Jay said, "I think I'm gonna be sick."

"Stop being overdramatic, Jay," said George. "You've seen plenty of dead bodies."

"Aye, boss, but they're normally dead before I see them killed." He pointed to the screen and shuddered. "That was fucking awful."

George agreed with the young DC. The pop of the skull as it shattered under the tyre of the car would haunt George for the rest of his life.

Tashan nodded at the screen. "Martha Lickiss' Ford Fiesta again."

"Which is why it's been handed over to us. Well, that and the victim is Brenden Steffen." George explained how Brenden was Martha's lover but was excluded from the investigation due to his solid alibi. The DI then asked, "Who could have killed him?"

"Other than the obvious, boss?"

"Who's the obvious, Jay?"

"Well, Geoff Lickiss."

* * *

"Yes. That's what I'm saying. I didn't know anything about an affair until that lass called me today," said Geoff Lickiss. They were sat in an interview room at Elland Road.

George furrowed his brow and leaned closer. "What lass?"

"Paige, something. Said she'd heard about the affair from one of Martha's mates. I laughed and said, 'What fucking mates.' Anyway, the bitch wanted a fucking quote. Asked me if I was angry about the affair."

"Paige McGuiness?" the DI asked through gritted teeth, and Geoff nodded. George made a mental note to speak with Paige McGuiness and ask which of Martha's mates had spilt the beans. Rather they'd missed something huge, or one of the friends they'd interviewed hadn't been entirely honest with them.

"But it fucking gets worse."

CHAPTER THIRTY

George said, "Explain."

"Well, the stupid bitch asked me if I killed him."

"And what did you say to her?" Wood asked.

"I told her the same as I'm telling you now," Geoff spat. "I di'n't kill him. Di'n't know the cunt even existed, but if I knew he was shagging my wife behind my back, then, of course, I would've."

"When was this phone call?" Wood asked.

"Today." He shook his head. "It's why I'm 'ere. To clear mi name, because I di'n't do nowt."

DS Wood said, "You've got to admit it doesn't look good, Geoff."

The man frowned. "I know, which is why I came to you first. When that little bitch accused me of killing that prick, I thought it'd be best to come and see you."

George smiled. "OK, Geoff, give us your alibi."

Geoff blinked. "What?"

"Where were you when Brenden Steffen was killed?"

Geoff looked confused again, a similar look plastered across his face as when they interviewed him before—complete bewilderment.

"I need to know which day he was killed to be able to tell you, don't I?" Geoff asked George. Then, when no reply came, he tried Wood. "When did he die, Sergeant?"

"You said you were here because you wanted to provide us with an alibi because you didn't kill Brenden Steffen," Wood said, sticking to the plan. "So please provide us with your alibi."

"But... But I need to know when he died, don't I?"

The man had no idea when Steffen died. And George believed him. Again.

***

Back in the Incident Room, George and the team were going through all the evidence they had on the hit-and-run, but everything they had so far only led them to one thing—that Geoff Lickiss was innocent.

"What do you think?" George asked, looking at each member of his team. George thought Geoff was innocent.

"I think he's innocent, boss," said Jay.

"Yeah, I think so too, but let's go through what we have, because shit keeps happening day by day," said George.

DS Wood stood up and pointed at the Big Board. "OK, on the night Hope Lickiss was murdered, her mother, Martha, and her sister, Faith, went missing from the farmhouse. We still haven't found Faith, but yesterday, Martha was dumped from her own Ford Fiesta outside St James' hospital. She'd been badly beaten and is currently in an induced coma."

Wood nodded at Jay, who stood up. "Tashan and I checked the CCTV footage and saw two black-cladded figures dropping Martha off in her car. That same car was involved in the murder of Rita Holdsworth, who was, according to the pathology report, drugged and abducted before being treated like a dog, and murdered in the cemetery behind Holy Trinity Church in Rothwell. Rita's car was then found in Springhead Park, not far from the church, burnt-out."

George asked, "Has the Fiesta been tracked down yet?"

"Not yet, boss," said Jay.

Wood added, "We still don't know where Rita was drugged. CSI have searched the house and there's nothing indicative of an assault or abduction. We also haven't been able to find either car on traffic cameras, which is disappointing."

"And that's the same for Martha, too. We've no idea where she was kept during the days that she'd been missing, and I have to agree that the assault must have been recent. If it was carried out the night Hope was murdered or even before we arrested Geoff, there's no way Martha would still be alive," George said. He pointed towards the board again. "Calder Park has her clothes, and they're carrying out tests to see if they can retrieve any environmental fibres and such. If they find anything, it'll lead us in the right direction."

"Why was Brenden Steffen killed?" asked Tashan.

"I have two theories," said George. "One, he knew something and was killed so he couldn't tell us. He may not even have known he knew something, but somebody wanted to shut him up. Two, they wanted to frame Geoff Lickiss again, because that's what the killer has been doing from the start."

"What if Geoff is working with two other people, sir?" asked Tashan.

"Go on," said George.

"I've been thinking, and whoever killed Hope, and abducted Martha and Faith, it must have been difficult to get them into Martha's Fiesta alone."

George considered Tashan's words. "I suppose, but if it is Geoff, who's helping him?"

"Well there's Tyrell Grant," said Tashan. "Perhaps Tyrell made a deal with Geoff because he was Faith's boyfriend. He abducted Faith and Geoff abducted Martha?"

"And Faith did have all that cash in her bedroom, which suggests she was involved with drugs, boss." Jay drew his tongue across his teeth. "And if Faith was involved with drugs, boss, then is she connected to the fire in Oulton?"

"Perhaps," said George. "You all know the grade two cottage

was the subject of arson. You also all know the doors were screwed shut, and two bodies were recovered from the scene. One was dead, the other barely alive." He shrugged. "But that doesn't explain why Tyrell, and a third person, would drop Martha off at the hospital."

"I've been thinking about that too, sir," said Tashan. "What if the third person is Faith Lickiss? What if she's been involved in all of this?" He shrugged. "There's no sign of a struggle involving Faith at the farmhouse, unlike the struggle involving Martha. And if we go back to my original theory, that Geoff was there to kill Martha, and he killed Hope by accident, then it's plausible."

"I appreciate what you're saying, Tashan, but we have zero evidence that Tyrell was at the farmhouse."

Tashan shrugged. "As my favourite detective always says, 'When you have eliminated all which is impossible then whatever remains, however improbable, must be the truth.'"

George grinned. "Fair enough."

"Going back to Faith Lickiss," Yolanda said, "What's her connection to it all?"

"The OSU was sent in to the cottage, and they removed cannabis plants from an insulated building to the rear of the cottage. We're still awaiting clearance to enter the burned structure."

Yolanda asked, "You think the cottage is where Martha and Faith Lickiss were held, then?"

"We're not sure," said George. "We have teams out looking for Faith still, but I think it's time to ramp up her disappearance on social media. I'll get the press office to issue yet another statement because we need to find her."

"Did we ever find out who the cottage in Oulton belongs to?"

asked Wood.

"I've checked council tax records," said Tashan, "but it's owned by a company, apparently. I've checked Companies House but got nothing."

"Could be fraudulent, which wouldn't surprise me considering the cannabis," said George. "Check with Land Registry and get back to me."

"Arthur Grady said we should check estate agents," said Jay.

"What do you know about him, Jay?" asked George.

"Only that he still hasn't come to give a statement yet as I asked," said Jay. "Otherwise, nice fella."

"OK, Jay, follow that up today. I'm aware other people called 999 that morning to report the fire; go and take statements from them after the meeting, see if we missed anything."

"Will do, boss." He made a note and then looked up. "So, who are we looking for now, boss?" Jay asked the DI.

George said, "The people in the balaclavas who abandoned Martha at the hospital. We find them; we find where they kept Martha. And who knows, Faith may be there."

Chapter Thirty-one

George sat at his desk and fired up his computer, then logged in. He checked his email and spent the next five minutes deleting ones that were of no interest to him. That left four. The first came from Yolanda, and attached was a short video file. It was footage of Brenden Steffen's death taken from a dashcam of a poor family heading to Toby Carvery for tea. George clicked on the attachment and watched the film several times. The more he watched it, the angrier he felt. The murder had been so brazen, yet they still had no idea who'd committed it. He froze the film with the hooded figure in full view, enlarged the shot and stared intently at the screen. It was a man with a beard.

"DS Wood," George said after standing and poking his head out of his office door, "come and take a look at this."

Wood got up from her desk and walked into the office. She looked at the screen.

"This guy look familiar to you?" asked George.

After narrowing her eyes and scrutinising the footage, she said, "Maybe." She pointed at the screen. "Long beard."

"Geoff Lickiss has a long beard," said George.

"It's not Geoff; his alibi's tight."

"Yeah, I know, but I feel like I've seen somebody else recently

CHAPTER THIRTY-ONE

with a long beard."

"There's Nigel Lickiss," said Wood with a shrug. "He has a long beard."

"But why would Geoff's brother want to kill Brenden Steffen?" George bit the inside of his cheek. "And obviously, there's Hope's murder and Martha's abduction. Plus, there's the death of Rita Holdsworth." George continued. "What's his motive?"

"I don't know, but I think we need to speak with him, anyway, especially if we consider what Faith's friends told you."

"OK," she said, heading for the door. "I'll get uniform to bring Nigel in then."

"Thanks, Izzy," he said, closing the email. Something was niggling at him, but he wasn't sure what it was. He stared at the screen briefly before opening the next email. Attached to it was a witness statement from a jogger named Hollie Bircumshaw. She'd been so close to the incident that she'd been covered in Steffen's blood. She gave a short description of a person wearing dark clothes with a hooded top. When pressed, she said she was unsure whether the culprit was male or female and made no mention of the beard George had seen on the dashcam footage.

George clicked on the following email to find it was another witness statement taken from a guy called Lenny Hirst. He'd been second at the scene and had used Hollie's phone to call triple nine. Lenny hadn't seen the driver at all; his concern for Hollie and calling the police, meaning he only saw that it was a navy-blue Ford Fiesta.

George's phone rang. "DI Beaumont," he said without looking at who was calling.

"DI Beaumont, it's Lindsey Yardley," the CSI said. "I've just sent you the results of the tests done on the plants found at the Lickiss farm," she explained.

The DI clicked back and then into the email at the top of the list. He scanned it quickly. "Angel's Trumpets? I've heard of them before."

"Yeah, you will have, George, because you can harvest scopolamine from them."

Earlier that year, George and the team had solved a case involving Scopolamine, a compound said to lead to hallucinations, frightening images, and a lack of free will, eventually leading to respiratory failure and death.

"So, someone in the Lickiss family was growing those plants?"

"Correct, DI Beaumont. Geoff Lickiss."

"How do you know that?"

"We got lucky, George," she explained. "Hayden found some equipment down in the bunker, and we managed to lift prints from it. Geoff is on the system, so it flagged him up. It's why I called you straight away."

"Thanks for that," George said, "but what if it's equipment he, say, used ten years ago, and the actual culprit planted it there?"

"It's a good question," Lindsey admitted. "But the equipment was regularly used and has scopolamine particles on it. Plus, his prints are overlaid, suggesting he was the only one who used them. If somebody else was using it, say with a gloved hand, the prints would be smudged, and they aren't."

"Is all of that in the report?" George asked.

"It is indeed, DI Beaumont."

The DI grinned. "Thanks, Dr Yardley," he said, ringing off.

CHAPTER THIRTY-ONE

He popped his head out of the door. "DS Wood, I know you said Geoff's alibi was tight, but did anybody check it?"

"No. Not yet," replied Wood. "Do you need me to go and check?"

George shook his head. "Delegate, DS Wood."

"Of course, DI Beaumont." She picked up her phone, and George headed back inside his office.

The following email was a statement taken by Cathy Hoskins. Jean Lickiss had been home alone the night Brenden Steffen was murdered, and whilst George didn't think she was involved, he needed to cover all the bases.

His phone rang again once he'd finished reading the statement.

"DI Beaumont," he said.

It was the office manager, Samantha. "Geoff Lickiss is here."

"Stick him in an interview room and turn up the heating," he said. "I'll be down in ten minutes."

* * *

George wasted a full hour with Geoff Lickiss and his solicitor. He'd hear 'no comment' in his dreams for a year.

"What a twat," he said, entering the floor that housed the HMET.

"He's afraid, though," Wood said. "Hence the 'no comment' interview."

"He should be afraid, the arsehole," said George, clenching his fists. "He's been a thorn in my arse this entire case—"

"George, calm down. The last thing you need is to get stressed. It's no good for a healing body."

He nodded. "Thanks, love."

"He was agitated, too, completely different to his initial interviews."

"Because he's guilty."

She smiled. "Yep."

* * *

DS Wood was tying and untying her ponytail, sighing at every failed attempt.

"You look stressed," George said.

"I am," she said, her smile not reaching her eyes. "I've spent ages trying to piece together what Martha was working on, hoping for a link between her family tree and Rita's."

"A lot of the work she'd completed on her laptop was to do with the course she was studying, but some of it was private work done on Ancestry.co.uk and imported into Word. She'd paid a subscription and had assembled two trees, but we can't currently access her internet history."

"An adopted one and a birth one?"

Wood nodded and pointed to the printout.

"Can we get access to her emails?"

"I can ask Josh to check it out if you think it's of any use."

"Be good to know who, if anyone, she was in contact with," the DI said. He pointed at the printouts. "How far had she got with the family tree?"

"Not far at all, actually," said Wood. "In both trees, she had some of Geoff's family mapped out and her marriage to him and the resulting twins. In the one titled, 'Adopted', she had Ted and Mavis Mook, her adopted mother and father."

George nodded.

"In the 'Birth' tree, she hadn't filled out any of her birth

CHAPTER THIRTY-ONE

family's information."

"So, she was struggling like we were?"

"Looks like it."

George scrutinised the printouts. His maternal grandmother had attempted a family tree many years ago, but she hit a roadblock because only the 1911 census was released and not the 1921 census. Martha shouldn't have had that problem, however, because George knew about the 100-year rule and knew the 1921 records had been released.

However, a cursory Google search told him the 1921 records were behind a rather expensive paywall. Instead of paying a modest subscription and having all the records to hand like with Ancestry.co.uk, the 1921 records were exclusive to Findmypast.co.uk, and each record you wanted to look at cost money.

For a genealogist who would need to check different records to ensure they had the correct family members, that cost would be an absolute nightmare.

So, no wonder Martha had hit a roadblock.

George looked at the printouts again and noticed something he hadn't earlier. He showed what he'd seen to Wood and said, "What do you know about these lines?"

On the 'Adopted' tree, a thick line connected Ted and Mavis Mook. Dropping down from the centre of that thick line was a thinner line connected to Martha. A similar thick line joined Martha and Geoff Lickiss. However, this time, the thinner line that joined to the twins was only connected to Martha and not Geoff.

"Thick line means married," said Wood. The thin line means a different relationship. And when a line drops down, it means next generation, so in the case of Martha and the twins," Wood said, pointing at the thin line, "it connects the mother to her two daughters." She pointed to the thin line dropping down from the centre of that thick line that connected Ted and Mavis Mook. "As you can see there, you have mother and father dropping down to their daughter."

George nodded and then pulled out his PNB. He drew a thick line connecting him and Isabella, and then below, wrote, 'unborn child'. He looked at Isabella and said, "Is this right?"

She shook her head. "We're not married—"

"Not yet," he said with a wink.

"We would have a thin line like this," she said, redrawing the tree. "And if you wanted to add Jack, then you would connect Mia to your left with a thin line and then drop down the middle of that line and put Jack."

George said nothing at that, and he watched as Isabella realised the meaning of his silence, wincing.

"I'm sorry—"

"Don't be, my love." He pointed at the single line that branched into two. "So, is this suggesting Geoff isn't the twin's father?" George asked, not wanting to discuss Jack. He still wasn't sure the boy was biologically his, not that it mattered. Jack was his boy, and he loved him more than anything. He knew that would change soon once his child with Isabella was born. Then he'd have two people he loved more than anything, with Isabella coming in at a close second.

"Possibly," Wood said with a shrug. "It could also have been done by mistake or even out of spite because she was angry with him. We'll have to ask her once she's in a fit state to talk."

"This is all very confusing," said George. "Any other theories?"

"Nope." She smiled, but her smile did not meet her eyes

again. "It's why I've been pulling my hair out."

"Keep going through it, Izzy. Something will turn up."

* * *

A knock at the door interrupted George. He was still searching on Google, hoping it would improve his genealogy knowledge. "Come in."

DC Jason Scott entered. "Boss, uniform has managed to find two witnesses who saw a shady character the morning of the fire. Both say he was covered in blood and stank of smoke."

"Could be our guy."

"That's what I thought, boss."

"Bring them in and take detailed statements," George said. "Then have a word with the DCI. He knows all kinds of shady people. See if he can think of anybody matching their description."

The DC nodded. "On it."

Chapter Thirty-two

It was nearing four in the afternoon, and the sky was devoid of clouds, a cornflower blue when George arrived at the burned-out cottage. Because of the drug links, the DCI had handed the case over to George, most likely hoping the DI would solve it for him.

Looking over at the wet embers, now cordoned with crime-scene tape, he cast his gaze across the mess. The roof had caved in. He could hear the water dripping from the bare beams of the old cottage as he was signed into the scene by a PC standing at the entrance.

The structure of the house had been deemed safe, but looking at it, George was unsure. Everything in sight had either been burned or saturated by fire hoses. CSI was going through everything. The sound of cameras clicking and water dripping was grating on his nerves.

Hearing voices from the rear of the cottage, George headed there first to find Lindsey Yardley and her team of SOCOs, who were busy bagging and tagging the plants found in the insulated outhouse. Just as well, the fire hadn't reached that far. Otherwise, the population of Oulton would have been stoned.

He walked up to Hayden Wyatt, who was standing with a

clipboard in his hand. When he saw George, the Yank grinned. "Hello there, DI Beaumont."

"Wyatt," George replied. He pointed at the plants. "Worth a few quid that lot."

"Indeed."

"Not very discreet about it, were they?"

The American gestured towards the front of the house. "Security was pretty tight, to be fair, so they didn't need to be. And anyway," he shrugged, "they're just plants if you don't know any different."

"Was the shed locked?"

"It was," Hayden said. "Thick, iron chains and a combination lock." He pointed at the bolt croppers. "Didn't stand a chance against the bolt cutters, though, DI Beaumont."

Wyatt became momentarily distracted by a colleague who was dragging another bag full of cannabis plants towards the marked van. The American's pen met his pad before he looked back up at George, but the DI was gone.

On the way back to his Merc, George's phone rang. He pulled it out and pressed the green button. "DI Beaumont."

"Boss, whilst you've been out, I've managed to speak to the pub opposite the cottage in Oulton and the Shell garage next door," said DC Jason Scott.

"OK."

"They kindly sent me CCTV footage of the morning of the fire, and, after going through the witness statements again and speaking with the Lidl worker and the Shell garage worker, I've isolated the time they saw the shady figure," Scott explained.

"That's very good, thorough work, Jay," said George.

"Thank you, boss," said Jay. "Anyway, I've picked up the shady guy on camera, and I went to the DCI as you told me to, and guess what?"

"Go on, DC Scott; the suspense is killing me."

"DCI Alexander knows the suspect, boss," Jay said. "Derek White. He's got a rather distinctive neck tattoo. That, his beard, and the fact the rest of him is covered in tattoos meant the witnesses identified him. DCI Alexander said he runs the Harehills gang, so God knows why he's in Oulton."

"That's brilliant news. And the two witnesses are adamant it's him?"

"As soon as they saw the images of Derek, boss, they picked him out."

"OK, ask the DCI to bring Derek White in. I'll head back to Elland Road now."

* * *

"You remain under caution," DI Beaumont said after they'd turned on the tape and reeled off the usual spiel. "Do you know why you're here?"

Derek White rolled his eyes. "Nope, so you'll have to enlighten me."

"You're here because we are treating the fire of a cottage in Oulton as arson," George explained.

White raised his brow. "And what's that got to do with me?"

"Two independent witnesses placed you at the scene, Mr White."

A look of mock shock crossed the man's face. "Not me." He smirked at George.

"It was you, Mr White," said DC Jason Scott.

The thug shrugged. "Prove it."

"I intend to." George slid across two documents to White

CHAPTER THIRTY-TWO

and his solicitor. "Document twelve is a statement taken by my colleague here, DC Scott, from a woman who works at Lidl on Aberford Road in Oulton," the DI explained. "She claimed to see 'a tall, broad, tattooed gentleman who sauntered around cockily and smelled of smoke. He had blood on his hands, a long beard and a fade.'" George raised his brow. "'He also had an owl tattoo on his neck.' See where we're going with this?"

"That could have been anybody," White's solicitor said. "And I must repeat that my client insists it's not him."

George grinned. "See, I would usually agree with you, but the witness was very descriptive when it came to the 'owl tattoo on his neck'."

"What did she say?"

"It's all there for you in black and white," said George. "But she said a 'barn owl'." He let that sink in for a moment. "If you have a look at document thirteen, you'll see we set up an identity parade where a police sergeant unfamiliar and uninvolved with the case showed our witness pre-recorded video footage of nine unrelated men of a similar appearance and age. She made a positive ID for number one." The DI gestured for the two men opposite him to turn over their pages, which they did. "Male number one should be familiar to you both."

George leaned back, a cocky but triumphant sparkle in his eyes.

"We both know identity parades aren't always reliable," the solicitor said. "None of these men have barn owl tattoos on their neck."

George nodded. "I agree with you, but men with barn owl tattoos on their necks are extremely rare." The DI grinned. "Would you agree with me that male number one is your client?"

"It is me in that picture," Derek cut in, "but that doesn't mean I was involved in this arson of yours." He nudged his head in the direction of his brief. "As he said, identity parades aren't always reliable."

"And as I said, Mr White, I agree that identity parades aren't always reliable, the key word being always," said George. "However, in this case, I think you'll appreciate the lengths we went to ensure our witness was telling us the truth."

A frown appeared on the brief's face. "What on earth do you mean?"

George slid across another four pieces of paper, two each for Derek and his solicitor. "Documents eighteen and twenty," George said. "Twenty details a second identity parade, set up by yet another independent police sergeant. This time, she picked male number six." He grinned. "Please have a look at document eighteen."

White shook his head. "Another picture of me. I'm guessing she picked me out again?"

"Bingo."

"But that's also unreliable, especially if you're using the same witness."

"Again, something we agree on," said George. He turned to Jay. "DC Scott."

Jason cleared his throat. "Independent witness two, a male in his thirties who works in the Shell petrol station on Aberford Road, Oulton, was also asked to attend virtual identity parades."

"Parades?" asked the solicitor, to which Jay and George nodded.

DC Scott slid across two sheets of paper, one to Derek White

CHAPTER THIRTY-TWO

and one to his brief.

"As you can see, for impartiality, we used two different police officers who were unfamiliar and uninvolved with the case and swapped the numbers of the images around." Jay pointed at the printouts. "The results are there for you to see."

After a moment, George broke the silence. "So, Mr White, tell me why you were seen by two independent witnesses, covered in blood and smelling of smoke, outside the burning cottage the morning it was burnt down?"

* * *

Detective Sergeant Josh Fry, now head of the digital forensics team, entered George's Incident Room after knocking on the door. He was a tall, lean man, usually unshaven, who wore black Ray-Ban rectangle glasses with such thick lenses that his eyeballs looked as if they were protruding from his face.

"Nice to see you, Josh," George said, "and congrats on the promotion." Despite the permanent yawn and a bird's nest atop his head, Joshua was the best-qualified person in Leeds Police HQ regarding tech. He'd studied Forensic IT at Leeds University and was George's go-to guy.

"Hardly a promotion when I was doing the job anyway, sir," Josh said with a grin.

"Fair enough." George smiled. "To what do I owe the pleasure?"

The DS cleared his throat. "I've downloaded the contents of Brenden Steffen's phone that CSI brought in, sir." He grimaced. "There were a lot of nude photos on there, and I must admit, it felt like I was snooping on the guy."

George knew how the DS felt. He was repulsed by the sheer

amount of information digital forensics could seize from a mobile phone within minutes of having it. That included location tracking, text messages, and photos, deleted or not. It felt very invasive to George to know such intimate details of a person's life—without a warrant and sometimes without the full context, understanding and knowledge, or even the consent of the phone's owner. It was as if someone was always watching, continuously tracking your every move, yet it was out of your control.

Yet, when solving murders, having data downloaded from a mobile phone was often the reason a case was solved rather than becoming cold.

George left the Incident Room, entered the shared office space and said, "The digital forensics team's retrieval of Brenden Steffen's phone revealed a series of text messages."

"What kind of messages, boss?"

"Messages from Martha, Jay," George explained. "DS Fry is putting them up on the whiteboard as we speak.

The team entered the Incident Room and sat down. Josh opened the transcript of messages on the laptop, which appeared on the whiteboard.

After a moment, the atmosphere in the room became charged.

"Holy shit!" Jay exclaimed.

"My thoughts exactly, Jay," George said.

Nobody said anything else.

There was only silence.

DI Beaumont broke the suffocating silence when he said, "Right, Jay, I need you to access Hope and Faith's birth certificates to see who was registered as their father."

CHAPTER THIRTY-TWO

* * *

Lindsey Yardley contacted George to advise they'd finished sifting through the ashes of the cottage, so George grabbed Jay, and they sped out to Oulton. On the way, the DI tried to ring Isabella to let her know why Martha had connected the twins only to her and not to her and Geoff.

Approaching the carcass, George saw the white suits gliding like ghosts in and out of the blackened shell.

"Proper weird situation is that cottage, innit, boss?"

Jay was driving, and George was reading emails in the passenger seat. He turned to his right. "What do you mean?"

"Well, with the number of cannabis plants in the shed, it's weird that they weren't stolen." He pulled up where a PC advised him to, then turned to meet the DI's eyes. "If this were gang-related, surely the Harehills gang would have stolen the plants."

George nodded. "I think that's why the DCI gave the case to us," he explained. "With Tyrell Grant and the money found in Faith Lickiss' bedroom, plus the fact that we found plants in the bunker at the Lickiss farmhouse, it's a safe assumption that the cases are linked."

"I just feel like we're missing something, boss," Jay said, getting out of the car. "Somebody tried to murder two men but only succeeded in killing one. Then, that person burned down the cottage and didn't take plants worth thousands of pounds. And we have Derek White in the area, too."

After finally admitting he was in the area, White was adamant he wasn't involved. He'd had a one-night stand with a lass who lived on Leventhorpe Way with her grandma. The grandma had found Derek in her granddaughter's bed that morning and had kicked him out. When further examined, White explained he'd punched a wall repeatedly and most likely smelled of smoke because he smoked thirty a day. Lindsey had sent a SOCO to the wall to take samples, but it would be a day or so before any results came back.

George shrugged at Jay's question and said, "The only thing I can think of, Jay, is that the culprit didn't know about the drugs."

"Then that makes it worse, doesn't it?" Jay shrugged, almost looking embarrassed. "It means White probably wasn't involved, and if he wasn't, then who was?" Jay paused. "Who would have a reason to attempt to kill two men?"

"I don't have the answers, Jay," George said, "but with any luck, Lindsey does. And if all else fails, we cross our fingers and hope Dr Ross can identify the victim. As you know, most murders are committed with a victim in mind."

In silence, the pair pulled on protective coveralls, overshoes and gloves. George opted for a mask, but Jay didn't. SOCOs had erected tents to cover as much of the cottage as possible, protecting evidence from the blistering heat.

George and Jay entered the charred remains of the cottage and bumped into Dr Lindsey Yardley.

"DI Beaumont, DC Scott," she said.

The two detectives greeted the crime scene co-ordinator before George said, "What's that?" He pointed to the scorched object in Yardley's hand.

"A bone," Lindsey said.

"A bone?" George took a step closer and held out a gloved hand. Yardley dropped the bone into it, then bent down and picked up another one.

"Is it human?" asked Jay.

CHAPTER THIRTY-TWO

George nodded. "These are the missing fingers," he explained.

Jay physically recoiled. "Jesus Christ. Fingers?"

"I'll collect everything and tag them, then inspect them later," Lindsey said, retrieving the finger bone from George and popping it into an exhibit bag. "I'll let you know of any findings."

"Thanks, Lindsey," George said. "Before we go, you got anything else for us?" George asked.

"As I said, I'll let you know."

"OK, fair enough," George said. "We'll let you get on with it."

Jay's phone pinged with a message as he and George returned to the squad car.

"Who's that?" George asked.

"Tashan, boss." He stopped in his tracks and continued reading. "Guess who owns the cottage?"

"I'm in no mood for guessing games, Jay."

"The Lickiss family."

Chapter Thirty-three

As soon as Jay and George arrived at Elland Road, the DI's phone rang. "DI Beaumont."

"It's Hayden Wyatt, DI Beaumont," the American said. "We've found a bag in the back garden hidden in the undergrowth."

"And?"

"There's a collar and a lead covered with blood."

George turned to Jay, who fired the engine back up. "You heard that?"

"Aye, boss."

George placed the phone back by his ear. "OK, we're on our way, Hayden. Thank you."

* * *

George and Jay arrived at the cottage in Oulton. It was George's third time that day and the constable's second, but it was all part of the job.

Again, a police constable showed Jay where to park, and both detectives alighted the vehicle and followed the track to the right to the back of the cottage. In the far back corner, on the opposite side of the cannabis shed, they could see a group of

CHAPTER THIRTY-THREE

officers and SOCOs mulling around the thick undergrowth.

At the sight of George and Jay, the officers stood back to allow the detectives a clear view into the undergrowth. It was clear an opening had been cut into it, and George could see Wyatt crouched over a black rucksack lying in the thick grass, taking photos.

"Once I've finished photographing it, DI Beaumont, I'll get it to Calder Park ASAP for you," said Wyatt.

One of the American's colleagues entered George's personal space and handed him an exhibits bag and a pen. "I need you to authorise a 24-hour turnaround and the Premium Charge, sir," the SOCO said.

"Give me a minute; I'll need to seek approval from the DCI." During his hunt for the Miss Murderer, he'd gone over budget and had been bollocked by DSU Smith. It was a lesson he'd never forget.

After calling twice, the DCI finally picked up, and George explained the situation. He put Atkinson on speaker and said Jay was there as a witness. Jay then watched as George ticked the box for a 24-hour turnaround and watched him sign again at the Premium Charge Acknowledgement box. "Thank you, sir," George said before hanging up. The DI turned to Wyatt. "Can you personally take this to Calder Park?"

"I can, DI Beaumont." The American looked around, presumably for Lindsey Yardley, but when it was clear she wasn't around, he stood up and took the exhibit bag from George.

"If Dr Yardley asks, I asked you to take it personally."

"Thank you, DI Beaumont, much appreciated."

George and Jay watched the SOCO power walk towards the front of the cottage. A moment later, they heard an engine fire up.

George turned to the SOCO, who had given him the exhibit bag. "What have you got left to do?"

"Very little, sir. We're almost finished and are just winding down."

"And the entire undergrowth has been checked?" asked George, pointing.

"Yes, sir."

"Thank you," George said as he walked away, Jay in tow.

When they got back to the squad car and DC Scott had fired up the engine, George turned to him and said, "Well, this proves the cases are now linked, Jay."

"I thought as much, boss." He shook his head in frustration. "But why would Rita Holdsworth's killer burn two men to death?"

* * *

On the way back to Elland Road, George called Dr Christian Ross to see if he'd carried out the PM on the man who died in the fire.

"He's currently on the slab, George," the pathologist explained.

"Can you tell me anything?"

"Only that he didn't die in the fire."

George frowned. "What?"

"Everything I've found so far suggests he was already dead before the fire started, George," Christian said.

"Such as?"

"I found a few nicks on his ribs, which, in my opinion, means he was stabbed. That, and the fact there was no smoke in what's left of the lungs, suggests he was dead before the fire."

CHAPTER THIRTY-THREE

George took a moment to digest this information. One victim was murdered and left to burn, whilst the other had their thumbs and fingers hacked off with a knife. The DI tried to put himself into the killer's shoes and concluded that the fire was started to draw attention to the victims. But why would a killer want to do that? Was the killer goading him? Were they that cocky, that sure they wouldn't be caught, that they wanted to draw attention to themselves? Was that also why they left the rucksack behind?

Again, there were so many questions but zero answers.

Or was the killer trying to deflect the blame? George had felt that right from the start, the culprit had tried to frame Geoff Lickiss. What if the culprit was trying to get them looking at gangs? It would explain hacking off the fingers and leaving behind the cannabis plants. The DCI had shared with George stories from his past when he was part of the drugs unit, sparing no detail when explaining how the gangs dealt with people who were skimming off the top.

"I'll email the preliminary results soon, son," Christian said, bringing George out of his mind and into the present. "I've some good news, though."

"Go on."

"I've identified him."

* * *

George called Isabella, wondering where she was.

"I'm on my way to Rita Holdsworth's house to have a look for anything interesting. Is everything OK?" she said.

"Yeah, I'm just calling you to update you on the PM of the body in the fire. He'd been stabbed numerous times and was dead before the fire," George said. "Or that's what Christian thinks, anyway, and he's usually spot on."

"What does that mean?"

"I'd have thought someone was trying to hide a murder, but whoever burnt down the cottage used an accelerant and ensured the doors couldn't be opened."

"So we'd classify it as murder anyway," said Wood.

"Exactly."

"I guess we've got to wait for the John Doe to wake up and let us know what happened then," she said. "Do we have the identity of the deceased?"

"We do. Dr Ross came through for us."

* * *

If you live by the sword, then you die by the sword, thought Isabella Wood.

The Haymer family were a bunch of scumbags, and Aiden was specifically a rapist, though he was never convicted. She'd worked on one of his cases when she was a DC working for the Wakefield branch. The last woman brave enough to come forward, the woman she was supposed to protect, had suddenly gone missing, and the judge threw the case out. It didn't help that the semen sample had vanished, either.

To Izzy, the Haymer family had somebody on the inside, loyal to the family rather than the police. And that was dangerous. Even more dangerous than Aiden was his brother, Alfie, head of the family—West Yorkshire's answer to the Mafia.

From working on that case, Isabella knew the Haymer gang were gun runners and drug suppliers. But it was also so much

CHAPTER THIRTY-THREE

worse than that. The gang was involved in prostitution, money laundering, identity theft and protection rackets.

DS Wood was glad Aiden Haymer was dead but also extremely worried because Alfie Haymer wouldn't let the murder of his brother pass without making waves. She only hoped he wouldn't make a bloody tsunami.

* * *

DCI Atkinson shuffled into the Incident Room, his suit jacket over his arm, and grunted, "Afternoon, DI Beaumont. Hot enough for you?"

Without looking up, George rang off and replied to the DCI. "Scorching, isn't it, sir?"

"Indeed."

"I've just received some information from Dr Christian Ross, sir," George said. "We have a name for the man who died in the fire. Aiden Haymer." George stuck up a picture of the man on a separate Big Board.

The DCI turned slowly and pointed a finger at the picture of the burned man. "I know him," said Alistair.

George turned. "How, sir?"

"You know my background, right?"

George did. DCI Alistair Atkinson was second in command, subordinate only to the Assistant Chief Constable, of a serious and organised crime crackdown called Programme Precision. Programme Precision was West Yorkshire Police's collaborative, multi-agency response to the threat of Serious and Organised Crime. Atkinson worked across West Yorkshire to tackle those involved in the spectrum of serious and organised criminality, including cyber-crime, money laundering, gang activity, serious violence, and County Lines activity. It was why the DCI was so interested in Jürgen Schmidt.

"Aiden Haymer is... was second in command to his brother, Alfie Haymer, who is head of the Armley gang."

"Why on earth would Armley's second in command be in a grow house in Oulton?" asked George.

"Gangs are always looking to expand, George," said the DCI. "It could be Aiden wanted to be in charge of a gang, so he decided to go rogue and start an operation in Oulton. Or it could be the Armley gang wanted to expand into Oulton." Alistair shrugged. "Schmidt's closest, though, so I would have bet on him being involved. And then you have Derek White who runs the Harehills gang." The man furrowed his brows. "If it wasn't White, then perhaps Schmidt was the one who burnt the cottage down?"

"It'd make sense, sir," said George. "Cutting off his brother's fingers and then burning the cottage down would send a message to the Haymer family."

"Great minds think alike, Beaumont, though the same could be said for Derek White."

"What kind of drugs are the Haymer family into, sir?" asked George.

"Everything, really. They don't discriminate. But they're big on heroin. They often cut it with cheaper products."

"Like talc, sir?" asked Jay. "Baby powder," he explained at the DCI's frown.

"Yeah, anything that mimics heroin is used, to be honest. Baking soda, sugar, starch." He shrugged. "I've even known powdered milk and caffeine to be used." He then closed his eyes. "I've also been involved in some horror stories involving crushed over-the-counter painkillers and rat poison.

CHAPTER THIRTY-THREE

Sometimes, what they cut the heroin with is worse than the stuff itself. And don't get me started on fentanyl."

"If you know about the Haymer brothers, then why haven't they been arrested, sir?" asked Tashan. It was the obvious question, which had an obvious answer.

"Well, Aiden disappeared over a year ago and went to ground. It won't surprise me if he's been operating out of the cottage in Oulton this past year. But obviously, someone got greedy, and somebody grassed."

"Could the Lickiss family be slap bang in the middle of it?" asked George. He explained the scopolamine and what Dr Yardley had found.

"Geoff Lickiss' name comes up a lot, or it used to, I should say. As he's aged, he's calmed down a lot, but it wouldn't surprise me if he's involved."

"Could Hope's murder and Martha's assault be drug-related, then?" asked George.

"It certainly could be, but you've linked the murder and abduction to Rita Holdsworth's murder, right?"

"Right."

"How is Rita linked to drugs?"

"She isn't, sir," George admitted.

"And then there's Brenden Steffen," said the DCI. "His only link is that he was shagging Martha Lickiss, right?"

"Right again, sir."

The DCI scratched his nose. "If you're entertaining the drugs idea, then all I can venture is that Rita and Brenden were killed to keep their mouths shut."

"Faith Lickiss is still missing, sir, and we found heroin at the Grant household, mainly in Tyrell Grant's bedroom. Apparently, he was in a relationship with Faith. She's fifteen, and he's in his twenties."

"How did you come to that conclusion, Inspector?" asked Atkinson.

"We found a big wad of cash in her bedroom, and we have photo evidence of them together."

"I remember now." He grinned. "Fair enough," said Atkinson. "Grant's name has come up in Precision meetings for sure, but he's small-time to tell you the truth. We don't know who he's working for." He licked his lips. "Have we identified Aiden's mate yet? The one in the hospital?"

"Not yet, sir," said George.

Alistair shoved his hands into his trouser pockets and strutted around the room's perimeter. "As soon as he wakes, arrest him and take a DNA swab, see if he's on the database."

"Will do, sir," said George.

"So, what are you doing next?" Atkinson asked.

"We're searching for Martha Lickiss' Ford Fiesta," George said. "That car links all three murders. And, if we find that car, we will hopefully find the two people who dropped Martha Lickiss off at the hospital."

"And the culprit, I assume?"

"Or culprits, sir, yes. Taylor Corbyn, Jean Lickiss' partner, is also missing. She had an issue with Martha Lickiss, as did Jean, because of her treatment of Geoff. It's enough of a motive for them to abduct Martha, but it doesn't explain why Hope, Rita and Brenden are dead, and Faith is missing." George continued. "And Jean Lickiss was home the night Brenden Steffen was murdered. DS Hoskins took her statement."

"And Geoff Lickiss?"

"I got DC Scott to check his alibi, sir," said DI Beaumont. He turned to the young DC, who was unusually quiet.

CHAPTER THIRTY-THREE

"It's legit, sir," Jay said to the DCI.

Chapter Thirty-four

Delighted that one of Leeds' most prominent criminals was dead, DCI Atkinson couldn't keep the grin from meeting his eyes as he lowered the squad car window, reached out, and pushed the buzzer. Alistair knew he was being filmed, so he tried to keep a straight face.

On the way over, he'd told George about some of the awful things Aiden Haymer had done over the years, things that could never be proved, things that had haunted the DCI's dreams for as long as he could remember. "It's a shame he was murdered before the fire got to him," Atkinson had said. "I hear burning alive isn't very pleasant. Aiden got a quick death, which he didn't deserve."

George had nodded at the DCI but hadn't really spoken. Not until they'd pulled up outside Alfie's house, marvelling at the wealth being on the wrong side of the ladder gave you. George didn't have electric gates or a lit driveway leading to an immaculately gravelled turning circle. And whilst he loved his Merc, the Ferraris and McLarens parked outside the garages were enough to keep Clarkson and co busy on their Amazon series.

"Jesus Christ, sir, we're in the wrong job."

"Fucking terrible what crime pays," was all the DCI said.

"Then again, look at the risk. You live by the sword; then you die by it."

George nodded at that.

"And your children will be relatively safe," said Alistair. "Rumour has it Alfie has a son who is kept in a bunker so rival gangs can't abduct him."

"Bloody hell."

"You know, Beaumont, you'd be good at this."

"Good at what, sir?"

"Working for Precision and tackling organised crime rather than running major enquiry cases."

"I don't think my body would be up to that, sir, to tell you the truth."

Atkinson nodded as he pulled up behind a sleek BMV, parking the squad car in the centre of the road, blocking the path of all other vehicles. It was petty, but the DCI was in a fucking good mood.

As they got out of the car, he turned to George. "Try not to laugh in Alfie's face, Beaumont, OK?"

"Gotcha," said George, "though, sir, I think you need to take your own advice."

"Yeah, maybe," Alistair said with a grin as they walked up the porch steps and underneath the columns. It was like all his birthdays, and Christmases had come at once. Before Atkinson knocked, the door swung open, and a man almost as wide as he was tall stood there. He was bald but covered with tattoos. "Now then, Bill. Mr Haymer's expecting me."

"Come in, Mr Atkinson."

"DCI Atkinson," he said, and this is "DI Beaumont."

Bill grunted and led the way into the lounge, a man who could have been Bill's twin taking over guard duty at the door.

The only difference between Bill and the newbie was that Bill was covered with tattoos, and the other guard had none.

Alfie Haymer stood by the empty fireplace, smoking a cigar, his eyes on them as they entered.

"We're here about Aiden."

"He's dead, isn't he?" Alfie asked.

DCI Atkinson cleared his throat, then nodded, trying to keep his composure. "That's correct, Mr Haymer."

"How?"

"There was a house fire, but the pathologist found a few nicks on his ribs, which, in his expert opinion, means he was stabbed. That, and the fact there was no smoke in his lungs, confirms that theory."

"Where?"

Atkinson gave him the address of the burnt-out cottage in Oulton.

Alfie took a long breath in through his nose, then exhaled, never keeping his eyes from the DCI.

"We'll be appointing DS Cathy Hoskins, a family liaison officer Mr Haymer, to keep you informed—"

"No." Alfie sucked on the cigar. "Who did it?"

Atkinson bit the inside of his cheek. "That's not something—"

"I want names, and now."

He moved towards the detectives, the tension palpable. Alfie Haymer wasn't a remarkable man, but his strong presence meant George struggled to breathe. It was a sweltering night, made even hotter by the fact he was wearing his suit jacket.

"Cigar?" Alfie offered both detectives.

Atkinson and Beaumont shook their heads, neither moving from the spot. Both were tensed up, breathing heavily, sweat

CHAPTER THIRTY-FOUR

dripping from their brows.

Not many people could intimidate George, but it appeared Alfie Haymer was one of them. He forced himself to remain loose in case he needed to react.

"Are you warm, gentlemen?" He didn't wait for them to answer. "Get the detectives a drink, Bill."

Atkinson held up a hand. "We're good, thanks, Mr Haymer."

"You come in here with bad news and reject my hospitality." He grinned. "If you weren't detectives, I would be offended right now."

George couldn't help himself and butted in, "We appreciate that you're upset, Mr Haymer, and we're doing everything we can. A liaison would be beneficial so we can update you."

Alfie trained his gaze on George, his eyes widening with each of George's words. When George was finished, Alfie simply said, "I'm not upset; I'm fucking angry."

"Hence why you want the names?" asked George.

"Correct."

"Do you know of anybody who would want to hurt Aiden?" George asked.

The entire room erupted into laughter.

Alfie shook his head and returned his gaze back to the DCI. "Brought a fucking joker with you this time, have you?"

It was clearly rhetorical, so Atkinson said nothing.

"I want names." He nodded at Bill. "If you have nothing for me, I'd like you to leave. Bill will show you out."

"Tell me about Geoff and Martha Lickiss."

Alfie immediately said, "Who?" then, as Atkinson was about to elaborate, Haymer said, "Is that who killed my brother?"

"I'm not saying that," the DCI said. "I just want to know whether you recognise the names."

"I don't." Alfie eyed his crew. Each and every one of them shook their heads. "We don't."

"Fine. CSI will be out shortly and will need to lock Aiden's room down," Atkinson explained.

Alfie frowned. It was only for a split second, but Atkinson's words had managed to breach the gang leader's façade. Eventually, he said, "For how long?"

"For as long as necessary, Mr Haymer."

Alfie nodded. "When can we have his remains back? We have a funeral to arrange."

"We're still investigating, which is why a family liaison—"

Alfie Haymer had said nothing, his facial expression doing all the talking required. Atkinson immediately shut up. Eventually, Alfie said, "You need to fucking listen to me because I can make things difficult for you."

The two men stared at each other.

George watched, clenching his fists.

Then, out of nowhere, Bill appeared behind George and whispered, "Don't fucking move," in his ear. For a massive guy, he was quick, quicker than George anticipated. Even fully fit, George was unsure he would have been able to react.

"You know full well how this can go, and my respect for you—that only exists because you're a detective—will only last for so long." He looked between the detective's eyes, searching for fear. "So, are we doing this, or are you going to get the fuck out?"

Alistair's face relaxed. A fake smile crossed Alfie's face. The gang leader even laughed.

"We'll be in touch," said Atkinson.

Alfie said, "Looking forward to it."

CHAPTER THIRTY-FOUR

* * *

"Who the fuck works, Oulton?" Alfie asked. He'd watched the detectives leave, knowing full well how much the knobheads were enjoying the death of his brother. But it was the first thing they had on the Haymer family, probably a fucking highlight of the DCI's career. And he didn't like the blonde dickhead, either. He looked dangerous. There was no fear in his eyes.

Perhaps he'd get his claws into the DI.

"Didn't you cunts hear me? I said, who the fuck works Oulton?"

Bill swallowed his drink and then shrugged. "Not us; I know that, boss."

"So how the fuck was he involved in a fire?" Alfie lit another cigar and decided he was going to get pissed tonight. He liked being drunk; it took away the shite parts of life and replaced them with warmth. "And who the fuck stabbed him?" Aiden was a hard man, sharp, and with no filter. He rubbed people up the wrong way most of the time, but he could also charm the knickers off a nun. "And find out about Martha and Geoff Lickiss, whoever the fuck they are!"

"I'll find out, boss," said Bill.

"Aye, I bet you fucking will."

* * *

Jean Lickiss had dismissed the family liaison officer. All she was there for was to snoop; anyway, Jean thought.

She had come to terms with the fact that Taylor had fucked off and wasn't coming back. Their relationship had been strained recently, though Jean couldn't tell anybody why.

Then again, it may have been something to do with Taylor's grandma. Recently, she'd been at her gran's house more than being at home, even staying over three or four nights in a row. It was like Taylor wanted to be away from her, Jean thought.

That or she was having an affair.

Jean didn't know what was worse.

She pulled out her phone and tried to ring Nigel, but the phone kept ringing and ringing before going to his answerphone.

"Fucking hell!" she screamed, throwing her mobile across the room.

Then she immediately rushed towards the mobile phone and snatched it up, calling her other brother, Geoff, this time.

But she got the same result and had to take deep, calming breaths to stop herself from launching the fucking mobile against the bastarding wall!

Why had she done it?

You weren't thinking straight, Jean, she told herself.

She was a glutton for punishment. Jean knew deep down inside that telling Geoff about Nigel had been the wrong decision, but she'd done it anyway.

Stupid cow.

***

George's respect for his DCI had grown exponentially after the meeting with Alfie Haymer.

"Do you think Haymer's telling the truth about not knowing Martha and Geoff Lickiss?" asked the DCI.

"He was a bit too quick to answer, sir, but he maintained composure. So, he's rather a fantastic liar or has an excellent memory."

"Or both," the DCI said. "Great liars need incredible memories so they can remember each lie they told."

George nodded. "Is he going to be a problem?"

"He already is, George, to tell you the truth." He indicated left and entered Elland Road. "Alfie's been on our radar for years, but we've never managed to get anything to stick." He pulled the squad car into a bay. "I shouldn't have mentioned the Lickiss family because I know what they'll do next."

"We have uniform stationed at the hospital, and I guess we can get Sergeant Greenwood to bring Geoff in. Unless you want to put Geoff under surveillance so you can finally get something to stick?"

The DCI stopped and turned on his heel, a grin on his face. "I told you you'd be good at this job." He scratched his chin. "I think getting Greenwood to bring Geoff in is wise, though, Beaumont," said Alistair. "Get on that ASAP. I'd rather him be alive than dead."

"Yes, sir."

Chapter Thirty-five

DS Isabella Wood arrived at Rita Holdsworth's house, not really knowing what she was looking for. It was late, and the summer sun was setting. It made her immediately regret not bringing George with her, but he was busy back at the station. Finding out about Martha's ancestry and the messages on Brenden Steffen's phone kept the DI busy.

Inside, she headed straight for the spare bedroom in the back of the house that acted as a study and started searching the desk drawers for anything useful.

After looking through a stack of pages and not finding what she wanted, Isabella checked the filing cabinet. Once she had a good bundle, she sat on the computer chair by the desk and flicked through them.

"Come on, Isabella, find something to help George," she muttered aloud. Rita Holdsworth had to know something that got her murdered, but Izzy had no clue what that was.

After wading through the chaos of paper for another half an hour, DS Wood was about to give up when she got a call from George.

"I'm heading home," he said. "How long are you gonna be?"

"Another hour, sweet. Are you OK?"

CHAPTER THIRTY-FIVE

"Yeah, just knackered," George explained. "I'm going to take some pills and then hit the sack if that's OK with you?"

"Of course, babe. I'll get something to eat on the way home." She paused. "Make sure you eat."

"Yes, boss," he said before hanging up.

She promised she'd only give it another half an hour before heading home herself. Isabella knew there was something, somewhere, and was desperate to find it.

Her phone rang again, it vibrating in her pocket. She looked at the caller ID. George. "Hiya gorgeous."

"Don't be home too late, beautiful," he said. "You can always go back to the house tomorrow."

She looked at the time. "Christ, is that the time?"

"Yep."

"OK, you're right; I'll come home now."

"Now?"

"Yeah, see you soon."

"I'm gonna take my pills now, so if I'm asleep when you get in, I'll see you in the morning."

Izzy laughed. George was a light sleeper, so even if he did take the pills, she'd definitely wake him up once she entered the bedroom. "Sweet dreams," she said and hung up.

Leaving the study, she headed through the living room to leave the bungalow and caught sight of a faded manila folder by the armchair opposite the TV. She hadn't seen it on the way in because of the angle, but now, on her way out, it was easily seen.

Her fingers tickled across the old paperwork, and she knew this was it. In this folder was the answer she was looking for.

* * *

Wood retrieved a plastic evidence bag from the car and carefully slid the folder inside. She needed peace and quiet to go through the folder, but a cursory glance had told her enough. There were sheets and sheets of family trees, each with detailed information on each member, like where they were born and when, where they were living now, if alive, and if dead, when and where they died. She even saw photos of graves as she flicked through, as well as birth and death certificates.

Rita Holdsworth had taken genealogy very seriously, and boy, was Isabella glad she did. Somebody in this stack of papers was their culprit, but who?

Her legs felt heavy as she hobbled towards her car, nodding goodnight to the PC guarding the tape they'd erected outside Rita's bungalow.

Wood clicked on her seatbelt and fired up the engine, shivering as if somebody had just walked across her grave. Her stomach was roiling, and she assumed she was hungry. The baby had also been very quiet that day. She thought with a smile, probably preparing its strength to meet the world.

Before driving away, Isabella locked the car doors and flicked on the light above her. Then, pulling out her mobile, she snapped some pictures of the extensive family tree and attached them to an email. Her engine was idling, the vibration soothing, the sound making her tired. Then, suddenly, there was a knock on her window, and Isabella quickly turned her neck to the right.

It was the PC guarding the tape. She pressed the button that wound the window down.

"Are you OK, ma'am?" he asked.

"Yeah, I'm just sending an email to my boss," she explained.

He flashed her his pearly whites. "It's getting late, ma'am;

CHAPTER THIRTY-FIVE

make sure you don't overwork yourself."

She scrunched her nose and gave the PC a small smile before saying, "Thanks."

"Have a safe journey home," he said, his voice masked as the glass rewound its way up.

On the way home to Morley from Rothwell, she thought about the case and the victims. They must be linked. All of them. But how?

They still weren't sure why Martha and Hope Lickiss were targeted, nor did they know Faith Lickiss' current whereabouts. Martha's boyfriend, Brenden Steffen, who admitted to having an affair with Martha behind Geoff's back, was killed, they assumed, because Martha had confided in him that the twins, Hope and Faith, weren't biologically Geoff's but somebody else's. They didn't know who that was yet, but that person must be related in some way to Rita Holdsworth and possibly to the Haymer family.

Isabella glanced at the folder sitting in the passenger seat next to her. It must have the answers they need.

Regardless, there was a killer in the family.

With a spring in her step, she reversed her car on the drive in front of George's Mercedes and then stepped out onto the path. Then, clutching the file tight to her chest, she walked towards her front door, pulling out her mobile phone so she could use the torch. Then, as she got closer, she gripped the folder in her left nook, held the mobile in her left hand, and pulled out her keys with her right.

She sensed nothing until the force of the whack to the back of her head caused her to stumble towards the door, the manila folder slipping from her grasp as she fought to regain balance. But with the baby, she was too heavy at the front, and she misjudged how fast she was going, twisting her ankle and landing on her right hip. She cried out in pain as a shadow reached down with a gloved hand and took the file, her keys, and her mobile. Then, it took off into the night.

* * *

Isabella staggered to her feet and, heart hammering, wildly glanced around. Where had the person gone? She couldn't hear a car screeching away, nor could she hear any shoes pounding the pavement.

Blinking, she struggled down the end of the drive and out into the road, her ankle killing her. That was when she glimpsed a shadow entering a ginnel just down the path.

She had a decision to make. Did she follow after the shadow or try to wake George by hammering on the door? It was that, or wake a neighbour and ask them to call triple nine for backup.

Isabella took a breath. By the time she did the latter two, the shadow and the manila folder would be gone. Plus, they had her keys and her mobile phone.

The pain cleared her head. Clearly, someone had ambushed her, desperately wanting the information inside that folder, so she decided to follow after the shadow. The adrenaline kicked in as she took off after him, the pain in her ankle subsiding.

She followed the shadow into Lewisham Park, trying to figure out where it was going. The park was dark at that time of night, and Isabella kept to the shadows, stalking her prey from the bushes.

When the figure reached the multicoloured basketball court, she knew it was time to pounce. "Stop! Police!" she yelled at the top of her voice.

CHAPTER THIRTY-FIVE

Swinging round, trying to see where the voice had come from, the shadow lost its footing on the grass and tripped up. Isabella heard a female voice scream out and was confused. She'd expected a male voice. Still, she sprinted towards the figure, not as oblivious now to the pain, the adrenaline running out.

It made her spring towards the shadow slower than she'd have wanted, and as she got closer, pain shot from her ankle, and she stumbled.

That was when the shadow finally managed to get to her feet.

The two women looked at each other, one a police detective, her identity on show, one a thief wearing a balaclava, masking herself from the world.

"Who are you, and what are you hiding?" Isabella asked.

The figure shook her head slowly, then pulled out a knife.

That was when Isabella regretted following the figure and wondered whether she'd have enough energy to turn back and limp back to the house to call for backup. The figure, unmoving, decided for Isabella, who began to walk backwards, dragging her leg, when another figure stepped out of the basketball court, silhouetted by the warped lights in the distance, lean and tall, clothed from head to toe in black, waving the plastic evidence bag containing the manila folder.

"Give me my file, my keys, and my mobile, and I'll leave," she said.

Silence.

The figures advanced, one step at a time, pincering her.

Shit! She was in no condition to take one of them on, never mind two. And she was unarmed, too.

Isabella held her stomach.

What was more important, protecting her unborn child or finding out the truth that Rita Holdsworth had been murdered for?

It wasn't even a question that needed answering. She needed to escape, and fast! She turned to the side and took a step back so they were creating a right-angle isosceles triangle. It meant she could see both figures. She said, "Just give me my phone and keys then."

But as the two black-clothed figures took more steps closer, images of George and Jack, alone without their fiancée or sibling, flashed in her mind. She would never see Jack grow up, and George would never get to hold their child.

What she'd done was irresponsible, and she was going to pay for it.

Isabella Wood closed her eyes as the figures got closer, now two or three steps away.

The tall, slim one punched her in the side of her head and for a second, her vision went dark before she could feel herself falling. And just as blood poured down her face to blind her, she glimpsed the glint of a knife before her knees hit the stiff grass. Isabella Wood had one last thought before she fell unconscious—that she'd failed her unborn child down already.

* * *

At the exact moment, Isabella Wood blacked out, Marie Beaumont awoke at the kitchen table, her legs cramping. She'd been dreaming about Rita Holdsworth and her children. George had asked her about Liz, and she remembered her as easily as she remembered most people, but the son alluded her. He'd been in the dream, too. Despite being older than Elizabeth, he'd always been shorter, which had always annoyed him.

Marie tried to remember his name, tried to access the dark hallways of her mind, but something was blocking her.

She sat up, letting her eyes wander through the darkness, picking up shapes that shouldn't be there. She blinked, hoping the shifting shadows were remnants of her nap, but they weren't.

The shadow said nothing to her; it simply watched. She was used to the darkness and the silence, but there was something unnerving about a person staring at you across a room, unspeaking, unblinking.

Marie wondered whether she hadn't woken up at all and was still asleep, dreaming a ridiculous nightmare.

But upon pinching her skin, she concluded what she already knew—what she was seeing wasn't a dream.

And then she clicked. She was losing her mind. She'd felt the same last week with the fuse box. Marie sighed.

"Yer aff yer heid, Auld Yin."

"No, you're not," the voice said back.

"You've finally come for me?" she asked.

"I have indeed."

Marie closed her eyes; she knew she would be sorry to die. She'd miss seeing her grandchild, Jack, and George and Izzy's unborn bairn grow into adulthood. She smiled sadly. She'd also miss the wedding. Marie looked up and met eyes with him.

Then, resigned to her fate, she flicked on the kitchen light and closed the curtains. For more than thirty years, she had kept his secrets. But perhaps now was the time to reveal them.

No matter what happens, the past always comes back to haunt you, she thought. And that was when she remembered

Rita's son's name.

"Hello, David," she said. "It's been a while, ey?"

Chapter Thirty-six

The chirping of birds woke DS Wood up. "Christ," she groaned, her hand shooting towards her forehead. "My head." Pulling her fingers back, she noticed they were covered with crusted blood.

She struggled to get to a sitting position before realising that she wasn't bound. In front of her, high up, a sliver of light peaked through a gap between a door and its frame.

Where the hell was she?

Then she recalled what happened—the two figures in the park.

Wood took a moment to ensure she had no severe injuries by running her hands down her body, fingers shaking as she struggled through the pain. Her head still thumped, and she could feel her pulse throbbing in her temple, but other than that, she was fine.

She was still dressed in her clothes from the night before, though they were now soiled with dirt and muddy water.

After parking her pain, and steeling her body with resolve, thinking of the baby in her stomach, Isabella stood up.

From the sliver of light, Wood determined that the walls and floor were made from stone, the floor tinged blue, with red graffiti on one of the walls. Above her were exposed, rotting beams that looked like they could come down any moment.

Isabella looked around the room, hoping to find a weapon, but other than a few ceramic tiles—which would do a job if necessary—there was nothing she could wield to defend herself.

While searching for a weapon, she noticed another wooden door, which was nailed shut. She wondered where she was. An outbuilding, perhaps? But where?

Her mind was blank.

She headed for the other door, the one allowing the sliver of light through, but every step she took caused her to wince because of her throbbing ankle. That, too, was locked, but not nailed shut, meaning somebody had trapped her there.

But who?

Her mind was fuzzy from the assault.

She knew for sure that there were two of them. Could they be the same two people who dropped Martha Lickiss off at the hospital?

* * *

Back at the station, George checked in with DCI Atkinson, who had activated a county-wide search for DS Wood. He'd woken up late that morning, the drowsiness from the painkillers to blame.

As soon as he realised Isabella was missing, and that her car was in the drive, he'd immediately contacted the station.

Jay met George in the open office of the HMET floor.

Pulling off his suit jacket, bundling it into a ball, and throwing it into his office, George looked at DC Scott and said, "What's this information you have?"

CHAPTER THIRTY-SIX

His tone oozed impatience, but Jay understood and didn't take it personally. There was a time he would have, of course, and would have replied with one of his defensive smirks, but he loved DS Wood as much as the rest of the team did and wanted to find her ASAP.

"One, Martha Lickiss is well enough to be interviewed, boss," Jay said. "And two, I managed to get a hold of Faith and Hope's birth certificates."

"Right, and?"

"It says Geoff is their biological father," Jay explained as he chewed on the end of a pen. He pointed to a stack of documents.

George sat down and scanned through the documents, his mind swirling with thoughts of Isabella. God, he hoped she and their baby were OK.

He thought the young DC looked stressed. In fact, looking around the shared office, his entire team looked stressed.

"Right, so that contradicts what Brenden's phone told us, doesn't it?" said George.

"It does, boss, but what if Geoff never knew? What if Martha had cheated on Geoff years ago and got caught pregnant." He shrugged. "She could have broken off the affair and told Geoff the twins were his?"

"Sounds plausible, but what evidence do you have, Jay?"

"Well, none, boss," the young DC said. "I was just thinking out loud, that's all. But what do they say, once a cheater, always a cheater?"

George mulled the information over, desperately wanting to leave the station and search for Isabella. "Have a look into the marriage records, Jay; see when they were officially married." George turned on his heel and was about to leave when another thought occurred to him. "We've still got Geoff in protective custody downstairs. Take Tashan and speak with him; ask him loads of questions about their early relationship."

Looking up, Jay asked, "What are you thinking, boss?"

"Something my mother mentioned," George explained. "She said Martha was much younger than Geoff when they got married, which obviously isn't unusual, and how my—my father knew Geoff before they had the twins. I guess what I'm asking is how long were they together before they got married, and how long after that did Martha give birth to the twins?"

"On it, boss," Jay said, eyes focused on his screen, his fingers poised.

"Ring me if you get anything," George said. "And—"

The door crashed open, and Alistair rushed in. "Martha's been talking."

"What's she said?" George asked.

The DCI said something, but George was thinking about Isabella.

Alistair shoved his hands into his pockets and frowned. "Are you listening, George?"

George turned around and nodded.

"She said Geoff's innocent," the DCI explained.

It was George's turn to frown. "But she said Geoff's name, dead, and baseball bat. We thought it meant he used the bat to kill Hope."

"Yeah, I know, but she was referring to something else. It was a code. It was supposed to help us figure out who attacked her and killed Hope."

"Well, who is it? Who killed Hope and attacked Martha?"

Atkinson grinned. "You won't believe me if I told you."

* * *

CHAPTER THIRTY-SIX

With a ceramic tile strategically near her hand, Isabella resumed the position she had been left in by her abductor and waited.

She didn't have long to wait.

The grinding of rusted metal, grating against rusted metal, alerted Isabella to the door in the corner, causing the hairs on her arms to stand to attention. She took a deep breath, her head throbbing, but she was ready to react.

Bright light spilt into the room, and despite shielding her eyes from the light, she made out the silhouette of a slight figure coming down the stairs.

"Faith?" Isabella asked, surprised. She's seen pictures of the young woman. Where Hope had strawberry blonde hair, Faith had dyed hers black.

"Please stop talking. Just be quiet, and you won't get hurt." The young woman gave Isabella an apologetic smile. "I mean it, Detective."

Isabella couldn't help but laugh. "You've already hurt me."

Faith shrugged and slid a plate of food across the uneven stone floor, keeping her distance.

"Faith, how on earth are you involved in all of this?" She pulled the plate towards her as Faith rolled a bottle of water across the floor. DS Wood pulled the lid off and greedily guzzled down the lukewarm liquid. "Do you know your sister's dead, and your mother is in the ICU?"

"You need to shut up because he's in a bad mood, and you don't want him coming down here." Faith risked a look towards the open door, then turned to look at Wood. "Trust me."

"Who is he?" Wood asked. Faith Lickiss looked scared and much younger than her fifteen years. Her hair was tied

277

back, and she wore no makeup. She was dressed in black jeans, a white T-shirt, and white Nike trainers. When Faith didn't reply, Wood asked, "Can you at least get me a pillow or something?" She pointed at her stomach. "I don't know if you've noticed, but I'm about ready to drop."

"Eat and drink and shut up." Faith stepped backwards, away from Isabella, never keeping her eyes off the detective. "I'll speak with him and see what we can do."

"Why am I here?" Isabella asked as the girl retreated up the stairs. "You'll gain nothing from keeping me here. Let me go." She winced at the pain in her head. "Please."

"You were just in the wrong place at the wrong time." Again, Faith offered Isabella another apologetic smile. "Plus, you had something we needed."

"What, Faith? What did I have that you needed."

No answer.

"I can help you, Faith. Get you away from him, whoever he is. You just need to help me. Can you do that?"

But the young girl didn't answer; instead, she slipped through the door and snapped the bolt shut.

Sniffing the cheese sandwich and checking the bag of crisps hadn't been opened, Isabella tried to understand everything that had happened since the murder of Hope Lickiss. How did Faith fit into the equation? And who was he? Geoff Lickiss? No, it couldn't be; they had him in custody because of the scopolamine. Though, for all she knew, George had released him.

But at the back of her mind, she knew Geoff was innocent. And whoever 'he' was, had also murdered Rita Holdsworth and Brenden Steffen.

But who was he?

CHAPTER THIRTY-SIX

She decided it didn't matter because whoever he was, Isabella had to figure it out. And quickly. Because it wasn't just her life that depended on it, and she knew exactly what 'he' was capable of.

* * *

"Wait, so we're looking for somebody else entirely?" George asked as they marched down the stairs to leave Elland Road. "Somebody we haven't even thought about?"

Alistair said, "She still can't talk fully, but her fingers worked pretty well, so she typed up the message." George nodded, and they headed towards a squad car. Atkinson got in the driver's side before George could protest. "Get in, Beaumont, now!"

George did as he was told and watched Jay and Yolanda get into a separate squad car, the young DC driving.

Then they were off and out onto the main road, heading towards the M621 and their eventual destination on Leeds Road.

"I've got Luke looking into specifics, George," Atkinson explained. "But Martha said Hugh Corbyn was the culprit."

"Who?"

Alistair grinned. "Martha's first love, and father of the twins."

George frowned. "What the hell have I missed?"

"A lot, by the look of it." He pulled off at junction seven and raced down Wakefield Road. "I think DS Wood figured it out, which is why they took her."

"They?"

"Hugh and Taylor Corbyn."

"But we looked into Taylor Corbyn. We found nothing. And

her alibis were solid." George was struggling to process the information. "Where are we going, anyway?"

"To the Corbyn farm on Leeds Road," the DCI explained. "The Corbyn family abandoned the farm years before Taylor was born. Taylor Corbyn is related to Rita Holdsworth, and that's the information DS Wood was looking into."

"But what if you're wrong?"

The DCI said nothing as he sped the car up Pontefract Road.

George couldn't see Jay and Yolanda's squad vehicle, assuming they must have taken a different route. "Why would Martha's first love assault Martha and kill their daughter?" the DI asked. "It doesn't make sense." He bit the inside of his cheek. "Plus, how is Taylor involved?"

"I don't have all the answers yet, Beaumont, but I'm sure DS Wood is at the farmhouse, OK?"

"Are you sure?"

The DCI shook his head. "I'm not, but do you have any other ideas?"

"No, sir."

***

Isabella Wood must have fallen asleep after eating the crisps and drinking the water because she awoke with a jolt and found a man standing over her, staring, tapping a long hunting knife against his thigh. The door was open, and the light was flooding in.

"Finally awake, are we?"

Isabella was taken aback. "You?"

"Yes, me," he snarled.

"You and Faith did all of this?"

"No, it was all me. Despite what she told you, I forced her to assist me."

"What do you want? Why did you abduct me?" Isabella attempted to focus her thoughts and tried to sit up straight.

"Because you know who I really am, don't you?"

Did she? She wracked her brains. Her head hurt still, and she couldn't think straight. She needed to buy some time. "I don't know what you're talking about," Isabella said. "Where am I?"

"Inside an outhouse of what should have been my rightful inheritance before my mother and father decided to abandon it."

"What?"

The man looked at Isabella suspiciously. "Did you not read the information in the file?"

"I had no time to read it. You attacked and abducted me, remember?"

"I was simply protecting myself and my family, Detective."

"By attacking an unarmed pregnant woman?" Izzy laughed. "You're a hard man, aren't you?"

"I've had a tough life if that's what you mean?"

"You're fucking insane."

Kit Holdsworth laughed.

Chapter Thirty-seven

"I'm a detective sergeant, Kit, so you need to let me go." She attempted a smile, but it showed as a grimace. "We can work all of this out."

Holdsworth laughed again, louder this time, with more menace. He took a step closer, the light from the door cloaking him, and he looked like the devil rising from hell.

Isabella shifted her position, hiding the ceramic tile, not allowing Kit to see it; it might be her only hope of getting out alive. Her thoughts were a jangled mess of everything she had worked on during the last week.

Then it clicked. "The information I had was on Rita Holdsworth family tree." She thought about the genealogy group meeting she attended at Blackburn Hall. "But you don't appear on it, do you?"

"Ah, so you are a detective after all." Kit grinned. "But you're wrong, I am on Rita's family tree."

"What do you mean?"

"I wasn't lying when I told you that Rita Holdsworth was a distant family member I was looking into."

"That much is obvious now," said Wood. "And it's obvious too that it was you who killed her."

"Ding, ding, ding. Congratulations. It took you so long to

figure it out. Your fiancé and team are extremely incompetent."

Wood rolled her eyes and shook her head. "Why did you kill Rita?"

"The question you should be asking is why I killed my grandma?"

"What?"

"You heard me."

"Rita Holdsworth is your grandmother?"

"Was my grandma."

Izzy frowned. "I don't understand."

Kit smirked and said, "Shall I enlighten you?"

As long as she kept Kit talking, Isabella thought she might get a chance to use her weapon. And if she knew George like she thought she did, he would be on his way soon. She just knew it. It would all click into place.

Or would it?

She'd emailed the genealogy information to the shared inbox, but that didn't mean anybody had looked at it. Or had she? Had she sent the actual email, or was it still stuck in her drafts?

She held her stomach and decided she had sent the email. Keep him talking. "Tell me your story. I want to know what happened to you."

"I suppose I can confess everything to you," he explained. "I took your phone from you, so you can't record me on it. And nobody knows I'm alive, nor does anybody know I even exist any more, so Faith and I will get away with it."

"What do you mean?"

With eyes filled with fury, he screamed, "Stop interrupting me, bitch!" Kit was swinging the hunting knife around, gesturing in a frenzy. Then suddenly, he stopped, and full of malice, he whispered, "Are you going to be fucking quiet now?"

Isabella gulped and managed to nod, one hand behind her back, her fingers gripping the ceramic tile. She may only have one chance, and she'd have to take it carefully. She watched intently as Kit stepped away from her, the knife still in his hand. Clearly, he didn't see Isabella as a threat, which would only work in her favour.

"Think very carefully about the family tree you found, Detective," Kit said.

Isabella did but couldn't really see where Kit was going with it.

"And remember, my name's not really Kit Holdsworth, though Rita is definitely my grandma."

She traced the connections in her head. Rita's daughter was Liz Brearley, Hope's teacher. Liz had married but didn't have children. Isabella said this to Kit.

"Rita had a son called Kit, who she was ashamed of," Kit explained. "Kit was my father. It's why I took his name, to try and fucking scare my grandma." He grinned. "And boy did it work."

"And your mother?"

"For now, that doesn't matter," Kit said. "What matters is Kit's son died."

"Died?"

"Well, he was murdered, or that's what the murderers thought," said Kit. "My mum and dad reported me missing, and you lot never found me. I'm sure you're aware, but prior to 2013, English law generally assumed a person was dead if, after seven years, there was no evidence that they were still alive, the people most likely to have heard from them had no contact, and inquiries made of that person had no success." Kit shrugged. "So, as far as the world is concerned, I'm dead."

"How do Martha and the Lickiss twins come into this?"

Kit grinned. "I thought you'd never ask."

The psycho took a moment to relax himself, ready to reveal his story. "My mum and dad were, at one stage, rather well off. Apparently, she was a farmer, and he was nothing but a pretty face. They fell in love, but Rita disagreed with the match."

"Hence why she was ashamed of Kit?" asked Wood.

"Correct, Detective. My mum and dad married anyway, and my father took my mother's maiden name as his surname. It was unusual but not unknown at the time. My maternal grandparents were lovely people, but they passed away tragically, and my mum and dad could no longer cope as farmers and wanted to sell up. My mother was pregnant with my sister, you see. And my dad was only a pretty face. In fact, I'm told he was fucking useless. And so, my mother chose him over the farm, and they left it to rot."

"Your inheritance?"

"Correct again, Detective." He held out his knife, pointing it at her swollen stomach. "But stop fucking interrupting me!"

A short moment later, he continued, chaotically licking his lips. Kit reminded her of Barty Crouch Junior from one of the Harry Potter films.

"Anyway, I was about to go to uni when I made a mistake." He shrugged. "Though, perhaps it weren't a mistake." He shook his head. "No, not a mistake. I did something I regretted at the time. I got a woman pregnant."

Isabella's eyes widened. She wanted to know who Kit had gotten pregnant, but the hand holding the knife was flailing around.

"That was over sixteen years ago," Kit explained. "And for sixteen long years, I was made to think that she had terminated my child... My children..."

Isabella felt pieces of the puzzle begin to click into place. She remained silent for a moment, resisting her urge to slip into detective mode. But she also needed to keep him talking.

"Faith and Hope?"

He nodded.

"You wrote the love letters?"

A look of surprise flashed across his face. "Martha kept them?"

It was Wood's turn to nod.

"Guess it was lucky I never signed them."

"You were scared of Geoff," said Wood. It wasn't a question but a statement of fact.

He shrugged. "Who wouldn't be?"

"Is that why you set him up?"

"Yes and no."

Isabella frowned.

"Haven't figured it out?" he asked.

She shook her head.

"I mentioned earlier that I was murdered. Or, specifically, I said the murderer thought I was dead." He paused and took a breath. "Geoff assaulted me with a baseball bat, bundled me in his car, and hid my body deep within the woods of Rothwell Country Park, thinking I was dead."

Now Martha's comment in the hospital made sense to Isabella. "In the hospital, Martha said the words 'baseball bat', 'Geoff', and 'dead' before she passed out."

He nodded. "I'm glad that was all she could say, as it led

CHAPTER THIRTY-SEVEN

you lot down the wrong way, didn't it?" He shrugged. "But there was always a risk it would come out," Kit said. "Faith and my sister went behind my back and dropped her off at the hospital."

"Your sister?"

"My God, you really had no idea, did you?"

Keep him talking, Wood thought. Keep wasting time. She shrugged and looked down at the stone floor. "Why did you kill Hope?"

A flash of anger crossed his face, and the man clenched his fists. A single, stray tear fell from one of his eyes. "It was an accident."

"How?"

"I was outside the farmhouse, watching and waiting. I'd been in touch with Faith for a while, and she was open to coming to live with me, but Hope had threatened to tell Geoff and Martha that I was still alive." He must have seen the look of shock on Wood's face and the twitching of her mouth as he held his index finger to his lip and shushed her. "If you want to know what happened, then fucking keep quiet."

Wood gulped, then nodded.

"OK, good girl." Kit took a deep breath. "I'll admit that the idea was to disappear with Faith, but I still wanted to give Hope a chance of coming with us. For sixteen long years, that bitch Martha had denied me my girls. And I was going to change that."

He started erratically licking his lips again.

"But that's when I saw Geoff. He walked into the farmhouse, and I watched him and Martha arguing through the window."

"So, the prints we found out back were yours?"

Kit nodded. "I watched them argue for a while, listened to

Geoff talk about Hope and Faith as if he owned them when they were mine! And then he left, so I looked around the shed for something I could use to kill Martha with."

"And you found the bat?"

"Oh, the irony." Kit grinned. "I slid into the kitchen, and from behind, I smacked Martha's head with the bat as hard as I could, only—only it wasn't Martha."

Isabella held her hand against her mouth.

Kit closed his eyes as more tears streamed down his face. "I'd killed my little girl, and it was all Martha and Geoff's fault!" He paused before continuing. "Then Martha entered the kitchen, and well, I'm sure you can imagine what happened next."

"You'll have to tell me, Kit."

"I told her who I was and took in the horror on her face as she realised I wasn't dead and knew all about her dirty little secret. That the girls were mine, and she'd lied about their termination." He licked his lips again. "She begged me not to kill her, so I hit her across her head and took her with me. The idea was to torture her before I killed her."

Still shocked by his confession, Wood asked, "So what of Faith?"

"Faith came downstairs to find me standing over the body of her mother and sister; she said she didn't want to come with me any more because I was a murderer. So I forced her to come with me. Threatened her. Locked her up in here until she complied." He shrugged. "As I said, she's innocent in all of this."

"You say Hope's death was Martha and Geoff's fault. Is that why you tried to frame Geoff?"

"He made it very easy," Kit explained. "He'd left his leather jacket on the newel post, so I left it there for you lot to find. Plus, he needed to pay for trying to murder me all those years ago. And for stealing my daughters."

"So why did you kill Brenden Steffen?"

A large grin stretched across Kit's face, stretching from ear to ear. "I was so happy when I found out Martha was cheating on Geoff with Brenden. Once a cheater, always a cheater. And I knew if I killed him, you lot would instantly look at Geoff. I obviously hadn't done a good enough job to frame him for Hope's death and Martha's assault; your fiancé saw to that, but I figured killing Brenden would highlight Geoff again."

"Which it did."

"Well, you're fools for falling for it," Kit said.

"Only we didn't, did we, because he came to us with a solid alibi," said Wood. "Where did you keep Martha before your sister and Faith dropped her off at the hospital?"

Kit spread out his arms.

"Here?"

"Correct. Faith helped me bundle her mother into the boot of Martha's car, and I brought both of them here."

"So your sister wasn't initially involved?"

"No."

"So what happened?"

"I murdered our grandma."

Isabella frowned. "I'm confused."

"Of course, you are because you haven't figured out who I am or who my sister is."

"Keep talking, and I may prove you wrong," she said with a grin. "Why kill Rita?"

"Because she was the only person who could connect my sister to all of this," Kit explained. "Plus, I was masquerading as a genealogy student, interested in Rita's family tree, remember. And, if you recall, that's how I got in touch with Brenden and Martha. How she didn't recognise me, I don't know, but being so close to her like that was so exhilarating."

"I still don't see how Rita was a danger to you."

"Are you stupid or what?" Kit asked, stepping closer and waving the knife at Izzy. "Rita was in regular contact with my sister, and believe it or not, my sister was the only one who knew I was still alive."

It clicked.

"You think your sister told Rita you were still alive."

"Finally!" He sighed. "I know for a fact she told Rita I was still alive because I heard my sister tell my grandma as such. I witnessed it. And so I had a decision to make. Kill my grandma or kill my sister." He paused. "Or, for all you know, I killed both."

"After she and Faith dropped Martha off at the hospital?"

"Well, that was the final straw, you see."

The man's cold-blooded tone got on Isabella's every nerve, and she desperately wanted to lash out with the ceramic tile, to smash it across Kit's head, as he had done to Hope and Martha. But she was too far away and knew she needed to bide her time. "So you killed your sister as well?" Wood asked, and Kit nodded. Isabella tried to understand what she was hearing and why Kit was so happy to divulge everything. Then she realised that Kit had no intention of releasing her alive; otherwise, he wouldn't be telling his murderous story. "You're a serial killer, Kit; congratulations."

"You don't know the half of it," he bragged.

"Care to share?"

"No."

CHAPTER THIRTY-SEVEN

"Why? You've killed your sister, your grandma, and your daughter. That's three right there. You tried to kill Martha, but unluckily for you, she survived." She raised her index finger into the air. "And you killed Brenden, which makes four. Am I going to be your fifth?"

Kit laughed. "You're forgetting the two men I burned to death."

Thinking about being trapped inside a burning building made Isabella feel nauseous. "So you're involved with all the drugs, then?"

"I am now, yes," he said. "My death afforded me some immunity, and with no legal ID, I had to do what was necessary to survive."

"What can you tell me about the scopolamine at the Lickiss farm?"

"Nothing at all, I'm afraid, but I can tell you who those two men worked for."

They already knew surviving man worked for Jürgen Schmidt and the dead man was Aiden Haymer, but she wanted to keep Kit talking. "Go on then."

"George Beaumont's nemesis, Jürgen Schmidt."

"What do you know of George and Jürgen?"

"Only that Jürgen wants to repay George for everything he's done," said Kit.

"Is that a threat?"

He snorted. "Not from me, dear."

"You do realise you've ignited a gang war, don't you?" Wood asked.

Kit narrowed his eyes. "Explain."

"You killed Aiden Haymer, Alfie Haymer's brother." She took a deep breath. "He was the one you stabbed to death."

"Shit."

Izzy grinned. "Are we missing anything?"

Isabella felt the heat of Kit's fiery stare as he said, "Only that I had Schmidt deal with Tyrell Grant because he was sniffing around my fifteen-year-old daughter."

Wood shook her head. "Why are you telling me all this?"

"It's obvious, is it not?"

"I want to hear it from you personally."

Kit grinned. "I'm going to butcher you and leave you for George Beaumont to find. Then I'll tell Schmidt what I did. He'll accept me as his right-hand man, and I'll be set for life."

Izzy's heart began to hammer in her chest, but she managed to maintain eye contact with the psychopath. "Before you do that, tell me who you really are." She gritted her teeth and tightened her grip on the tile behind her back. Then she kept watch as Kit continued his silent march up and down the confined outhouse, silently praying for the knowledge to know when to strike.

Chapter Thirty-eight

Keep him talking, Izzy, keep him talking, she thought.

Kit was walking around, brandishing the sharp hunting knife, the blade glittering in the fading light. Isabella felt no fear for her own life but feared for that of her baby. It was the adrenaline, she was sure, but the calmness that made her settle and focus on the tile worried her.

"Tell me your real name, Kit!" Wood demanded.

"Should I tell her?" Kit asked as a girl walked through the door.

"Well, it doesn't look like she's gonna guess, Dad."

From the look on Faith's face, it appeared Kit's insanity had wormed its way into her.

Isabella held her breath. The atmosphere in the room had changed. Was it time for her to die? Was George going to be too late? She had to stall. "Who did your father marry, Kit?"

Kit stopped pacing and tapped the dull edge of the knife on his knee. "You still haven't figured that out yet?" He frowned. "It was there, in black and white."

The tapping ceased. All was silent. She couldn't make a sound; she couldn't give herself away. The ceramic tile was heavy and might have made a sound as she scraped it across the stone floor. She prayed for a way to get out of the situation.

"In the family trees Rita had created?" she asked. Keeping Kit talking seemed the only way to stall the inevitable. "Which was why you were following me last night?"

"Correct. The family tree."

"But if you were legally dead, then I wouldn't have made the connection, anyway, would I?"

"Probably not, but it was a risk I wasn't willing to take. Plus, Faith was worried about implicating her aunt."

Wood turned to the girl, who looked like she was crying. "Your aunt? I didn't know Jean was involved in this."

"You've still no idea, have you?" asked Kit.

"I have my suspicions."

"Bullshit!" Kit started tapping the knife against his thigh. Then he started laughing maniacally. "If you knew, you'd have said already."

"And you would have mentioned Taylor Corbyn," Faith added, her tiny voice echoing around the room. She took a step closer to her dad.

"What's Taylor got to do with this?" asked Wood.

The girl took another careful step forward. "Everything," Faith advised. She pointed at Izzy's stomach. "Boy or girl?"

"We decided we wanted to be surprised," Wood explained.

Faith took another step. "We need to let her go, Dad."

"What the hell are you talking about?" Kit asked. "We've admitted to everything; she can't leave."

Isabella met eyes with Faith, pleading for her safety. The young girl nodded. "I'm tired, Dad. I've had enough. I didn't kill anybody, and I helped you under duress." She pointed towards the second door. "Leave, Dad, please. Escape. You've got your revenge. Let the lady and her baby live."

"She knows too much, Faith," Kit said, turning to his

daughter. He pointed towards the open door. "Go to the car, love. You really don't need to see what I do next."

With his back to Isabella, he had no idea that the detective had suddenly stood up with the ceramic tile in her hand.

But Faith could see her.

It was now or never.

Faith said, "You're right, Dad. I don't want to see or be involved with anything you do any more."

"I've done all of this for you, you ungrateful little cow!" he screamed at his daughter.

With all of his attention on Faith, Isabella took her chance and, stepping forward, brought down the tile on Kit's head with both hands.

But as she brought the tile down, Kit had turned towards Isabella and, seeing the tile, stepped back slightly, throwing Isabella off balance, the tile glancing Kit's shoulder before shattering on the stone floor.

Isabella saw her life flash before her eyes as, with a shriek, Kit lunged, thrusting the knife towards her.

Isabella stepped backwards, then decided to throw her body sideways at the last minute.

But it was too late.

"You bitch," Kit yelled.

The world went slow.

A scream pierced the muggy air.

Isabella wondered whether the scream had come from her own throat.

There were more screams.

And the sound of sirens.

Car doors slammed.

Footsteps pounded on the ground.

People were shouting.

"George!" Isabella shouted, just as her vision turned black.

Chapter Thirty-nine

With Jay and Yolanda in tow, George crashed through the door and flew straight for Isabella with just a sideways glance at Faith Lickiss, who was on the floor, unmoving. Hugh Corbyn or Kit Holdsworth, whatever his bloody name was, was in the corner, hugging his knees to his chest and sitting on the floor.

Turning her over on her side, he whispered, "Izzy?" She was covered in blood. He lowered his ear to her mouth.

A faint breath.

"Thank God."

"It's not my blood, George," she breathed.

He said nothing, holding her in his arms while waiting for the paramedics to arrive. George watched Alistair check Faith for a pulse and saw him shake his head towards Yolanda. Jay handcuffed Hugh.

"Is she—is she dead?" Hugh cried.

"Shut your mouth," DCI Atkinson ordered.

They were waiting for Greenwood's uniforms to arrive, who'd take Hugh Corbyn to Elland Road to be processed before being interviewed.

Then, two paramedics entered the outhouse. George whispered in Wood's ear, "The paramedics are here; you're going to be fine."

"I love you," she told him.

"I'm so sorry," he replied.

"Not your fault."

George said, "I'm never letting you out of my sight ever again." He kissed her on the forehead, but she winced.

"Good," she replied. "I wouldn't have it any other way."

The two paramedics checked Faith over first, but she was already dead. Her father had killed her, providing the same fate as her twin.

Then they came over and checked Wood's vital signs.

"Is she going to be OK?" George asked, not letting Isabella go.

"She appears to be fine," one said. "But we want to make sure the baby is OK, so we need to get her out of here now."

"Then what the hell are you waiting for?" George shouted.

Within a few minutes, they had Wood strapped to a gurney, a cannula inserted into her arm, a blood pressure cuff on the other, and an oxygen monitor attached. Then they were gone.

George, still trying to still his racing heart, looked at DCI Atkinson for permission to follow his fiancée.

"Go, Beaumont," he said. "We can handle things here."

"Thanks, sir," he said, jogging after the paramedics.

* * *

Detective Superintendent Jim Smith was pacing the incident room when George arrived. "Any news, George?" he asked.

"They have her hooked up to a monitor, but it looks like our baby is fine, sir," George said. "The nurse explained Isabella haemorrhaged, and they may decide to carry out a caesarean section."

CHAPTER THIRTY-NINE

"Then what the bloody hell are you doing here, George?"

"She's fine for the moment, and my mother is there with her. They haven't decided what to do yet, sir. And when they do, I'll be the first to know." He scratched his beard. "I don't want to be here, trust me, but Isabella needs closure. She'd be here herself if she could. She told me to be here."

"That woman always did work too hard."

"Ain't that the truth." George smiled. "Did they find anything at the farm?"

"Not yet," Smith explained. "Jay and Tashan are there with uniform. Luke will be arriving when his shift starts."

"Isabella said they should find the genealogy reports they stole from her. It should explain everything, including how Kit Holdsworth is Hugh Corbyn." George paused. "Hugh also admitted to killing his sister, but obviously, Isabella didn't know he was referring to Taylor Corbyn. We'll need to ask him where her body is."

"DCI Atkinson is interviewing him with DS Williams as we speak, George." Smith took a sip of his drink. "It'll all come out."

"According to Izzy, Kit's responsible for all the murders, even the two in the cottage."

"As I said, George, it'll all come out." He shook his head. "Get off to the hospital, you idiot!"

George stood in front of the Big Board as Jim Smith left the room. Kit Holdsworth, born Hugh Corbyn, was the son of Kit Holdsworth and Emily Corbyn, who'd been classified as legally dead fifteen years ago after he went missing suddenly. Beaumont knew from Isabella that Geoff Lickiss, and perhaps Martha, was involved in that attempted murder because Hugh was in love with Martha.

That, and Martha was pregnant at the time Geoff attempted to murder Hugh and she presumably knew Hugh was the father but never said anything to Geoff. According to Izzy, Martha had told Hugh she had aborted their child, a blatant lie, which had been the catalyst that started everything.

Yet all Hugh had managed to do was kill his family with his own hands. He'd killed his twin daughters by accident, but the murder of his grandma had been premeditated. He'd murdered his own sister, too.

Then there were the two men in the fire, and the Yank, Brenden Steffen, taking the killer in the family's body count to at least seven, eight if you included Tyrell Grant.

George wondered just how many more lives Hugh Corbyn had destroyed.

Chapter Forty

Geoff Lickiss admitted to growing Angel's Trumpets but wouldn't say who he was growing the product for. He simply said, 'No comment,' whenever he was asked that question.

So, they had nothing to charge him for.

The plant was not illegal to grow in the UK, and the scopolamine harvested from the plants was not a controlled substance under the UK Misuse of Drugs Act 1971, so they struggled to get any charges to stick.

That was until they received a 999 call from a concerned neighbour about an odour that 'smelled like death'.

After forcing entry, they found Nigel Lickiss, Geoff's brother, dead, the crime scene reminding DC Blackburn and DC Scott of Edmund Flathers and Andre Harding.

During that case, people had been killed by the seeds of Angel's Trumpets, which had been ground down into a powder, by Johann Gruber, despite his continued protestations that he was innocent.

George's team did an incredible job, with Yolanda taking a starring role and finding the CCTV that proved Geoff Lickiss had killed his brother.

Dressed in a white Tyvek suit, Geoff Lickiss cut a gloomy figure in his cell. DC Scott left him there and headed upstairs to the office with Tashan.

"What an unpleasant bastard," said Jay. "Bloody 'no comment' this, 'no comment' that." With every step they took, Jay smacked his hand against the railing as they ascended the stairs.

"Lindsey will find something," Tashan said. "Then we can nail him for the murder." He clapped his friend on the shoulder. "And his DNA should be in the house."

"But why did he do it?"

"I dunno, mate," Tashan said. "But if we play it right, we can find out."

"I don't have a brother, but if I did, I don't think I could murder him."

Tashan grinned. "I have three, and let me tell you, they're annoying little shits."

Later, when DC Blackburn and DS Williams interviewed Geoff Lickiss, the man eventually admitted, "The fucking paedo had pictures of my girls in swimsuits on his laptop. Scum like that don't deserve to be alive."

So, Tashan arrested him. The CPS authorised a murder charge, especially after Yardley and her CSI team found forensic evidence linking Geoff to the crime scene, and he was remanded in Armley Nick until his trial.

George promised himself he would look into Johann Gruber's case again to see whether Gruber was as innocent as he'd always insisted.

* * *

Geoff Lickiss spent his first afternoon in HMP Leeds in serious trouble, which started just after he stepped out of his cell. He turned left to walk down the narrow corridor to the weights room. He made an error in judgement and bumped into another inmate, their shoulders touching. He looked down at the guy and apologised. That was his mistake.

It was a terrible mistake, and he didn't understand why. But he'd broken a rule. He'd disrespected the other inmate in front of another. The guy he apologised to was short and stocky, covered with tattoos. The tattoos were gang tattoos, but Geoff didn't know. He smiled but didn't move forward. He should have just walked on and hoped for the best. But he didn't.

Instead, he said, "I'm Geoff Lickiss; sorry about that." He held out his hand to shake.

Another bad mistake. Lickiss hadn't known that anything awful was about to happen. There was a hot pain, and then Geoff's wrist broke. The short, stocky man's left hand had seized it, twisting both hands and snapping it like a thin twig. It all happened in a blur, a shattering noise and an explosion of motion.

Karma.

Geoff tried to scream, but it was too late. The other inmate had already managed to get one of his giant hands clamped over his mouth, with the other around his neck. He couldn't move.

"What are you looking at?" the guy said. Geoff was on his knees in agony at the pain, his right wrist mangled. He could hardly breathe with the hand over his mouth. At that point, Geoff Lickiss understood what had happened and how he had fucked up. What are you looking at? That was a universal phrase for shit is going to get worse, and it was not a phrase you wanted to hear, especially in prison. "I can't hear you," he said mockingly.

Geoff was shaking his head, trying to get out of the lock that had been snapped shut around him. The guy's arms and biceps were hugely muscled. "Nothing," he managed to say when the bigger guy removed his arms, but he soon realised he had made the situation much worse.

"You looking at nothing? Bro, you calling me a nothing?" He stabbed his finger into Geoff's chest. "You hear this, Jimmy; he's calling me a nothing. Shall I show him how a nothing behaves?"

Geoff got up on his feet and tried to move on, but it was way too late. He felt the gang member's stare on his back and gave up on going to the medical office, that's if they had one. So he walked back into his cell and laid down on his bunk in absolute agony.

Finally, there was peace and quiet.

But it didn't last long.

Something huge blocked the light from the cell entrance, causing a shadow. Geoff Lickiss opened his eyes.

That was when he noticed the smell. The air was sour. It smelled of sweat, dirty hair and stale urine. It reminded him of the lions at the Yorkshire Wildlife Park.

Three men entered the cell, one of them the man with the tattoos who had broken his wrist. The man cracked his head from side to side and moved closer.

Geoff gritted his teeth and said, "Wait. Don't you know who I am?"

The guy's friends, who were all stocky small guys with the same tattoos, laughed. They all had short hair and the same look in their eyes.

"Of course we do," the gang leader said. "Geoff Lickiss, right?" He stepped closer.

CHAPTER FORTY

"Wait," Geoff said again.

But the gang members didn't wait. The two lackeys each grabbed an arm, pinning Geoff to the spot, as the ring leader stepped closer, a shiv in his hand.

"You don't have to do this," Geoff pleaded. "I know Jürgen Schmidt. I know him very well."

But the leader stepped even closer, their noses touching, the smell of sweat heavy in the air. He grinned and said, "Hugh Corbyn sends his regards."

Geoff was medevacked by helicopter to the LGI and was operated on to try and save his life. Then he was handcuffed to a cot in a secure intensive care unit, unconscious. The doctors and surgeons weren't sure when, or if, he would ever wake up again. A few of them said they didn't care. They'd heard whispers of the crimes he had committed in his youth.

Epilogue

George Beaumont looked at himself in the mirror, adjusting the light-blue scrubs, turban cap, and mask to make him look presentable.

They'd called him in because Isabella was going to have an emergency caesarean section. She was haemorrhaging because the placenta had detached from the womb, endangering her and the baby.

The DI entered the theatre, and Izzy was laid on a gurney, the epidural already in place. He watched as the anaesthetist talked Isabella through the procedure.

"I love you," George said as the surgical team sprayed Isabella with a spray to ensure she was numb.

"I love you more," she replied.

"Can you feel anything?" the surgeon asked, and Izzy shook her head.

"I doubt that you love me more," George said as the staff rubbed iodine across her swollen stomach.

"Well, it's not a competition."

One of the team members erected a light-blue curtain the same colour as George's scrubs.

George grinned. "You made it one first."

"Because I always win."

He gripped her hand. "Can you feel anything?"

"Nope. I don't think they've started yet."

EPILOGUE

George looked to his right and noticed the surgeon had blood on his gloves. He asked the surgeon, "Is everything OK?"

"Yes, I'll only be another minute or so," the surgeon replied.

"Wait, so you've started already?" asked Isabella.

The surgeon nodded.

And it was then that George heard his child's tender but vociferous cry, a miracle to his ears.

As he wiped a bulbous tear from his face, not keeping his eyes from Isabella, she nodded at him. It was permission to leave her and go to the scales to cut their child's cord.

As soon as the midwife had done their checks and swaddled the baby, she handed the child to George, who then headed back to Isabella and held their child across Izzy's chest.

Isabella then looked up at George, smiling proudly, and asked, "Is it a boy or a girl?"

Find out in the next novel, *The Stourton Stone Circle*, out early October.

Family Tree

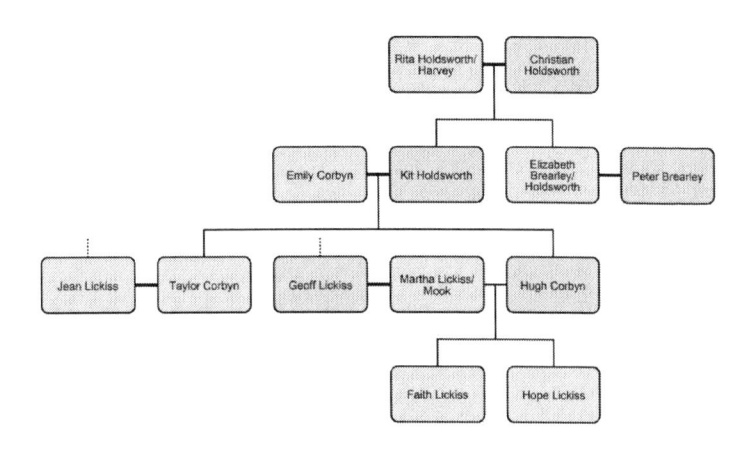

- Rita Holdsworth/Harvey — Christian Holdsworth
  - Kit Holdsworth (m. Emily Corbyn)
  - Elizabeth Brearley/Holdsworth (m. Peter Brearley)

- Taylor Corbyn (… Jean Lickiss) — Martha Lickiss/Mook (… Geoff Lickiss) — Hugh Corbyn
  - Faith Lickiss
  - Hope Lickiss

Also by Lee Brook

The Detective George Beaumont West Yorkshire Crime Thriller series in order:

The Miss Murderer

The Bone Saw Ripper

The Blonde Delilah

The Cross Flatts Snatcher

The Middleton Woods Stalker

The Naughty List

The Footballer and the Wife

The New Forest Village Book Club

The Killer in the Family

Pre-order The Stourton Stone Circle

More titles coming soon.

Printed in Great Britain
by Amazon